ISBN: 978-0-992-26850-3

Under Fire

Rachel Amphlett

In memory of
Stephen Davies
whose valuable contributions will be sadly missed

Prologue

Grant Swift pulled his keys out of his pocket and glanced through the glass doors of the atrium in the large industrial building. His fingers flexed around the handle of the battered briefcase in his hand, the black leather peeling and faded to grey.

Sleet poured off the covered walkway, the force of the downpour echoing through the building's reception area. Grant jumped as a gust of wind shook the glass doors and sent debris tumbling across the landscaped path which led towards the car park.

'Going to make a run for it, Mr Swift?'

Grant turned to the reception desk, manned by a solitary security guard who had looked up from a half-completed Sudoku puzzle. He pushed his scarf under his coat collar. 'If I miss our anniversary dinner this year, I might as well look for a new home.'

The guard laughed, reached across and turned up the radio. 'I reckon you should take your chances then. Better you turn up soaked and frozen than late.'

'That's what I thought.' Grant swung the briefcase over his head and pushed his way through the glass doors, the sound of a top forty radio station echoing in his wake. His feet kicked up torrents of water as he ran through the puddles on the concrete footpath. His breath fogged in the air.

As he neared his car, a late-model silver Mercedes saloon with a personalised plate reading 'GEN1US', he swung his arm up and pointed the key fob at the door. The indicator lights flashed once. Wrenching open the door, he threw his briefcase onto the passenger seat and launched himself into the driver's seat. Pulling the door shut, he sat stunned, watching the sleet streak down the windscreen.

'Jesus,' he murmured, 'bloody English weather.'

He shivered. His last assignment had been on a project in the Middle East. Two months later he was ruing the day he'd accepted a contract with the organisation and returned to the United Kingdom.

He ran his hand through his sodden black hair, shivered as cold water dripped down the back of his neck, and then glared as a pool of water spread under the briefcase and over the upholstery of the car.

He shook his head, put the ignition card in its slot and started the car. The engine purred to life, the instrument panel lighting up like a primed jet fighter. Grant leaned forward and adjusted the temperature controls. The fog on the inside of the windscreen began to clear as he fastened his seat belt and switched on the headlights.

Flicking on the wipers, he put the car into drive and swung away from the complex.

A mass of architecturally-designed glass and steel, the organisation's headquarters was the centre-point of the new business park. Its three storeys towered above the neighbouring offices, all designed to fit in with the tree line of the surrounding countryside. Twenty miles from the centre of London, the intention was to create an oasis of calm for the software engineers who had descended on the place nearly two years ago.

Grant fidgeted in his seat, got comfortable and pointed the car in the direction of the city. With the weather worsening, an hour's drive had just turned into two hours and he was definitely going to be late. Twenty minutes later, he was on the road heading west, the traffic nose-to-tail while he did his best to avoid being blinded by the rear fog lamps the idiot in front of him had switched on.

The traffic slowed to a crawl and he craned his neck, trying to peer over the vehicles in front of him, He saw the red and blue flashing lights of emergency vehicles and groaned. He glanced down as the phone began to ring in its cradle and flicked a switch on the steering wheel.

'Don't divorce me yet.'

A throaty chuckle emanated from the other end of the line. 'That bad?'

'I'm about forty minutes away, tops,' he lied.

'I thought as much.' A pause. 'I'll phone the restaurant and tell them we'll be there at eight o'clock, okay?'

'Sounds like a plan.' He checked his mirrors. 'I'll take the next exit. It's a bit of a diversion but at least I'll be on the move. I can't see this lot going anywhere fast.'

'Okay. Be safe.'

'Always. Love you.'

'Love you too. See you when you get here.'

Grant ended the call. Checking the mirror again, he indicated left and began to pull across to the left lane. Headlights flashed in his rear-view mirror. He squinted and angled his head so his eyes could adjust. He calculated the exit was only about two miles away and, sure enough, within a minute or so he passed a green sign pointing to the left. He started indicating half a mile before the slip-road began, easing himself out of the traffic and then edged the car down the ramp away from the dual carriageway.

The van behind him slipped into the wash from his tyres and followed him down the road. Glancing in the rear-view mirror, Grant smiled. Obviously someone else had had enough of the tailback.

As his car descended, he allowed it to pick up speed around a curving left-hand bend, and then slowed as he passed through the green traffic lights at the end of the slip-road. He steered the car across a right-hand turn and pulled up at a T-junction.

The force of the sudden impact from behind threw him forward, his body straining against the seatbelt. He blinked, shocked. Clutching the steering wheel tightly, he quickly corrected the car as it veered towards the middle of the road. The headlights behind him flashed once. He groaned, drove the car across the junction and pulled up on the opposite side of the road, cruising to a halt.

The road was deserted, and no traffic passed the two vehicles. A street lamp flickered above the Mercedes, its light shimmering across the wet tarmac.

Fantastic. He punched the steering wheel with the palms of his hands, put the car into 'park' and unclipped his seatbelt, his heart hammering between his ribs.

As long as the idiot's got insurance. Reaching down to the glove compartment he popped the lid open, took out a small notebook, then felt further under the dashboard and pulled out a ballpoint pen with the end chewed off. Closing the lid, he put his hand on the door handle.

He glanced in the wing mirror and froze. A silhouetted figure emerged from the other vehicle, a coat pulled up over its head, running towards his side of the car. Grant pressed the button to lower the window and blinked as rain blew in.

The figure slowed to a halt at the car door and bent down. In the bad light, Grant could just make out a bearded chin, a hood covering the upper part of the face, while rain cascaded down the figure's back. The man shouted over the noise of the storm.

'Sorry! My wife's at home – expecting our first. Tried to stop but the brakes seized up. You okay?'

Grant held out the notepad and pen. 'Give me your insurance details – I'll write mine down for you.'

The man nodded and opened his mouth to speak.

Without warning, the passenger door was wrenched open. Grant turned, astonished, as another man pushed the briefcase onto the floor and lunged for him. Grant yelled, pulled on the door handle, then felt an arm thread around his neck. He coughed, gasping for breath.

The man in the hood leaned further through the window and murmured in his ear. 'Don't struggle – you'll only make it worse.'

The other assailant held a syringe in his hand, the needle upright and primed.

Grant kicked his feet helplessly at the floor of the car, his toes clipping the throttle pedal. The man with the syringe grinned, his short cropped salt-and-pepper hair glinting in the low beam from the light above the car door.

Bile rising in his throat, Grant tried to prise the hooded man's grip away from his throat. The salt-and-pepper-haired man grabbed his wrist, yanked up the sleeve and plunged the needle into the vein in the exposed skin.

Grant opened his mouth to yell – fear, pain, frustration – and immediately the hooded man clamped a hand over his jaw, silencing him to a muffled cry.

The other man relaxed, sat back in the passenger seat of Grant's car and watched him, his eyes gleaming.

Grant's head started to spin, his heartbeat pounding in his ears gradually slowing, echoed by the rain drumming on the roof of the car. Black dots appeared before his eyes as the hooded man's grip slackened and he fell back into his seat.

A muffled voice. 'He'll be out in sixty seconds.'

Sixty seconds? What happens after sixty seconds? The drowsiness began to claim him. Grant blinked twice, fought to lift his chin from his chest, aware his head was drooping.

The man with the salt-and-pepper hair lifted Grant's briefcase out of the passenger footwell of the car, opened it and began sifting through the contents before he snapped it shut and shook his head at the other attacker.

'Nothing here. We'll take him with us. Let's go.'

Grant's body sagged as the car door was opened. The hooded man reached in and, checking over his shoulder for any unwanted witnesses, slowly began dragging Grant from the vehicle.

'No…,' Grant murmured. Dammit, what had they given him?

Before he passed out, he was lifted into the back of the vehicle and a blanket laid over his body. The musty aroma of oil assaulted his nostrils, while the hard steel floor of the vehicle dug into his spine.

Then darkness.

Chapter 1

Arizona, USA

Dan Taylor walked slowly across the parched earth. Dressed in a dark green Kevlar armoured jacket, with matching trousers and black lace-up boots, he paced towards a small malevolent object lying on the ground.

Across the barren plain, a late afternoon haze began to settle, liquefying the blue cloudless sky. In the distance the haze parted to reveal a long ridge of hills, scorched brown by the past summer's heat. A few scrubby trees broke the monotony of the landscape, providing rare shade among the parched grasses and dust.

As he approached the object, his pace slowed. Almost reverently, he walked carefully around the object in a clockwise direction, kicking small stones and pebbles away from it.

He stopped, appraising his work as a thin cloud of dust settled in his wake, and stared at the device which lay glinting in the sun's rays. A sigh escaped his lips as he waited for his heart rate to slow down from the fierce beating between his ribs. As it calmed, he carefully crouched down in the dirt, flexed his fingers and reached out to the explosive ordnance.

His eyes blinked rapidly behind the protective visor covering his face. A bead of sweat trickled down his forehead, threatening to run into his eyes, but taking off the visor and wiping his face wasn't an option. He shook his head slightly, flexed his bare fingers and re-focussed his attention on the device on the ground next to him.

Dan rocked back on his heels away from the object, unzipped a pocket on the front of his jacket, and extracted a small set of pliers. Re-zipping the pocket, he held the pliers up to his face, nodded, then bent back down until his eyes were level with the device.

He'd studied a similar object yesterday, only then it wasn't activated and had sat benignly on a work bench while he'd methodically stripped it apart and tried to unlock its secrets.

This time it was different.

He remembered what he'd learned yesterday, which wires could be safely cut, which wires had to be left alone. And how much explosive power lay hidden under the layers of metal.

Pushing aside any thoughts of what could happen, he reached out and gently slid the pliers over the dry packed earth towards the object. Usually, any bomb disposal team would use a specially-designed robot to neutralise a threat.

The problem was, some devices were placed where robots weren't an option.

Between the dirt and the shiny surface of the device, Dan saw a space, about a centimetre wide. A thin yellow wire protruded from the device, just visible to the naked eye. Pulling back the pliers, he crouched on his haunches for a few seconds, thinking. He then lowered himself onto the dirt, laying prone on the earth and wriggled forwards, reaching out with the pliers once more, his head tilted to one side.

Carefully, he applied pressure to the pliers, the claws slowly closing in on the yellow wire. As the teeth bit into the coloured plastic covering, he stopped breathing.

Above him, he could hear the distant roar of a jet engine as an airliner spewed contrails across the azure sky. He waited for it to pass, until the silence returned to the landscape and the only sound was his heartbeat echoing in his ears.

Another heartbeat, then he cut the wire. Breathing out slowly, he pulled the pliers back, his heart racing.

Suddenly, a high-pitched whine began emanating from within the object.

Dan's eyes opened wide. In one fluid motion, he stood up and began running away from the device as fast as he could, towards a piece of red tape which fluttered in the breeze between two fence posts.

In his mind he counted off the seconds – from habit rather than any knowledge of how much time he actually had.

It was going to be close.

Approaching the red taped-off area, he dropped to his knees and skidded under the temporary boundary, sliding into a shallow trench crudely dug into the earth just hours before, crouched down and burrowed his head in his arms.

The explosion rocked the landscape. The ground boiled and rolled upwards, lifting soil, shrubs, and rocks into the air. A small flock of crows scattered and squawked as dirt and fragments of stone fell back to earth, raining on his body, showering him in a layer of dust.

Then silence.

Dan slowly raised his head and looked over his shoulder. A thick dust cloud masked the area where he'd been crouched next to the device. Standing up, he scowled as fragments of dirt slipped under his collar and down the back of his neck. Dusting himself off, he swallowed as the ringing in his ears began to fade, and then turned around at a shout from behind him.

Two large white four-wheel drive vehicles parked a further hundred metres away framed a shaded area, a tarpaulin strung between them acting as a temporary respite from the bright winter sunlight. A swathe of red tape fluttered in a slight breeze, marking the outer perimeter of the temporary no-go area.

Dan began to walk towards the vehicles, awkwardly at first as he eased out the kinks in his limbs and wondered how many bruises he'd have the following day. As he approached the cordon, another man rounded the back of one of the four-wheel drive vehicles, tucking a mobile phone into the back pocket of his jeans, and then folded his arms, waiting.

'Nice work,' he said as the dusty figure approached him.

Dan removed his protective visor and frowned, running a hand through his brown hair which had grown long over the previous summer, compared with the buzz cut he'd preferred while in the British Army. He stopped and turned, looking at the ruined landscape behind him, a thread of smoke trailing into the blue sky above. He turned back to the man standing next to him.

'That,' he said, pointing over his shoulder at the smoking crater in the ground, 'is a very nasty piece of kit, Chris.'

The man next to him shaded his eyes with his right hand and nodded. 'Apparently they were found on a guy apprehended at a checkpoint on the Israeli border. Hezbollah of course...'

'Had the Israelis come across anything like this before?' asked Dan.

Chris shook his head. 'No, that's why they shared a few with us – and why we called you. Figured we'd work out how the hell to disarm them and test their capability to see what we're up against.'

Dan nodded. Since leaving the British Army after being injured in an IED blast in Iraq, he'd started to dedicate himself to learning everything he could about new terrorist weapons to make some sense of what had happened to him, and try to save someone from going through the same hell he'd lived through.

Although his nightmares had gradually faded, it took only a news report to flick the switch for him to have sleepless nights for weeks. Working as a consultant to the British Army and using his skills as an EOD operator, he found the work satisfying and cathartic.

For the past few months, he'd teamed up with Chris Lewis, an ex-SEALS munitions expert pensioned out of the US Navy following a training accident which had left him with two fingers missing from his left hand.

Dan turned and walked over to one of the four-wheel drive vehicles. Under the shade of the tarpaulin, he began to strip off the layers of Kevlar body armour.

Chris followed him into the makeshift tent, and helped him lift the heavy protective jacket over his head. Dan almost staggered with the effort. As Chris dumped the jacket on the ground, Dan pulled off his boots then wriggled out of the armoured trousers. Underneath, he wore blue jeans and a black polo shirt, both faded from years of wear. While Chris put the Kevlar body armour onto the back seat of one of the vehicles, Dan re-laced his boots, then strode over to a mini-refrigerator hooked up to a small generator and took out a soft drink. Popping the lid, he drained half the contents in three gulps, and then belched.

He put the can on top of the refrigerator. On the floor next to it, a tarpaulin spread out over the ground held a display of butchered metal, wires, and detonating devices.

Bending down, he pulled gloves over his hands, and retrieved one of the pieces of stripped parts. He turned it in his fingers, his blue eyes squinting at the parts, trying to work out how they'd been designed.

He turned and held it up to Chris. 'It's almost like a small limpet mine, but with a directional blast mechanism.'

Chris crouched down. 'How come the one we just detonated tore a fucking great crater in the General's paddock?'

'That's exactly what I'd like to know.'

Both men looked up as a shadow passed over them, and then stood and looked at the smouldering hole in the ground.

'Rogue one?' suggested Dan.

The newcomer rolled up the sleeves of his denim shirt, twitched the baseball cap on his head and scratched his ear. 'Some rogue.'

In his late sixties, General Bartholomew 'Bart' Collins retired from the US Army, bought acreage in the middle of Arizona and continued to fight terrorism in his own way, which provided both the US and British armies, and any consultants such as Dan, the opportunity to team up with other experts and pool their knowledge.

Dan looked over the General's shoulder and frowned. 'I didn't hear you pull up. Where's your truck?'

A deep rumbling snort from behind one of the vehicles pre-empted the General's response.

He smiled. 'I didn't buy a ranch so I could drive all day son. I was out for a ride – saw the explosion and thought

I'd better head over here to make sure you were both still in one piece.'

Dan turned, stretching his back, and looked at the General who was frowning at the crater.

'What are you thinking General?'

The older man turned. 'There are some very nasty bastards out there.' He shrugged, unhitched his horse from the four-wheel drive vehicle's bull bars and launched himself into the saddle with the agility of someone twenty years younger.

'Sorry about your paddock,' said Dan.

The man shrugged. 'Shit happens. I was going to plough it over this year anyway. You've saved me a job.' He glanced at his watch. 'You'd better clean up here and head back to the house before Wendy serves dinner.'

Adjusting the reins between his fingers, he looked down at Dan. 'I'll see you both in the study for drinks and a full debrief at eighteen hundred hours,' he said, and gave the horse a swift kick.

As the horse cantered off, Dan gave the General a casual salute, and turned back to the task of tidying up. He bent down and began to gather the pieces of the dismantled explosive device, folded away the notes he'd made, tucked them into his back pocket and then started to put each piece of the device into its own separate plastic bag.

Chris used a permanent marker pen to label each bag before placing them into a metal container the size of a large toolbox. Dan threw the last bag towards Chris, stood up, then pulled off his gloves, balled them up and threw them in the passenger footwell of the vehicle.

They pulled down the tarpaulin which had been providing shade all day, rolled it up, and stored it in the back of one of the vehicles. Finally, they bent down and tested the weight of the metal box.

Dan glanced up at Chris and nodded. 'On three.'

They carefully lifted the heavy box into the back of Dan's four-wheel drive vehicle, and pushed the door shut.

Dan ran his fingers through his damp hair, a bead of sweat trickling down his neck as he surveyed the test area, checking they'd picked up everything. 'I'll follow you out,' he said to Chris, who nodded and started the first vehicle.

Climbing into his vehicle, Dan threw the empty soft drink can and toolkit onto the passenger seat, swung the door shut and started the engine. He let it idle for a minute, rolled down his window, then swung the truck out onto the rough track and followed the cloud of dust behind Chris.

As he steered the truck along the narrow track towards the General's house he glanced over at the winter landscape. He was already tanned from spending the previous six months in the barren vastness of Arizona.

Despite its remoteness, the small town where he'd based himself was friendly enough.

Which was just as well, given he was staying in the only available guesthouse.

Chapter 2

Grant Swift opened his eyes. Darkness enveloped him. Blinking, he felt his right arm under his body and realised he was lying on his side. His shoulder hurt where his body weight had been rocking with the motion of the van. Shaking his head, he tried to clear the heavy sensation behind his eyes. The hood scratched his face, and when he brought his hands up to his head to try to remove the rough blindfold, he found his wrists had been bound tightly together, the weakened circulation deadening all feeling in his fingers.

His heart thumped in his chest as his mind devoured and tried to process what had happened. How long had he been unconscious? Where was he?

He strained his ears. He was travelling, the undulating rhythm of the vehicle broken by the occasional pothole, while his body swayed with the motion of each bend in the road. He recalled seeing a van parked behind his Mercedes – *how long ago?* – and then… and then…

Realising he had probably been bundled into the back of the vehicle, he blocked out the noise of the van's engine and concentrated on the sound of two voices coming from the front seats. Conversation appeared to be minimal but a radio played. A series of advertisements were on, the upbeat jingle of a large chain of clothing stores playing behind an excited voiceover. Shortly afterwards, the radio station's own jingle played before another top forty song began. Grant repeated the radio station jingle in his head. He recognised it, but couldn't quite remember where he'd been travelling to at the time.

He winced as he attempted to shift on the hard floor of the vehicle, and tried to sit up. He panicked, kicking out, his leg banging against something hard and metallic, which clanged loudly.

A voice from the front of the van carried over the drone of the engine and radio. 'He's coming round. How far is it?'

Another voice, muffled. 'Not long. Keep him quiet.'

Grant tensed. He could see nothing through the hood pulled over his head, but he sensed someone approaching, then smelt the man's foul body odour as he leaned over him.

'Please, no…,' whispered Grant.

Urine trickled between his legs, and he closed his eyes, embarrassed. The cold steel floor of the vehicle made his muscles and joints ache. He tried to shift position, get some circulation back into his legs curled under his body.

A hand clamped down on his shoulder. 'Be still.'

Grant whimpered as the man inserted another needle into his arm, and felt his world sinking beneath him.

***

As he floated in and out of consciousness, Grant had a sensation of being carried by two people – his head had rolled back, and he felt a firm grip on his wrists and ankles. He tried to lift his head. His throat was parched and he desperately needed to swallow, but his neck was at an awkward angle and he started to cough violently. A voice swore. The grip on his wrists tightened, and he heard a door being kicked open before he was hauled through the opening.

He turned his head left and right, trying to hear or smell something to tell him where he might be. He gasped as he was lowered to the ground. Cold tiles bore into his exposed skin where his shirt had come untucked from his suit trousers. From his left, he could hear a scuffling sound then the jangle of keys, before one was selected and he heard it being inserted into a lock. The lock turned with a soft squeak, and he heard another door being opened. A faint *click* – he guessed a light switch – then he was picked up once more.

He panicked and began to struggle as he felt a sensation of descending. Both of his captors cursed.

'For fuck's sake!' said the voice at the end of his feet.

Grant fell, his shoulders and knees taking the brunt of the wooden stair treads. Instinctively, he pulled his head and hands into his chest to protect them. He cried out as his left ankle bent awkwardly and the back of his head hit against a balustrade.

Then he was lying on his back, crying silently, while above him he could hear the chuckles of his captors.

'That had to hurt,' laughed one.

'The boss said no bruises,' chastised the other.

'Well it was his fucking fault.' The first voice had taken on a whining tone. 'We didn't do anything.'

A sigh. 'Let's take a look at the damage.'

Grant heard footsteps descending towards him. He cringed, turning away from the noise and eased himself up onto his hands and knees. He tried to stand up but his ankle gave way under his weight. He cried out as he crashed to the ground, his knees slapping against the hard stone floor. Again, he raised himself up and began crawling away from the voices.

'For fuck's sake! Stay still or you're going to end up head-butting the wall!'

A hand grabbed him by his shoulder and forced him to the ground. Suddenly, the sack was ripped off his head.

Grant blinked against the harsh light of a suspended light bulb swinging backwards and forwards from the ceiling above him. He turned his head to avoid the glare then gasped as his eyes met those of one of the attackers. A black mask now covered the man's face. Grant frowned, trying to recall the faces of the men who had attacked him in his car. Whatever drug they had forced into his system had blurred the details of the attack and he couldn't remember.

'Who the hell are you?' he croaked.

A snort emanated from behind the mask. The man turned and called up the stairs to the other. 'He'll live. A few scratches. Probably have a couple of bruises on his face by tomorrow but nothing too bad.'

'What about his ankle?'

Grant turned at the sound of the other man approaching and squinted up at him. He was shorter and skinnier than the first kidnapper.

Grant cried out as the man kicked his ankle.

'Can you move it?'

Grant tentatively turned his ankle left and right. 'It's sore. Twisted. Not broken,' he gasped.

'Good.'

The man bent down and flicked a knife in Grant's face.

'Don't!' he pleaded.

The man laughed, grabbed Grant's wrists and pulled the knife through the bindings, turned, pushed his colleague in front of him and began to walk up the stairs.

'Wait!' Grant crawled unsteadily to his feet, reaching out for the wall to balance. 'Who are you? Where am I?'

The larger man stopped and turned halfway up the stairs to face Grant. 'No questions.' He turned back and climbed the stairs.

Grant heard the door being slammed shut and locked. He blinked then turned and surveyed the room.

A thin mattress had been shoved up against the far wall, a pillow and blanket thrown haphazardly across it. Grant wandered over and picked up the blanket. It was covered in hair and smelled of dogs. He threw it down in disgust and glared at the stained pillow.

He scowled at the grey metal bucket which had been placed in one corner of the room, and noticed a bottle of water next to it. Bending down, he unscrewed the plastic cap and drank half the contents to quench his terrible thirst.

He re-capped the bottle and glanced up at the light bulb which swayed gently from the ceiling, then looked for its power source. He sighed and leaned against the wall in frustration. A light switch, rather than a pull cord. The kidnappers had thought of everything.

I can't even hang myself.

Grant lowered himself onto the edge of the mattress on the floor, and slowly began to rock backwards and forwards, his arms hugging his knees while he closed his eyes and tried to fathom what the hell he'd done wrong.

Chapter 3

Turning the glass in his hand, Dan savoured the bourbon aroma as ice cubes clinked against the crystal surface.

'Cheers,' said the General, holding his glass in the air.

'Cheers.' Taking a sip, Dan relished the taste as it burned his throat. He hardly drank following a long dependency on alcohol after Iraq, but when he did now, it was with the knowledge it was a pleasure not a crutch.

He looked up as the door to the living area opened and Chris walked through.

'Get over here, son,' said the General. He stood behind a bar built into a corner of the living area, filling a glass with more bourbon which he passed to Chris, who gratefully accepted it.

'Thanks, General.'

The General moved from behind the bar and walked across the large living area to a stone fireplace which dominated the far wall. He bent down, picked up a couple of small logs and tossed them into the grate, sending sparks flying up the chimney. Standing up, he grinned at Dan who was easing himself into one of the armchairs next to the fireplace. 'Arizona winters are fine during the day but they can turn damn cold at night.'

Dan smiled. 'I'd still take them over an English winter any time,' he said. He stared into the flames, mesmerised and calmed by the flickering light. He started slightly at movement out of the corner of his eye, then relaxed as the General's dog, a golden retriever by the name of Ripley, brushed against him and padded her way to a space on the hearth rug.

The General's voice broke his reverie. 'So – what do you make of those new IEDs?'

Dan shook his head and frowned. 'Too high tech to be thrown together by a backstreet bomb-maker,' he said. 'Looking at the one we dismantled, the parts are too well machined.'

Chris wandered over and flopped down onto an adjoining sofa. 'You're saying they're mass produced?'

'Not on the scale you're imagining, no,' said Dan, 'but certainly made in large quantities I would think.'

The General stood with his back to the fire, swirling his drink around in the glass. 'Is that what determines which ones are directional, and which are more destructive?'

'I'm not sure yet,' said Dan, who took a sip of his drink before continuing. 'We did notice the one we dismantled had a blue band around it. The one we armed and tried to neutralise this afternoon didn't. Whether that's the signature of two different bomb-makers, or a deliberate attempt to identify the clout of each – I think we'd have to take a look at that.'

He broke off as the living-room door opened and a willowy blonde walked in. She approached the General, and gave him a light kiss on the cheek before turning to the others.

'Hi, Dad – hey you two,' she grinned. 'We heard you from here this afternoon – Mom swore blind the kitchen window nearly fell out of its frame this time.'

'It wasn't that bad, Anna,' Dan smiled.

Chris laughed. 'So says the guy who had his head between his hands kissing dirt a nanosecond before it went off.'

'Really?' Anna's eyes opened wide with concern. 'You're okay?'

Dan nodded sagely. 'It's been a while since I've nearly been caught out, but yes, I'm okay.'

'Will you have nightmares?' Anna blurted out, and then blushed as she realised her error. 'I mean, sorry, but…'

Dan held up his hand. 'It's okay, don't worry. I hope not, but we'll see. Hopefully if I relax tonight, I'll be fine.'

Anna smiled awkwardly, her green eyes sad.

'Help yourself to a drink love,' said the General as he pushed her in the direction of the bar.

Dan watched Anna as she moved smoothly across the room. She was of average height, slim and moved easily, almost gliding across the space, and totally oblivious to the effect she was having on her father's visitors. Dan shook his head as he saw Chris grinning at him, and then glanced up as he saw the General wave his finger at him.

'Not a chance in hell,' growled the General. 'She finishes university first.'

Dan put his hand up in surrender and tried to look innocent. 'Don't know what you're talking about, General.'

He was saved by a familiar call through the house. 'Come and get it!'

'That woman,' said the General shaking his head, 'would have made an excellent colour sergeant.'

Dan drained his drink, stood up and stretched. Bending down, he scratched the dog behind its ears then followed the others towards the dining-room.

***

His stomach full after another enormous dinner cooked by the General's wife, Dan opened the back of the four-wheel drive vehicle and pulled the heavy metal box of dismembered bomb parts towards him. Chris took the handles at the other end, and between them they lowered it out of the vehicle to carry it across a wide yard towards a large barn with double doors.

One of the doors was already ajar. Dan and Chris slipped through the opening, breathing heavily with the weight of the metal container. They walked towards a low bench to one side of the barn, and lifted the box onto the surface.

Dan stretched his back and turned. The barn had once contained stabling for horses along its eastern side, whereas the western side had housed a tack room and office. Since the General had undertaken his new cause, the horses and tack had been moved out to new stables built on the other side of the main house half a mile away, and the barn converted into a large open workshop.

Along the sides, steel shelves had been built against the walls of the barn, their surfaces covered with metal parts, wires, and various boxes with labels on the front of them listing their contents. A floor-mounted rack system held an assortment of rifles, while near the door, several workbenches were laid out – including the one Dan and Chris were using to conduct their research into the new explosive device they'd been working on.

Two men sat at one of the other workbenches, each meticulously cleaning an assault rifle. As Chris made his way back to the house, Dan wandered over to the two men, nodded and sat down at one end of the table.

'More toys, Hatton?' he asked.

The older of the two men nodded, his grey-flecked hair glinting in the overhead lights. 'Yeah.'

Dan looked around the motley collection of guns on the table. 'How long were you out there for this time, Steve?'

The other man glanced up, his young age masked by the years of combat in his eyes, a look Dan himself was well aware of.

'Six months. Didn't get extended this time,' he said. 'Back for six weeks then I head off again.'

'Where exactly did you find this stuff?' asked Dan.

Hatton glanced quickly at the man next to him, and then back at Dan. 'Can't say.'

Dan grinned. He knew damn well the marines had a tendency to bring souvenirs back from their tours of duty, and the men in front of him were no different. He guessed a few of the rifles would end up in private collections.

He turned as another four-wheel drive vehicle slid to a halt in front of the barn, and Anna climbed out, running towards him. He stood up, frowning. 'What's wrong?'

'There's an urgent call for you,' she said, handing him a mobile phone. 'He wouldn't say who it was.'

Dan reached for the phone. 'Hello?'

'There's a plane at Phoenix waiting to bring you back to London,' said a familiar voice.

'What's going on?'

'I'll explain when you get here. What are you doing?'

'Working with General Collins.'

'Wrap it up, hand it over, do whatever you need to. Get here as fast as you can – you're now working for me,' David Ludlow barked. Now the head of a covert agency formed to protect the United Kingdom's energy security, he still behaved as he had when he was Dan's commanding officer in the British Army.

The phone went dead. Dan looked at it in the palm of his hand, his heart hammering in his chest.

Time to leave.

Chapter 4

Dan peered out of the small window in the fuselage as the Airbus A-380 dropped out of the holding pattern it had been in for the past twenty minutes to begin its final approach into Heathrow. Heavy grey cloud filled the air while large globs of water clung to the glass, streaking down it as the aircraft continued its descent.

He'd slept surprisingly well during the flight. The usual terror-inflicted nightmares brought on by his past as a bomb-disposal technician in the Middle East with the British Army had been kept at bay with careful use of the airline's free alcohol policy.

The cloud broke and he watched as the countryside passed beneath them. The aircraft lined up over the M4 motorway then followed the concrete expanse of the road to the outskirts of London before banking and lining up for the busy airport. A metallic scraping from below the fuselage emanated through Dan's seat as the under-carriage was lowered.

He closed his eyes, ignoring the grey skies. Thirteen hours ago, he'd been sitting in the air-conditioned confines of Phoenix airport, waiting for his flight to be called.

The aircraft shivered as it passed through a last-minute air pocket, the turbulence bumping it over the change in wind direction. The pilot made a correction to the aircraft's descent then lowered it to the runway. A slight bump, a roar as the reverse thrust fought with the wing flaps to slow the aircraft, and they were down.

Dan loosened his watch, shook it off his wrist and adjusted the time. Eight o'clock on a bitter Thursday morning in one of the most over-crowded cities in the world.

Fighting his way through the crowds in the arrivals lounge, Dan grabbed his old kit bag from the carousel, walked through Customs and out to the taxi rank. He jumped back as a black diplomatic car drew up to the kerb next to him.

The back window wound down and a familiar face peered out. 'Put your bag in the trunk. I'll be shot at dawn if you get mud on these seats,' said David Ludlow, and wound up the window.

Dan grinned. He threw the bag in the trunk and opened the back door, sliding in next to David. The car eased away from the kerb and powered through the traffic.

Dan turned to face his erstwhile superior. 'Is the department providing a free taxi service now?' he asked.

'You wish,' said David. 'I'm on my way to a briefing with the new Minister for Energy. Figured I'd bring you up to speed on the way so you can hit the ground running. We haven't got a minute to lose.' He pulled a briefcase from the opposite seat onto his lap. Flicking the two brass catches, he opened the case and reached in, taking out two manila files.

'Okay, what have you got?' asked Dan. He stifled a yawn, and rubbed the rough stubble which covered his face after the long journey.

'We've got two problems,' began David. 'First, you and Mitch are joining me at a Committee hearing with the Prime Minister behind closed doors tomorrow morning to explain what happened last time we worked together.'

'Committee hearing? Sounds serious.'

'It is. Both the Prime Minister's office and the Ministry of Defence are demanding reassurances from me that I know what I'm doing and why we didn't alert them there was a bomb heading their way.'

'Would they have believed us?'

David shrugged. 'Notwithstanding the fact we had to move fast and couldn't afford to wait for them to make up their minds whether to believe us, or sign however many pieces of paper to get us the sort of back-up we'd have needed for an assault on a ship at sea, we are accountable for our actions.'

'Hell of a thing to come home to.'

'I realise that, but you're going to have to help me explain why a civilian – you – became involved in the first place. Otherwise, I'm not going to be able to use you to help me investigate the other issues I'm dealing with.'

Dan stared out the window. Sleet dashed the glass surface. Pedestrians hurried along wet footpaths, their umbrellas buffeted in the bitter wind that whipped through the city streets. Grey clouds cast a darkness over the capital, and Dan immediately wished he was back under the winter sun in Arizona. He blinked and turned his head to stare at the tinted glass that separated them from the vehicle's driver. 'What's the second problem?'

David was silent as he looked out the car window. He drummed his fingers on the leather upholstery, lost in thought, before he spoke. 'One of the Government's key advisors on the latest North Kent coast LNG expansion project has gone missing.'

'When?'

'Last night. The man's a genius apparently, and forgetful at the best of times according to his wife, but the fact she spoke with him less than two hours before he was due to meet her at a restaurant for their wedding anniversary raised concerns.'

'She reported it to the police?'

David nodded. 'This morning. The news filtered through a couple of Government agencies before it reached us. It's recorded as low priority as a matter of precedent in the event he does turn up based on his past habits, but we're keeping an eye on the situation just in case.'

Dan looked across at the other man. 'If you're going to be put out of action by a Government Committee tomorrow, why are you pursuing this? Don't you want to wait and see what happens? You could end up having to hand your investigation over to someone else.'

'I'm well aware of that – but my concern is the longer the investigation isn't pursued, any potential adversary of ours is further ahead. I'd rather carry on regardless, as they say.'

'Has anyone seen a ransom note?'

David shook his head. 'Not yet, which is why I want you to attend a gala tomorrow night that the British Trade Commission is throwing to coincide with this week's energy conference, in case the engineer's disappearance *is* linked to the project. I want you to keep your ears open, find facts and give me some leads. I've got a team of analysts who are geniuses when it comes to looking at financial records, intelligence communiqués and the rest, but I need someone on the ground who can read people and quickly assess situations. You'll be there in a support role to the security detail for one of the Qatari Sheiks who's in talks with the British Government, so it'll give you a chance to wander around the place. Don't draw attention to yourself. Just watch and listen, then report back to me.'

'What's the energy conference about?'

'It's the annual World Petroleum Conference – last year's was held in Houston. Given this country's own gas fields are nearly extinguished, the Government felt that it would be a good idea to put together a bid to hold this year's event here in London. We're already buying a lot of gas from places like Qatar so it's an opportunity to strengthen those ties with a view to signing a new gas contract within the next two weeks.'

'Who are we watching?'

'A Qatari national by the name of Sheik Masoud Al-Shahiri. Iran is trying to muscle in on some of Qatar's long-standing gas contracts and the Qataris are politely trying to ignore them. It's really a case of making sure the Qataris aren't bullied out of continuing their supply contracts with the UK. It'd be an absolute disaster for foreign policy if we lost them and had to start from scratch with Iran. Can you imagine what the Americans would say?'

Dan laughed, despite the seriousness of what David was saying. 'That'd be an interesting phone call.' Pausing, he glanced out the window. 'What are you expecting the Iranians to do?'

'Since their embassy in London was closed down a few years ago, they've been relegated to a section of the Omani embassy. The Government here limits how long each delegation can stay, but the Iranians are always looking for opportunities to ruffle some feathers while they're here.' He pointed to the briefcase. 'In there is a briefing paper about the Sheik's background, as well as some photographs.'

Dan opened the case, fanning through the pages of information inside. 'Are the delegates expected at the conference?'

'No. We've banned them from attending the gala but I'm sure they'll find a way to use it to whine about the latest UN sanctions against them.'

"So, if you've got a security detail crawling over the place, why do you need me?'

David sighed. 'Because it's the same old story,' he said. 'The firm in charge tomorrow night was the cheapest bidder, so it won the contract. None of its personnel have ever done any proper close protection training or have any of your expertise. There's one bloke who spent some time working for a news team in Libya, but that's it. The rest have done so-called training courses and think they know the job.'

Dan shook his head. 'And of course their clients think they're in safe hands.'

David nodded. 'That's why I want you there. The Sheik has brought some of his own security people but the contractors will be running the show. The guy they've put in charge is an idiot but I can't shift him. I can however put someone in there to keep an eye on him.'

'You mean I'm babysitting the operation?'

David frowned. 'You're babysitting their client. Anything that happens to the contractor's team isn't our concern.' He peered out of the car window, and used the sleeve of his woollen coat to rub the condensation off the glass.

'What about transport?'

'It will depend on the outcome of the Committee hearing. If we're still operational after tomorrow morning, we'll give you a car. If you need to travel out of the country, let my assistant Philippa know so she can organise passports and make the necessary arrangements. You need to phone me daily to keep me updated on your progress as the Prime Minister expects the same from me.'

David leaned forward in his seat and banged his fist on the glass between them and the driver. The driver nodded and steered the car to the left, pulling up at the kerb.

'This is where you get out,' he said. 'Your accommodation is about half a mile from here.'

Dan looked out of the window. The road was a four-lane street with avenues leading from it, lined with three-storey Georgian terraced houses, their doors opening directly onto the footpath. He turned to David, who held out a set of keys.

'Number thirty-four Eaton Terrace is a safe house we sometimes use. There's a secure line connected, a small office – you've got exclusive use of it for the duration of this investigation. The pass code for the door is your birthday. Change it after you enter the building. Put these documents in the safe once you've finished reading them. Make sure you're at the Select Committee hearing an hour before the press is due to arrive so we can avoid a scene.' He reached into his coat and drew out a plain manila envelope which he handed to Dan. 'Your credentials for the conference centre tomorrow night are in there. Mitch will be in touch – Philippa sorted out his travel arrangements so I don't know when he's going to get here.

I want you two to work together to find out what's going on.'

Dan grinned. Mitch Frazer was another member of the bomb disposal team he and David had belonged to during the British operations in Iraq at the turn of the century, and another acolyte in David's shadowy new world of politics and espionage.

'Just like old times then.' He took the key. 'Who stayed there last?'

David shook his head. 'Can't say. He didn't stay long – he insisted on moving to a friend's house south of the river. He left that one in body bags.'

Dan raised his eyebrow. 'Plural?'

David nodded. 'Plural. Housekeeping said it was a bitch to clean. Needless to say, we arranged for that property to be sold. I think some sort of retired rock musician lives there now.' He shrugged.

Dan shook his head in disbelief, took the briefcase and climbed out, collecting his kit bag from the trunk. As he slammed the lid shut, the car sped off and flashed its brake lights as it turned left, away to Downing Street.

Dan scanned the street for any signs of trouble. He pulled up the collar of his jacket and walked away from the kerb, head down against the sleet, his eyes flicking left to right as he searched for anything that seemed out of place. He walked quietly, listening for the sound of footsteps behind him.

At the end of the street, he turned into the avenue and repeated the exercise. He passed the house and continued to the end of the street before he stopped and leaned against the wall of a large square brick Georgian building on the corner. He glanced back up the street, then to his left towards the main road.

A bus splashed past, Dan catching a glimpse of only three passengers on the lower level of the red double-decked vehicle. The inside of the windows were steamed up, with the people inside mere shadows.

He turned and began a slow walk back to the house.

'Home sweet home,' he muttered, jogged up the concrete steps to the front door of the house, turned the key and punched in his security number.

Chapter 5

Closing the front door behind him, Dan heard the locking mechanism click back into place, and began to explore his new temporary home.

The building was three storeys high, typically Georgian in design, with a basement sectioned off from the street outside by heavy wrought iron bars. Hitting a light switch to the left-hand side of the front door, Dan glanced around at his immediate surroundings. The hallway and lower level of the house had been decorated in neutral tones with carpeted floors. A staircase to the right of the hallway led up to the next storey.

To the right of the front door, he found a large study with a mahogany desk, a leather chair each side of it, and a window that faced out to the street. Net curtains provided privacy from the street. Dan strode over to the window, glanced out, then pulled the thick velvet curtains closed and turned to face the room. A laptop computer and printer sat on the desk. He noticed a modem near the wall behind the desk, its red light blinking in anticipation. A three-seat sofa stretched along one wall, facing a fireplace, while the back wall housed a large bookshelf that bowed slightly in the middle from the weight of the books lining its shelves.

He smiled when he saw the painting that hung slightly skewed above the fireplace. It depicted a nineteenth-century early morning hunting scene on the Berkshire Downs, with the Uffington White Horse rising up in the distance. Wandering over to it, Dan pulled out the painting slightly from the wall and was rewarded with a smooth *click*. The painting gave way, swinging aside to reveal a wall safe.

Dan grinned. He'd save that for later once he'd had a chance to read through the files David had given him to read.

Easing the painting back into place, he stepped out of the room and across the hall. Pushing open the next door, he discovered a dining area which opened out at the back of the room and moulded perfectly into a large kitchen which took up the back of the house. In the far corner, a solid door led out into a back yard, while a large centre island contained a gas hob and food preparation area. The kitchen sink and a dishwasher lined part of the back wall under a window with its blinds already closed to the back yard.

Turning back to the hallway, Dan bent down to pick up his kit bag, and began to climb the stairs to the first floor. At the top of the stairs, an open doorway on the right led through to a lounge area which encompassed the whole side of the building. A large plasma television and entertainment system stretched along one wall, with a sofa and two large armchairs opposite. A window looked out over the back yard. Dan pulled the blinds down across the front and back windows and wandered back out on to the landing. On the opposite side of the house, he found a bathroom and bedroom. He continued up the stairs to the top storey and located the master bedroom at the front of the house, with its own bathroom and a walk-in wardrobe. Dan grinned and threw his kit bag on the bed. Mitch could have the bedroom on the lower level.

Opposite the master bedroom were two more bedrooms, sparsely decorated compared with the rest of the house. He pulled the doors closed and returned to his room to unpack.

After putting his clothes into the enormous walk-in wardrobe, Dan kicked his kit bag out of sight under the king-size bed and wandered over to the bay window that wrapped its way around the room. He pulled back the net curtains and glanced each way along the street below. The grey sky was fading to black over the horizon and the buildings opposite cast shadows across the street. Doorways and entrances to alleyways provided perfect cover for a resourceful watcher, but after five minutes, Dan couldn't spot anyone who appeared to be anything other than the normal neighbours he'd expect in such a street.

He let the net curtain drop back into place, pulled the blinds shut, then remembered he had planned to investigate the contents of the basement. He jogged down the stairs and, not seeing a door in the hallway, retraced his footsteps to the kitchen. He glanced around until he saw what he was looking for.

He wandered over to the far wall and opened up a floor-to-ceiling cupboard door. He was slightly surprised to see a steel door blocking his way.

A combination lock stuck out from the surface of the door, a green digital display blinking in the twilight of the cupboard space. Dan typed in his birth date. The digital display flashed twice before the locking mechanism released with a *hiss*. Dan held down two buttons until the system requested a new password from him. He typed it in quickly, hit the 'set' button, and used the kitchen pedal bin to prop open the door. After he pulled a cord just inside the doorway, the area illuminated to reveal steps to the basement.

Descending the steps, Dan looked around in amazement. The room covered the area of the house above, the nearest wall containing a series of thin metal drawers.

Striding over to them, he pressed a button on the right-hand side of a drawer, and stepped back as it slipped smoothly out of the wall cavity. Inside, a display of handguns lay in a foam lining. Dan smiled, picked up a Sig Sauer, turned around and sighted it across the length of the room.

He swallowed, lowered the gun and walked towards the opposite wall. Closed circuit television monitors set into the nearest wall blinked sporadically, as their images swept through the property and the exterior.

Dan found the controls and experimented with the camera settings, soon finding two which could only have been concealed in street lamps at either end of the avenue.

Satisfied, he turned back to the armoury and searched through the drawers until he found the Sig's magazines. Slipping one into the gun and a spare into his back pocket, he climbed the stairs, pushing the gun into the back of his jeans. Reaching the top of the stairs, he closed the door and checked his watch.

Time to recce the venue.

Chapter 6

As the taxi drew up to the kerb, Dan leaned forward and handed the driver the fare.

'Keep the change,' he said, and opened the door.

He'd arranged for the driver to stop a couple of blocks away from the hotel being used for the conference and where the next evening's gala event was to be held to walk the perimeter and get a feel for what was taking place around him, before stepping into the mayhem of a full security detail and introducing himself to the man in charge.

A faint mist swirled across the footpath as he walked along the street, remnant of the late afternoon storm of rain and sleet which had cleared the smog from the city air. He sniffed, the faint stink of the river reaching his senses.

He took one last look up at the buildings which surrounded the square before he stepped off the kerb and began to walk across the cobblestones towards the security cordon.

A group of protesters had pushed their way to the edge of the temporary fencing and were hanging placards and hand-painted signs over the barrier. He could vaguely hear some sort of chanting emanating from the group. As he walked closer, he could read the signs.

'Free Iran. Stop the Sanctions.'

He approached one of the suited security guards and held his identity card up. After having his credentials checked, Dan put the card back in his pocket, glanced along the length of the cordon, and then back at the security guard.

'Who's in charge?'

The man nodded over his shoulder, careful not to dislodge his earpiece. 'Over there. Goes by the name of Mike Browning.'

Dan thanked him and ducked under the security rope strung between two metal posts. He walked up to the man the guard had pointed out who had his back to Dan, talking to one of the other plain clothed security detail.

Dressed in a dark suit like the others, he had broad shoulders and severe close-cropped silver grey hair. Slightly shorter than Dan, the man looked heavy-set but deceptively light on his feet. He sensed Dan approaching and turned as he drew level with him.

Dan didn't wait to be asked. He extended his hand. 'Dan Taylor – David Ludlow suggested I contact you.'

The man took the proffered hand. His grip was strong and he squeezed Dan's hand hard. Dan ignored the manoeuvre and held the man's gaze until he spoke.

'Browning.' He gestured towards the doors of the complex. 'Step in here where we can talk in private.'

Dan followed the other man as he stalked along the red carpet laid out for guests and pushed his way through the mahogany-framed glass double doors into the lobby. He caught the door and scowled as Browning let it fall back in his face.

He followed Browning through the lobby, down a darkly painted narrow corridor into a small office. As Browning entered the office, he clicked his fingers at three security guards who sat at a desk, monitoring the hotel's closed circuit television screens.

'Out.'

The security guards jumped up and quickly left the room, the last closing the door behind him.

Dan shook his head slightly in disbelief as Browning made a show of stalking around the room, seemingly collecting his thoughts while the closed-circuit camera screens continued to blink.

Browning suddenly stopped pacing, bent down next to a desk in the corner and picked up a black canvas bag. He unzipped it and pulled out an earpiece and radio microphone set. He turned to Dan and thrust the equipment at him. 'Before you get any ideas, you're here as an observer and that's it. I'm in charge. You don't even take a shit tomorrow night without asking me first, is that clear?'

'Clear,' Dan replied as he fitted the earpiece and tapped the microphone to test the volume on the pack. 'Anything else, or can I go now?'

Browning snorted. 'Just remember, I'm watching you.' He put two fingers to his eyes then used them to point at Dan, who turned to leave the room.

'Wouldn't want you to get nightmares from working tomorrow night,' said Browning. He sneered. 'Although London is a bit more cultured than the Middle East.'

Dan turned back towards the other man and in two strides had his face in front of the head of security, his blue eyes blazing. 'At least I was there, arsehole.'

Browning pushed Dan away. 'Piss off. You might be here because you're the current favourite but stay out of the way of my operation.'

Dan glared at him, and then walked out of the office, slamming the door behind him.

One of the security guards who had been looking at the video screens before being ejected from the room leaned against the opposite wall of the corridor. He grinned at Dan.

'Bit of a tosser, isn't he?'

'Putting it mildly,' said Dan, and wandered back into the lobby.

Ignoring the hotel staff hurrying through the rooms around him, Dan began to make his way through the building, starting with the lower levels.

Opening a door marked with a fire exit sign, he walked quickly down the steps, pushed open another door, and found himself in the hotel's underground car park.

On two levels, the concrete basement structure spiralled under the hotel. Dan guessed it would house over one hundred cars at full capacity, but noted as he walked through the empty bays that Browning's team had cleared all vehicles from the area to eliminate the risk of any potential bomb threats.

Dan wandered across to the entry and exit barriers and found two security guards with semi-automatic rifles held up to their chests, one facing the car park, the other scanning the small lane at the rear of the hotel. He nodded an acknowledgement to them as he flashed his identity card and stepped out into the lane.

Craning his neck upwards, he scanned the buildings opposite the hotel as he walked the perimeter. He reached into his pocket, pulled out a small notebook and pen and began to write.

At the rear of the hotel, he found a narrow alleyway. He glanced up, saw the barrel of a rifle pointing over the side and held up his hand in salute. The gesture was returned, and he continued along the alleyway, turning his head left and right as he walked.

The exterior reconnaissance complete, Dan spent the next two hours walking through the hotel kitchen, conference rooms and six levels of plush accommodation, noting that none of the rooms were occupied – another threat averted.

Satisfied with his tour of the building, he returned to the ground floor and knocked on the door of the hotel's CCTV suite. Browning was nowhere to be seen, and the security guard who opened the door gestured to Dan to take a seat in one of the spare chairs pushed up against the wall.

'How did you get on?' he asked.

'Not bad,' said Dan. 'Do you mind if I ask a few questions to help get my bearings before tomorrow night?'

'Fire away.'

'Have you got the schematics of the hotel and the building next door?'

The security guard stood up and reached behind the CCTV monitors, pulling out a large roll of paper. He unravelled it and handed it to Dan, who put it on the floor in front of him and crouched down. He flattened the edges of the paper with his palms and ran his hands over the plan.

'What security have you got next door?' he asked.

'Two on the door, two on the roof,' said the security guard. 'It's a private residence of eight apartments. The residents have been compensated for parking elsewhere for the next forty-eight hours.'

'Good. I'd like to see another two of your men on the ground level though. Keep the garage doors locked and have them run regular checks between the garage and the basement.' He tapped the plan. 'We don't want anyone blowing a hole through the basement there into this one.'

The security guard nodded. 'Not a problem.'

Dan frowned and pulled the hotel schematic closer. 'What's the depth of this sewer drain?'

The security guard knelt down. 'According to the hotel manager, that's an old one and it's blocked between the entrance to the car park and fifty metres past the hotel here.' He stabbed the page with his finger. 'During the hotel renovations five years ago, the construction team filled it with rocks and earth.'

'Do you have a guest list?' said Dan, leaning forward and rolling up the plans.

'Hang on.' The guard turned towards a table strewn with paper and passed a document to him.

'Thanks. What about staff members?'

'Here somewhere.' The security guard took the plans from Dan, tossed them onto the table, then rummaged around until he found what he was looking for. 'There it is.'

'Can I keep these?'

'Sure.'

'Any last minute changes?'

'No – if anyone goes sick or missing between now and the gala, the hotel manager is under strict instructions not to replace them.'

'Good.' Dan folded up the pages and put them in his pocket, then glanced at his notes. 'You'll need more than one man on the roof,' he said. 'The fire exits on the rear of the building are great for us to use if the shit hits the fan, but could be used in an attack after a fast rope descent.'

The security guard glanced over his shoulder at his colleague, then back at Dan. 'That might be a problem,' he said. 'We're at maximum capacity now. I don't know if the company has any more personnel available.'

Dan snapped his notebook shut and turned to leave. 'Then you'd better hope we don't have a problem tomorrow night,' he said.

***

After taking a convoluted route back to the safe house which involved two underground stations and a bus stop, followed by a half mile walk, Dan shut the front door behind him and switched on the light. It flickered once then illuminated the long narrow hallway that stretched through to the back of the house.

He followed its path to the back door, checked the deadbolts as well as the thin cotton thread he'd pulled from his shirt hem and placed in the jamb. It didn't hurt to have an early warning system in place which didn't rely on the numerous electronics that ran the building.

Satisfied, he turned to walk back to the front of the house when he detected a faint *thud* on the floor above him.

Steadying himself, he put a hand on the wall next to him and carefully removed his shoes, placing them on the floor. He drew his gun out from under his jacket and held it tightly while he shifted along the hallway to the base of the staircase.

The staircase was marble, with a thick carpet lining the middle, allowing little chance of a creaking stair tread to give him away. Dan inched close to the wall near the first tread and cautiously peered upwards, straining his ears. From the second floor landing, he could hear faint voices. He frowned. He couldn't remember leaving the television on.

He flattened himself against the wall and began a slow, steady climb up the curving staircase, keeping his gun in a two-handed grip facing upwards in front of him. As he climbed, his eyes kept searching the flight of stairs above him, looking for a sign of the intruder.

Thud.

He froze. Forcing his heart rate down, he breathed slowly and deeply through his nose. He counted to ten and resumed climbing.

As he approached the top of the first flight of stairs he dropped to a crouching position and crawled up towards the landing. The sound of the television was clearer now.

Dan glanced around, reminding himself of his surroundings. He peered in the direction of the bedrooms and saw only darkness. A glow emanated from the living area as the television images illuminated the ceiling and walls of the room.

He stood up and inched across the carpet, pushing his back against the wall. He crept closer to the doorway to the living area. He breathed out slowly, willing his heart rate down.

Suddenly, there was a loud *creak* as someone got up off of one of the heavily padded armchairs.

Dan looked around the passageway. There was nowhere to hide. He stepped back and raised the gun in front of him as a shadow fell on the open door of the living room.

'Freeze!' Dan yelled as the figure appeared.

The man dropped the empty beer can in his hand to the floor and turned around slowly to face Dan, his hands in the air above him.

'Jesus Christ, I nearly shit myself!' Mitch Frazer lowered his hands and glared at Dan. 'What the hell were you trying to do – give me a heart attack?'

Dan lowered the weapon carefully, pushed the sweat out of his eyes, and glared at Mitch.

'How the hell did you get in here?'

Mitch bent down to pick up the beer can rolling around on the carpet. 'I've got my own password, you idiot.'

Dan shook his head. He leaned against the wall to steady his shaking legs. 'Jesus, that was too close.'

'Tell me about it,' said Mitch. He held up the empty tin can and grinned. 'Do you want a beer?' he asked.

Dan glanced at him, wearily rubbed his hand over his face and nodded.

'Yes. Hell yes.'

Chapter 7

Dan looked up as he and Mitch approached the Victorian buildings, his eyes gazing over the red brick edifices topped with elaborate gargoyles and tall chimneys.

'Feels like being back at Oxford,' he murmured.

Mitch grinned. 'Just don't pull any of the pranks you said you used to. We might not leave.'

David looked over his shoulder at them and frowned. 'One day perhaps, you two might just grow up.' He turned and continued to stalk across the gravel path.

They entered the furthest side of the quadrant and stopped in front of a large double door, its worn oak panelling weathered from years of exposure to the elements. David stopped and turned to face Dan.

'You need to be aware if this goes wrong, you and I will be facing trial and prosecution. Keep to the facts, don't let your emotions get involved, and we might just be okay.' He turned back to the door and knocked.

Dan noticed the security cameras above the door moving from side to side, appraising the small group on the steps. Whoever monitored the camera feed seemed satisfied and a few moments later there was a *click* before the door swung inwards.

A security guard, his gun at the ready, stood in the doorway glaring at them. 'Security passes,' he said.

The three men handed over their passes and fell silent as the documents were inspected. After a short period, the guard handed back their passes and stood to one side, pushing the door open for them to enter.

'There are cameras throughout the building,' the guard said. 'Don't go anywhere you're not authorised to. We'll be watching you.'

David glanced at Dan and Mitch. 'This way,' he said and, turning, headed across a wide hallway and up a broad wooden staircase.

The stairs wound round back and over the hallway they had just entered, curving towards the left and right of the building. David hurried left at the top of the stairs and, without checking Dan and Mitch were keeping up, strode through a doorway into the bowels of the building. A long wood panelled corridor stretched before them, their footsteps muted by a crimson plush carpet dappled by the grey light streaming through a series of high windows set into the left of the walls.

As they walked past, Dan glanced through the windows to the quadrangle below. Four civil servants scurried across the courtyard, clutching documents to their chests with one hand while desperately trying to flatten hairstyles back into place against the vicious wind.

David stopped at an oak panelled door and turned to Dan and Mitch.

'Best behaviour, okay?'

Dan nodded.

'Let's do it,' said Mitch, grimacing as he straightened his tie. 'Before this thing chokes me.'

David rapped twice on the door. There was movement behind it, and then it swung inwards. A tall man dressed in a grey suit, blue shirt, and contrasting tie stood before them, absent-mindedly running his fingers through his grey-flecked light brown hair, then stood aside to let David in.

'Glad you could make it,' the man said, and turned back into the room.

David followed him, Dan and Mitch on his heels.

Dan could feel his heart pounding in his chest. He didn't often feel nervous around people, but he was growing more and more aware how desperate their situation was becoming. He forced himself to unclench his fists and concentrate on what was being said.

The man moved to a conference table set in the middle of the room, which had eight seats around it. Two were already taken. A cup and saucer at the head of the table suggested the Prime Minister had already settled into his anointed place before David's team arrived.

As Mitch closed the door behind him, the men began to drift back to their places. The man flicked his hand towards the spare seats, indicating to Dan, David and Mitch they should join the group.

While they settled into their chairs, the man who had opened the door made the introductions.

'Gentlemen, we know who you are but let me formally introduce you to the Prime Minister, Mr Edward Hamilton. To his right, we have Vice-Admiral George Moore, Second Sea Lord to the British Navy. My name is Hugh Porchester and I'm the Secretary of State for Defence's representative,' the man finished.

The Vice-Admiral was the first to stand and offer his hand to David, then Dan and Mitch. He was tall, a little over sixty, and wide enough to suggest he'd spent time in his youth as a rugby player.

Dan sat down after shaking hands with the Prime Minister, who held his gaze a fraction of a second too long, as if trying to fathom the man in front of him.

All the time, the Defence representative ignored the three men and busied himself with the documentation he had laid out on the desk between them.

The Prime Minister turned to him. 'Hugh – why don't you start the proceedings?'

The man nodded courteously at the Prime Minister, leaned forward and flipped open a leather binder on the desk in front of him. He cleared his throat then glanced up at the three men who sat opposite him.

'Gentlemen,' he began pompously, 'the Prime Minister has called this meeting so Mr Ludlow can help us, shall we say, *fill in some gaps*, in relation to a bomb scare a while back in the city and explain how two members of the public, namely you Mr Taylor,' he turned his gaze to Dan, 'and Mr Frazer became involved.' He glared at Mitch before looking down at the contents of the leather binder and removing a series of photographs, which he threw on the table.

Dan ignored them.

The Defence Secretary's representative then pulled a large ring binder towards him, opened it up to a section about three-quarters of the way down, folded his hands over the page, and looked up at Dan.

'Now, Mr Taylor,' said Porchester. 'Perhaps you could enlighten us as to how you managed to get yourself entangled in this mess.'

Dan cleared his throat, and stared at the man. 'A friend of mine was killed. His ex-wife asked me to help her investigate as she didn't feel the police were seriously looking into the possibility her husband had been murdered. Instead, it was made to look like he took his own life. We followed his research notes and it led to us being contacted by Mr Ludlow.'

Porchester looked down at the file in front of him, saying nothing. He flicked the pages back and forth before clearing his throat and looking up at Dan once more.

'Were you forced to work for Mr Ludlow?'

'No.'

'So you, a civilian, were quite happy to put yourself in danger, not knowing the consequences of your actions?' asked Porchester.

'It was the right thing to do,' said Dan. 'There was a madman with a bomb and no-one else in your Government seemed to give a rat's arse at the time. In fact, I seem to remember one of your colleagues was, in fact, assisting him.'

Porchester quickly looked down at the page in front of him. He reached out for the glass of water in front of him, took a delicate sip and placed the glass back on the table.

Dan waited, his heart pounding in his chest. Not from fear, but sheer anger and frustration he and his colleagues were being questioned in such a way. He met Porchester's gaze when the man finally looked up again from his notes.

'How are the nightmares?'

Dan blinked. 'What?' The question was unexpected and threw him for a second. 'Fine. Why?'

'Well,' said Porchester, leaning forward in his seat, 'we have to look at the fact that a mentally disturbed person was left to dismantle a bomb.'

Dan stood up, his chair falling backwards. He leaned over the desk towards the other man, who visibly shrank in his chair.

'Now you listen to me you bastard,' he snarled. 'I served this country proudly and I don't need you trying to second-guess what the consequences of my experience in Iraq had on me. I don't need your sympathy and I don't need your back-handed accusations. Just because you completely missed the opportunity to get your name in lights because you were too busy scratching your arse to wonder how a weapon heading your way got missed by your department, don't blame me. I did what I had to. I'd do it again.'

Dan turned around, picked up the chair and set it straight. He caught David's glance as he sat back down and folded his arms in front of his chest. He glared at Porchester, who was trying to appear unflustered by Dan's outburst and busied himself with his documents and files. Dan glanced down and noticed the man's hands were shaking. He smiled inwardly but continued to glare at Porchester.

The Prime Minister coughed. 'Perhaps, gentlemen, we should take a short break.'

There were murmurs of agreement around the table.

'Excellent – we'll meet back here in fifteen minutes. Mr Ludlow – perhaps I could have a brief word with you in private before you leave?'

Dan pushed his chair away and stood up. Mitch grabbed his arm and propelled him out the door, then didn't let go until they were halfway down the corridor. They stopped at one of the windows which overlooked the quadrant below.

Mitch ran his hand over his eyes. 'That went well.'

Dan shook his head as he watched the people below scurry back and forth.

'They're a bunch of idiots,' said Mitch. 'Instead of congratulating you and David on a job well done, they're going to hang you out to dry, aren't they?'

Chapter 8

Hassan Nazari straightened his blue silk tie, pulled his pale grey suit jacket sleeves down over pristine white cotton cuffs, and turned to look at his profile in the full-length mirror.

He raised his right hand, flattened his jet black hair, noting the grey highlights, then smiled, perfect teeth glinting through a neatly trimmed beard. His eyes travelled down his reflection. When his gaze reached his shoes, he grimaced inwardly. To him, the uplifts in the soles appeared too high. Too obvious. He shrugged, gave himself a reassuring smile, then turned and held out his hand. A briefcase was handed to him, his assistant avoiding direct eye contact.

'Is it all here? The original lease agreements for the farmhouse as well?'

'Yes sir.' The assistant bowed slightly and moved to the side.

Nazari looked at the two large men dressed in black suits who stood guard in the hotel suite – one just inside the door, the other to one side of the large window that provided a birds-eye view of the city. They were the only two people on his staff taller than him. Broad-shouldered, calm, imposing, wearing matching suits and black gloves – and carrying nine millimetre guns. On paper, they were noted as bodyguards, though often their job description stretched a little further than the title suggested.

'Are you both clear on what you have to do? Mustapha?'

The man at the door looked Nazari in the eye and simply nodded. Nazari turned to the man standing next to the window, and raised his eyebrow. 'Ali?'

'Yes sir.'

'Then let us proceed.' He tested the weight of the briefcase in his hand, strode across the room, and handed it to the man next to the window. 'Ali, take this.' He then watched as the bodyguard pulled a cloth from the inside pocket of his jacket and began to wipe all traces of Nazari's fingerprints from the briefcase.

Hassan turned to a man hovering nervously on the periphery of the room and beckoned him closer. 'Ibrahim, come here,' he commanded.

The man licked his lips, and took a couple of paces nearer to Hassan. A bead of sweat pooled on his forehead, which he wiped away as his eyes flickered over the gun in Mustapha's grip. In his late thirties, his cheap suit jacket was creased. He pushed the sleeves up his arms before running his hand through his dark brown hair. Unfastening the top button of his shirt, he kept his distance from Hassan, who noticed the odour of fear emanating from the other man, and smiled.

'It is alright Ibrahim, there is nothing to be scared of,' he soothed. Reaching out, he put his fingers around the man's arm, failing to notice Ibrahim's top lip curl up slightly in distaste.

'In our business,' continued Hassan, 'there is very little room for error, misjudgement, or,' he said, turning to glare at the assistant, 'treachery.'

'Treachery?' Ibrahim asked. 'When?'

Hassan watched the assistant wither under his stare and nodded to himself. 'Yes, treachery,' he whispered. He turned to Ibrahim. 'You would never betray us, brother, would you?'

Ibrahim shook his head and blinked.

'Good, good.' Hassan smiled tightly. 'We are too far along in our plans to stomach failure or a change of heart. Unfortunately, my assistant here does not show your faith or tenacity.' He beckoned to the second of the two bodyguards. 'Mustapha, if you please.'

The man stepped away from the door, an uninterested expression on his face. He calmly reached into his jacket, put away his gun, and pulled out a long piece of coiled wire. He slowly began to wind it around his fingers, twisting it methodically as he walked towards Hassan's assistant.

Hassan walked across to the window and gazed out at the cityscape below. He raised his eyes to the sky, noting the grey-yellow clouds which threatened snowfall before the afternoon was over, closed his eyes and inhaled deeply.

'Sir? Mr Nazari?' The assistant finally spoke. 'Is there a problem?' He turned, trying to face Mustapha, his eyes wide.

Mustapha, who was easily four inches taller than the assistant, quickly slipped his hands over the man's head and pulled the two ends of the looped wire together.

The assistant's hands flew to his neck, his eyes bulging while he tried to work his fingers under the wire which held him. A thin, reedy, choking sound escaped from his lips. Blood gushed from between his lips as he bit through his tongue, tears rolling down his cheeks.

Ibrahim closed his eyes and turned his head, trying to block out the sound of the other man slowly choking to death.

Mustapha's biceps twitched, the wire tightened once more and the assistant's head fell forward.

'No problem,' smiled Nazari as his assistant's body slumped to the floor. 'Not any more, at least.' He looked at Mustapha, who was slowly re-coiling the wire. 'Make sure you tidy up.'

Mustapha nodded, tucked the wire into his pocket and beckoned to the second bodyguard.

'Come,' said Hassan and led a sweating Ibrahim past Ali, who was fanning out a black plastic sheet on the floor, rolling the assistant's body onto it. They stepped out of the room and into an adjoining suite. 'Let them clean up in peace.'

He shut the door behind them and sat down on one of the pristine white three-seater chairs, before signalling Ibrahim should sit opposite. While the other man lowered himself onto the chair, Hassan smiled to himself, elegantly crossed one leg over the other and relaxed into the upholstery.

'Now,' he said, and watched Ibrahim as he sat down and perched nervously on the edge of the chair, his arms resting on his knees. 'Let us talk about *you*.'

***

As Dan and Mitch filed back into the conference room and sat down, Dan caught the Secretary of State for Defence's representative staring at him, and did his best to avoid the man's gaze. Instead, he leaned forward and reached out for a glass of water, ignoring his heart thumping between his ribs.

As the men settled around the table, the Prime Minister raised his hand and indicated to Porchester to begin taking notes.

'Mr Taylor, it seems you were caught up in events beyond your control,' the Prime Minister began. 'However, the fact remains you were *very* lucky in that instance.'

Dan risked a glance at the Prime Minister and forced himself to breathe slowly. He bowed his head, began to fold his arms across his chest, then thought better of it and placed his palms on the table in front of him.

'Upon discussing the evidence in front of me, and taking into consideration the account of Mr Ludlow, and the advice from the Secretary of State for Defence and the Vice-Admiral, I am unfortunately left to conclude that prosecution would be deemed appropriate in the circumstances.'

Dan stared at the Prime Minister. His mouth went dry and the sound of his heart echoed in his ears. His hands slipped from the table into his lap as he swallowed, fighting down bile.

The Prime Minister sifted through the documents in front of him. 'It seems you acted recklessly at times, often with little regard for the people around you in your relentless pursuit of the explosive device.' The Prime Minister sighed and leaned back in his seat, watching Dan.

'However,' he said, 'it does seem incredibly unfair to pursue such a course of action against someone with a prior service record like yours, who averted a terrorist threat against this country. I am therefore left with one other choice.'

Dan held his breath.

The Prime Minister leaned forward. 'After further discussion with the other members of this Committee, I have decided to grant you a reprieve.'

Dan breathed out, his relief echoed on the faces of David and Mitch.

'There are conditions to this reprieve,' said the Prime Minister, glancing at Porchester and the Vice-Admiral, who were both nodding in agreement. 'I understand from Mr Ludlow that you are currently required to assist him in assessing a potential threat against our Qatari colleagues.' He paused and glanced at David.

'In the circumstances, your reprieve is conditional upon completing these investigations to a satisfactory conclusion and ensuring the possibility of any imminent threat to this country is effectively eliminated.'

Dan nodded. 'Yes sir.'

The Prime Minister held up a warning finger. 'If you fail to prevent such an attack, the reprieve will be rescinded immediately – do I make myself clear?'

Dan swallowed. 'Yes sir.'

David waited until the murmurs around the table settled, then turned to the Prime Minister. 'Sir, if I may be so bold – we do have some pressing issues to work on. Perhaps you could let me have my orders?'

Dan frowned and glanced sideways at David.

The Prime Minister appeared to suppress a smile before speaking. 'Certainly, David.' He turned to the men sitting either side of him. 'Actually gentlemen, this meeting was convened to serve *two* purposes. Firstly to provide clarification with regard to the last terrorist threat, which was,' he nodded at David, 'successfully thwarted by the hasty actions of Mr Ludlow's team. Secondly, having spoken to both the heads of MI6 and MI5, and the new Minister for Energy, the British Government wishes to build upon that success and provide funding to you, David, to develop the proposal you brought to me some months ago.'

Porchester frowned and leaned forward on the desk. 'Excuse me, Prime Minister, but *what* proposal?'

The Prime Minister smiled. 'David – perhaps you'd like to elaborate for the benefit of the Committee?'

David nodded. 'After our last result,' he said, 'I was able to convince my superiors that a new agency was worthy of funding. After all, we proved the United Kingdom's energy assets are a major security concern – both from a natural depletion of resources, but also by threats from individuals, organisations and, potentially, other countries.'

'Because our operations last time were almost compromised by a leak within the Ministry, outwardly we've been disbanded. Redundancies, people moved out to other agencies – you get the picture. I was then given the task of rebuilding the group – handpicking individuals I could trust. We plan to move our headquarters out of the city centre and away from Government influence. We've distanced ourselves completely from the Prime Minister's office. Occasionally I'll brief him, but I'll do that under the auspices of an expert reporting alongside MI5 or MI6 – acting as an advisor to them.'

'Black ops,' murmured Dan.

David shook his head. 'Not quite, but close. On an 'as needed' basis. Yes, we will have people in deep cover, but selectively. Often they'll tend to try to influence behaviour, rather than constantly reporting to us, for us to then take action. Not all those people will be employed by the agency as staff either – we'll bring in people best suited to address the tasks at hand as consultants. And they'll be fully culpable for their actions.'

'What's the designation of this new team?' asked the Admiral.

'The what?' Porchester frowned.

'Its name,' said David, 'has already been assigned by the Prime Minister. It's the Energy Protection Group. Suitably innocuous, gentlemen, don't you think?'

Dan glanced up and looked at the expressions on the other men's faces.

Porchester began to bluster. 'But... Prime Minister... you can't just create a new agency using ex-military personnel and members of the public!'

The Prime Minister smiled. 'Of course I can. It's exactly how SOE, MI5 and MI6 were created. A gap in our intelligence capabilities was realised and the necessary funding appropriated to plug that gap. Mr Ludlow's team has already proven it reacts quickly to situations and, without having to wait for a Parliamentary Committee to approve everything it does, it will be able to better serve this country.'

'However,' he said, looking at Dan and Mitch. 'I'll remind you that if you fail to obey orders and subsequently fail to prevent an attack on this country, you *will* be held fully accountable. No Committee hearing next time.'

'Agreed,' said David, and stood up before Dan could interrupt. 'So, gentlemen – if you'll excuse us,' he signalled to Dan and Mitch to stand, 'we'll get back to work.' He shook hands with the Prime Minister who was smiling broadly, turned to the Vice-Admiral, nodded at him, winked at Porchester, and left the room with Dan and Mitch in tow.

'Holy shit,' said Mitch under his breath as they left the room. 'We're under fire from all sides.'

Dan smiled. 'Never let it be said that it's boring around me.'

Chapter 9

Dan stood at ease, a comfortable pose not easily forgotten, but perhaps slightly out of place wearing a three-piece suit and standing in the reception area of a five-star hotel in Mayfair.

His eyes scanned the reception area as he waited. The polished grey slate floor reflected light from the chandeliers above, while four receptionists worked behind the granite reception desk, answering telephones and talking to guests in hushed, practised tones, their black uniforms set off by coloured ties in the hotel group's signature green.

Opposite the wrap-around reception desk, two sets of black leather sofas were grouped around low glass-topped coffee tables, a water jug set on each, four glasses turned upside down at its base. Beyond, double panelled doors were propped open, the distinct *clink* of crystal glasses emanating from the innards of the dimly lit hotel bar.

Dan watched a couple of businessmen enter the bar, the elder of the two slapping the younger man on the back and laughing as they disappeared from view. He turned his attention back to the lift doors, and glanced up at the arrows pointing up and down above each. The left-hand side was showing a 'down' arrow. He waited.

Presently, there was a soft musical note as the lift finished its descent, and the doors slid smoothly open.

A slight pause preceded a stocky, well-dressed man of Middle Eastern origin, whose eyes swept the room then fell on Dan. The man turned back to the lift, nodded once, and led his employer out into the lobby, followed by a second bodyguard.

Dan drew himself up to his full height. Sheik Masoud Al-Shahiri was not an overly tall man himself, but the sort who demanded respect. His perfectly coiffed hair was jet black, all traces of grey wiped away, while he carried himself with the amused demeanour of the quietly confident, super-rich influential tycoon his reputation supported. As he drew closer, Dan noticed Al-Shahiri's eyes never stopped moving and instead, they constantly switched from one side of the room to the other.

Dan suppressed a smirk. Either the man didn't trust the capabilities of his own security detail or he was simply keeping a watchful eye out for the next business opportunity.

As he approached, Al-Shahiri appeared to relax a little. He stood and looked at Dan, which meant he had to raise his chin a little. A small scar on the man's chin, no longer than a centimetre, echoed the old path of a knifepoint.

Al-Shahiri smiled ruefully before he spoke, a soft resonant voice which carried well without volume. 'So Mr Taylor, you're my security's security tonight?' he asked.

'That's correct, sir,' replied Dan.

'Hmm.' Al-Shahiri glanced away, raised his hand and signalled to his two bodyguards to distance themselves from the ensuing conversation. He turned back to Dan. 'Let us sit.'

Dan pointed to the sofas against the furthest wall and indicated to the Sheik to take the one with its back to the lobby. He waited until the man had made himself comfortable, and then sat opposite him, still watching the lobby and the exits.

The Sheik smiled. 'Good, good. I can see you haven't forgotten your training.'

Dan arched an eyebrow. 'Unlike some practising in the field of personal protection, mine's a little more ingrained.' He leaned forward, picked up a water jug from the glass table between them, and poured two glasses of water, pushing one towards the Sheik.

The Sheik laughed. 'And not afraid to speak your mind. Excellent. David said we'd get on.'

Dan frowned. 'I'm not here to be your friend. Someone somewhere thinks you're in enough trouble that you need more than your usual security around you tonight. And given my Government has a vested interest in your latest gas project, you don't get a choice in the matter.' He nodded in the direction of the two bodyguards standing a little way from the Sheik and glaring at anyone who glanced in his direction. 'How long have those two been with you?'

The Sheik glanced up sharply. 'Since they were teenagers. I do not suspect people in my own household of plotting against me, Mr Taylor.'

'Why ever not? Surely in your line of work, everyone could be a threat?'

The other man shrugged. 'Simply because these men's families depend on their allegiance to me.' He stared unblinking at Dan.

'So where do *you* think a threat will come from?'

The Sheik impatiently waved a hand across his face. 'Business. Always business. Some people just don't know when to stop, when to – what is the saying?'

'Quit while they're ahead.'

'Exactly. Exactly. Always more, more, more.' He sighed, oblivious to the irony of his comments. 'My country is entering the biggest phase of expanding our natural gas exports. We're pouring billions of dollars into projects where our business partners will make extensive profits over the next twenty years.' He shrugged. 'As you will appreciate, there are some who want to ruin us, to teach us a lesson for dealing so openly with the West. There are others who simply want some of our business for themselves.' He sighed. 'Throw in a handful of the usual crazy people and there you go – take your pick of suspects.'

'Any specific threats recently?'

The Sheik waved his hands dismissively. 'What you British call sabre-rattling, that's all,' he spat. 'Comments to the press, opinions on regional television news, the internet. Trivial matters.'

Dan looked around the hotel lobby, watching guests and staff moving around as he listened. 'Have your men recce'd the venue today?'

The Sheik looked over his shoulder and beckoned one of his men over. 'The venue – was it satisfactory?'

The man glanced at the Sheik, straightened up and looked at Dan. 'There are two main entrances. One open to the public, the other is a side access for caterers and waiting staff. There is a small car park underneath the building which we sealed off after all staff vehicles were accounted for. The entrance to that is at the back of the building and we have two men stationed at the barrier. We'll have four men with His Highness at all times.'

As the man finished, the Sheik waved him away, then glanced at Dan. 'Well?'

Dan shrugged. 'Not bad. But he missed the possibility of an attack from the roof. I've advised them to increase the number of men there, as well as on the building next door. I don't believe Browning's done a complete check of the guest list or what other bodyguards might be present.' He reached slowly into the inside pocket of his jacket to not alarm the Sheik's bodyguards and drew out a folded A4 piece of paper. He held it up between two fingers to show the security men, before he slid it across the table to the Sheik. 'These are my recommendations.'

The Sheik frowned, leaned forward and picked up the piece of paper. He unfolded it, read it, folded it back up and held it over his shoulder to one of the bodyguards. When the Sheik looked back at Dan, his eyes were sparkling with amusement.

'You are very good,' he laughed, shaking his finger at Dan. 'Very good.'

Dan leaned forward and slammed his hand on the glass surface of the coffee table, making the empty glasses jump against the water jug with a loud crash. Immediately, the Sheik's two security men were by his side. Dan ignored them, and glared at Al-Shahiri.

'This isn't a game,' he said. 'It might be for you, but there are going to be people there tonight, myself included, who are expected to defend you with their lives if something goes wrong. It would *help* therefore if you could start to take this a little more seriously.'

Silence surrounded the table. The Sheik looked across at Dan and stroked his moustache, apparently deep in thought. Finally, he leaned forward, managed to look a little contrite, and smiled. 'Shall we be on our way?'

The Sheik stood up and turned to leave the lobby, flanked by his two bodyguards.

Dan lingered on the leather sofa, collected his thoughts, shook his head then stood up.

The Sheik glanced over his shoulder to the nearest bodyguard. 'Make sure those notes are distributed to the rest of the team and have them briefed immediately.'

While the group walked through the lobby and out to the waiting cars, Dan allowed himself a small smile.

Chapter 10

Ras Laffan gas facility, Qatar

Rashid Nasour yawned as his hand automatically reached for the mug of coffee to the right of his workstation.

The screens in front of him flickered, two showing live video links to the busy liquid natural gas port glowing under overhead floodlights, the other two displaying the supervisory control and data acquisition programme Rashid and his team used to operate the ebb and flow of the enormous gas production and export facility on the edge of the Qatari empire.

He scowled as the liquid touched his lips, noting the office coffee tasted bad enough when first poured, let alone when it had grown cold. He glared at the viscous liquid at the bottom of the mug, cursed and pushed his chair back, one of the wheels squeaking audibly. He grunted to himself, bemoaning the fact he worked at a multi-billion dollar facility and still had to put up with a squeaky chair. He ambled across the office to the small kitchen provided for the employees. As he walked, lights turned on automatically – all part of the state-of-the-art offices the organisation had built to house the control centre for the export facility. He finished making the coffee and took a tentative sip. It still tasted lousy.

He wandered over to the large floor-to-ceiling window which served as an observation deck for the office workers. A few chairs were scattered around the floor space directly next to the window, offering an opportunity for the control teams to sit and watch the activity below during their meal breaks. Rashid pulled one of the chairs closer to the window and sat down, cradling the mug between his hands.

He scanned the sea out beyond the port. Two large natural breakwaters acted as filters for the enormous LNG tankers which entered the approach channel leading to the port. He could see a tanker coming into the port, its bulk sitting high in the water while its storage tanks remained empty.

Rashid lifted the coffee mug to his mouth and blew gently across the surface of the liquid, then stood and wandered back to his workstation, letting his gaze fall back to the computer monitors. The screens flickered with a constant stream of measurements and data, issuing reports from each of the LNG processing plants as natural gas entered the facility, became super-cooled, then pumped out through a series of jetties to the LNG tankers ready to transport the volatile cargo to Qatar's clients throughout the world.

He leaned back in his chair, scratched his ear and looked up at the display of CCTV screens which covered the wall above his desk.

He jumped as a hand grasped his shoulder.

'Relax, Rashid, it's only me.'

Rashid turned in his chair as a man in his early twenties threw himself down in the chair next to his and began to log into the system.

'I swear you're going to give me a heart attack one day, Adil,' Rashid growled.

The young engineer laughed. 'You're old, but not that old.'

'Where the hell have you been anyway? Your shift started an hour ago.'

'I overslept. You won't tell?' Adil glanced at the older man.

'If you get caught, it won't be because of me. But I won't lie for you if you're caught.'

'You're lucky I made it in at all.'

'Was she worth it?'

Adil laughed. 'Yes. If her father catches me though, I'm a dead man.'

'If *your* father catches you, you're a dead man.' Rashid shook his head.

Adil glanced at his computer as it went through its start-up routine, then bent down and picked up the carry bag tucked under Rashid's desk and tested the weight. 'What did Shareen cook us for supper tonight?'

'Nothing for you,' said Rashid. 'Not even leftovers.' He smiled and turned back to the CCTV screens.

'It's not fair you know,' complained Adil. 'She always gives you far too much.' He gently shook the bag before putting it back under the desk. 'All my mum gives me is…'

'Not now.' Rashid held up a hand and frowned, looking back at the screens. Each one flicked spasmodically in turn, and then settled as if nothing had happened.

'What was that?' asked Adil, getting out of his chair and standing behind his colleague.

'I'm not sure.' Rashid reached out and moved the computer mouse slowly across his control screen. The pointer juddered as he moved it from left to right, the cursor moving backwards for every forward movement Rashid made. He lifted his hand off the mouse and both men watched in amazement as the cursor travelled backwards across the screen.

The screen displayed a schematic of the gas facility – a working drawing of the parts and systems which enabled the Qataris to super-cool the gas into its liquid state then pump it onto the waiting ships.

Rashid rolled up his sleeves, inched his chair closer to the desk and began typing a string of commands. He hit the 'enter' button and sat back, satisfied.

He blinked.

Adil gasped as the text started to disappear.

Rashid glanced down at the keyboard – nothing touched the 'delete' or 'backspace' buttons. He looked up at the screen and watched in amazement as the mouse pointer began to click on a set of valves within the pumping system, repeatedly turning them on and off in rapid succession.

'What is this?' asked Adil, his hands gripping the back of Rashid's chair. 'What's going on?'

Rashid shook his head. 'I'm not sure.' He looked up at the other man. 'Who's working in the main control centre tonight?'

Adil leaned across the desk and picked up a clipboard with a roster sheet attached to it. He checked his watch, then glanced down the page. 'Here you go – Samir's up there.'

Rashid leaned forward and picked up the phone. It rang twice before being picked up, the man at the other end breathless. 'Yes?'

'Are you doing this?' asked Rashid.

'No! What's going on?'

'I'm coming up.' Rashid put down the phone and turned to Adil. 'Come on – let's go.'

Both men ran to the stairs leading up to the next level, Rashid clearing them two at a time. As he rounded the top stair, Samir came running towards him. 'Whoever it is has changed the automated settings for the vapour return arms on the jetty,' he said, his breath labouring. 'If the valves keep getting turned on and off, they're going to fail and we won't be able to stop the gas flow.'

Rashid pushed past him and ran to the man's desk. He pulled up the view of the controls data and read through the strings of information in disbelief.

Samir and Adil stood either side of his chair, their eyes searching the data for clues.

'We've been hacked,' said Rashid. He turned to Samir. 'Get onto Engineering and IT – tell them what's happening.'

The other man nodded, moved away to another desk and began making phone calls. Adil looked down at Rashid and pulled out his mobile phone. 'I'll get on to Operations at the jetty. They might not be seeing this at their workstations.'

Rashid nodded, and glanced out the window behind them. His eyes opened wide. 'You had better hurry – look!'

Adil followed his gaze and watched as the large LNG carrier eased itself against the jetty. The ship's enormous bulk towered over the facility, its lights ablaze as it slowed to a halt.

Rashid gave the younger man a hard shove. 'Make that call – they can't start pumping gas into that ship until we've sorted this out.'

Adil nodded and sat down at the desk next to Rashid. He prayed someone would soon pick up the phone at the other end, knowing it was only a matter of moments before the highly pressurised liquid gas began to pump into the ship. 'Rashid – no-one's answering!'

'Here,' Rashid leaned over and typed a command using the keyboard next to Adil. He pointed at the screen as it burst into life. 'Take over from them – you can use the controls here and do it.'

Adil nodded and began typing in the data, strings of information flashing across the screen as he typed.

'*What*?!'

There was a crash from beside him and Adil looked aghast as he turned to see Rashid standing up at his desk, his chair over on its side behind him. The man gripped the desk with both hands, his knuckles white as he stared up at the screens. Adil followed his gaze.

On the CCTV monitors, the LNG ship listed heavily to its port side, tipping slowly towards the jetty it was moored alongside.

Chapter 11

Grant screamed as the hammer fell onto his outstretched fingers.

'The code,' hissed the man at his ear. 'Tell us the code.'

Grant took a deep shuddering breath. 'I can't!' he said. 'I can't remember!'

He strained at the bindings which held his arms securely to the wooden chair, kicked at the ropes which bound his ankles to the frame, then vomited onto the floor when he saw the remains of the little finger on his right hand.

The man glanced up at his colleague, who was breathing heavily through his black mask, his eyes wide.

'Do it again.'

'No!' Grant twisted on the chair, trying to move his hands away from the fall of the hammer.

His scream echoed off the walls of the basement, cutting through the dank air.

'Please,' he whimpered. 'No more. I can't…'

His head fell forward, a sigh escaping his lips.

The man next to him straightened, grabbed a fistful of Grant's hair and tipped his head back.

'Shit. He's fainted.'

He turned, reached down for a bottle next to his feet and tipped the contents over Grant's face.

The engineer spluttered, opened his eyes and coughed violently, his head falling across his chest as he brought up the water that had assaulted his lungs.

The other man rolled his sleeve back, glanced at his watch, and raised the hammer once more.

'We're running out of time.'

'Hold on.'

The man next to Grant crouched down. 'Hey. Grant.' He patted the engineer's face, forcing the man to focus. 'Don't pass out on me. What's the code? That's all we need, Grant. The code. Tell me.'

Grant's head fell forward, a sob choking his voice. 'I can't remember. The drugs – I can't focus.'

'Maybe this will help.' The man stood up, took the hammer from his colleague and waved it in Grant's face.

The engineer started to hyperventilate, his eyes wide. 'Please, no…'

The man smiled as he tossed the hammer from one hand to the other. 'Come on, Grant. They don't pay you *that* much. Tell us the code.'

Grant frowned, then lowered his head, his mind racing. What *was* the code? Why couldn't he remember?

'I'm waiting, Grant.' The man's soft voice burrowed into Grant's brain, turning his bowels to liquid.

'Christ.' The man stepped back as Grant shit himself, the stink filling the small underground room.

Tears streamed down the engineer's face. 'I can't remember!' he sobbed. 'Whatever you gave me – I can't remember!'

The man tested the weight of the hammer in his hand, stepped around the chair and pulled Grant's hand free of its bindings.

'Try harder,' he said, and swung the hammer down.

***

'Something hit it!' Rashid continued to stare at the screens in shock.

'What do you mean something hit it?' demanded Adil. 'There's nothing else near it!'

Rashid frowned. 'Something definitely hit it – I saw it! The tanker moved, like… like it was *shoved* or something..!'

He broke off suddenly. 'Quickly, quickly!' he said, waving a hand at Adil. 'Shut down the outbound pipes so no gas goes out to that jetty!' He pulled his chair upright and sat down, wiping his forehead with his hands.

Adil began typing in keystrokes, all his graduate training jumbling in his mind as he tried to recall their emergency drills at the facility.

'We've already got gas travelling through that pipe, Rashid! What do I do?'

Rashid pulled his own keyboard towards him and began typing furiously. 'We'll redirect it, loop it round to the overflow pipeline and send it back into the facility.' He pointed at the telephone on the desk between them. 'Call them now. Warn them it's coming back their way.'

Rashid glanced up at the computer monitors and gasped in disbelief as another string of data appeared across the screen. The cursor stopped at the end of the line of text, blinking ominously.

He read the data string, his mind automatically translating what the hacker had typed, then began typing in a counteractive command. He shook his head in frustration as the hacker started to delete the text as fast as he could type in the commands.

'Rashid – hurry! The gas is flowing already!' urged Adil, his hands gripping the desk.

'Phone the processing plant – tell them to stop it – *now*!'

Adil nodded, picked up the phone and hammered in the four digit number for the processing plant, his hands shaking.

Both men glanced up as Samir ran towards them. 'IT are onto it – they say it's definitely a virus in the system,' he said.

'It doesn't matter now,' said Rashid and pulled Adil's keyboard towards him. 'We're going to have to try the emergency procedure.'

Adil frowned. 'That hasn't been tested under stress yet,' he said, the phone to his ear. 'Are you sure?'

'Have you got a better idea?' Rashid opened up a programme on the computer's desktop and typed in a user name and password. As the programme window opened, he quickly scrolled across to a red button on the screen which simply said *FIRE*.

He glanced at Adil, who nodded, then depressed the button.

The schematic on the screen flickered, and a white box appeared on the screen, a red line tracking across its length, timing the progress of the new anti-virus programme.

'Come on!' urged Rashid. His eyes remained glued to the red line, his heart beating so hard in his chest it made him feel sick.

The red line reached the end of its progress bar, the white box disappeared from the screen, and the schematic appeared once more.

Rashid tentatively moved the mouse across the screen, anticipating the hacker's return.

Nothing.

He watched the command screen for the new software, its red *FIRE* button blinking calmly on and off. Rashid glanced up at the CCTV screens above their computer monitors. Alarms howled through the facility, their urgency echoed in Adil's voice as he spoke to the people in the processing plant. His heart hammered in his chest and, as he removed his fingers from the keyboard, he noticed his hands were shaking. He blinked as a bead of sweat ran from his forehead, the sound of alarms from the jetty carrying through the facility as emergency crews began pouring over the stricken ship.

Wiping his eyes, he looked at Adil, shook his head and glanced at the new software displayed on the monitor which he'd launched on the system just in time.

'That was close. That was way too close.'

Adil frowned and pointed at the CCTV monitors. 'We still have a huge problem down there.'

Rashid followed his gaze and saw the collapsed jetty, fires spreading around the stricken ship's hull while the facility's fire and rescue crews helped people from the deck. A helicopter hovered above the wreckage using its searchlight to help find crew who had dived into the deep water of the port.

He shook his head in disbelief. 'We're going to be out of action for weeks.'

Chapter 12

Dan shielded his eyes from the bright lights exploding from the camera flashes as the limousines cruised to a smooth halt. He glanced over at the Sheik's bodyguards and nodded. One exited the car away from the cameras, peering up at buildings then scanning the crowd for any sign of threat towards his employer. He was joined by the other men from the first vehicle who walked to the media side of the car, glared at the photographers, and then eased the car door open.

Dan slid across the leather seat and held up his hand to the Sheik. 'After me.'

He eased his large frame out of the car and raised himself up to his full height, seeking out potential threats. He turned, slowly, peering over the roof of the car. His eyes rested on one of the bodyguards who nodded in return, before they each returned to their observations of the surrounding area.

Satisfied, Dan leaned down, rested one arm over the top of the car door and spoke quietly to the bodyguard sitting next to the Sheik.

'Now. Quickly.'

He turned his attention to the Sheik and looked him in the eye. 'No stopping. You can talk to whoever you want once you're safely inside.'

The Sheik pursed his lips, displeased, but nodded in agreement.

Dan straightened up, beckoned the bodyguards towards him and indicated they should form a barrier between the press and their employer.

As the Sheik stepped out of the car, there was an almost perceptible surge forward by the photographers, all trying to capture the elusive perfect shot.

Dan glared at the photographers nearest to him and concentrated on ushering the Sheik forward and through the doors of the conference centre. It was only a few metres between the car and their destination, but to Dan, it felt like a marathon. His heart racing, he felt the responsibility for the other man's life on him like a weight, slowing him down.

Finally, they reached the double doors of the building. Dan used his shoulder to push open the doors before the concierge could do so, and stood holding them open for the Sheik, flanked by the four men protecting each side of him as he swept past.

The man at the rear turned and faced the photographers as the doors swung shut behind them and held up his hand. *Enough.*

Dan breathed out, the cacophony of the international press corp replaced with the bedlam of a party in full swing. He got his bearings, nodded to a familiar face working security for the venue, and watched the Sheik and his retinue as the crowd parted before them.

He wandered over to the bar, ordered a soda water and turned, leaning back against the wooden surface as he sipped his drink. Although he'd only been ordered to provide back up to the security team, years of training meant he wouldn't relax until the Sheik was safely back at his hotel.

As the room filled, Dan glanced to his right, catching a movement in the crowd, and spotted a waiter making his way towards the Sheik.

Dressed in the hotel uniform comprising a dark suit, white shirt, and red tie, he was of average height, with brown hair and dark brown eyes. He held a tray of drinks in his hands, a mixture of alcohol and fruit juices to suit the differing tastes or religious tendencies of the eclectic crowd.

As he drew nearer the Sheik, Dan noticed the waiter was sweating, his eyes darting around the room as he walked. His gaze fell momentarily on Dan, and then he looked away, back at the Sheik.

Dan frowned and eased himself away from the bar, his heart starting to beat faster. He edged closer to the Sheik, keeping a respectable distance between the man and his entourage, but making sure he slipped into the natural perimeter the Sheik's bodyguards had adopted.

The waiter approached the Sheik, glancing at the nearest bodyguard as he did so, then began to offer drinks to the Sheik and his guests.

A woman moved into Dan's line of vision. He side-stepped to his right, and saw the waiter holding out a smart phone to the Sheik.

'There is a phone call for you sir,' he murmured, bowing slightly.

The Sheik excused himself from his guests and reached out for the phone.

'No!' Dan pushed past the bodyguards and an overweight man in a grey suit. 'I'll take that,' he ordered.

The Sheik's head turned at the interruption.

The waiter's face fell, a look of shock in his eyes, the phone still held out to the Sheik's wavering hand.

Dan snatched it away and put it to his ear. 'Who is this?' he demanded.

'Watch the video,' said a disguised voice.

The line went dead. Dan looked down at the phone in his hand and heard the distinctive trill of a message being received.

'What's going on?' the Sheik asked.

Dan shook his head. 'I'm not sure.' He held up the phone to the Sheik and showed him the message which had appeared.

Watch this.

Dan glanced at the Sheik, who nodded, and pressed 'play'.

The screen lit up with a fiery scene – a television news report showed a ship capsized against a port jetty, while searchlights from helicopters scanned the surrounding waters. Fires swept around the hull of the ship and fire crews aimed jets of water across the structure. An excitable television reporter mouthed silently while a ticker line appeared below his face. *Ras Laffan port facility attacked in Qatar.*

The Sheik eased the smart phone from Dan's grip and watched the video, his lips pursed. He held up the image to Dan.

'This is my family's facility,' he said hoarsely. 'What's going on?'

Dan looked up and watched as the waiter stood in the middle of the floor where the Sheik had left him and appeared to search around the room, craning his neck from side to side, before turning and hurrying towards the corridor which led to the rear of the building.

Dan turned to the nearest bodyguard. 'I've got a bad feeling about this. We're taking him back to the car *now*. Don't let anyone come near him. *Go*.'

The bodyguards began to push the Sheik towards a side entrance, the leader with a hand cupped around his throat microphone, speaking to the drivers of the limousines, telling them to meet the Sheik's group outside.

Dan threw himself against a fire exit door, and pulled the Sheik down a set of concrete steps, just as the two limousines screeched around the corner of the building and slid to a standstill below them.

He jumped the last two steps, wrenched open the back door of the first limousine, checked inside, then turned and grabbed the Sheik.

'Get in – quickly!'

Dan stood to one side as two of the bodyguards leapt into the car with the Sheik, the others making for the second vehicle. Both cars launched away from the steps towards the street.

Dan ran back inside, heading towards the main reception area.

A commotion near one of the waiters and a crash reverberated around the room as a tray of drinks hit the floor, splintering glass everywhere. Then a scream, and the crowd parted as the waiter came charging through the guests.

Dan frowned and looked over his shoulder. He tuned into the voices over his earpiece, frantic stilted phrases.

'We've got the stairs covered… he tried to escape through the car park… he's coming your way!'

The waiter pushed past Dan, who turned to grab the man as he ran. The man's jacket slipped from Dan's grasp as he ran through the crowd. Dan cursed and pushed past people, gaining on him.

The waiter looked around in desperation then pushed his way through the panicked crowd, stumbling over people as he fled the room.

Dan's height gave him an advantage – he could see over people and noticed the man was heading down the corridor, past the office where Browning's team had based themselves. He pushed a woman out of the way, sending her towards the front doors, towards safety. A man elbowed his way past Dan, grabbed the woman and propelled her forward.

Dan looked over the man's head and saw the waiter facing them. His mouth was open in an 'o' of shock.

Dan realised too late what was going to happen.

As one of Browning's security men reached under his jacket, Dan yelled. 'Gun! Everybody down!'

Screams filled the air as the guests ducked as one, scrambling for the floor of the lobby, while Browning sprinted towards the waiter.

Dan drew his own weapon from under his jacket, glanced down at the human carpet, and jumped over people as he pushed his way towards the security guard. *He wasn't going to make it.*

'Don't shoot!' he shouted. 'We need him alive!'

The security guard raised his gun, sighting it on the waiter.

'No!' Dan yelled. 'Stay down!'

He felt the gunshot echo around the enclosed space a split second before he heard it.

Browning and the waiter collapsed in a tangle of limbs on the floor.

Dan frantically pushed his way through the swelling number of people now stampeding towards the front doors of the hotel. He glanced over a woman's head and saw the waiter pushing Browning's still form away from him.

The waiter stood, dazed, and then saw Dan heading his way. He turned and bolted down the corridor.

'Move! Move! Get out of my way!' Dan thundered.

He reached Browning at the same time as the security guard who had fired his weapon. The man's face was pale.

'I didn't see him running – I was aiming for the waiter!' he said, his voice shaking.

'You shouldn't have been waving your gun around here in the first place,' growled Dan. He dropped to the floor next to Browning and rolled his body towards him, then swallowed as he saw the damage the bullet had made to the man's rib cage.

'Is he dead?' asked the security guard, dropping to a crouch.

'No,' said Dan, and glanced at Browning's face as he heard a gurgling sound. Blood had started to bubble from between the man's lips. Dan turned the man's head gently to one side, and then spoke to the security guard. 'Stay with him.'

Dan looked around him and down the corridor. He turned back to the lobby and saw two security guards running towards him.

'Follow me!' shouted Dan, pointing down the corridor. 'He went this way!'

Dan ran down the corridor, pushed open an emergency exit door and bolted down the stairs, his jacket flying open. He gripped the handrail as he jumped off one flight, slid across the landing and launched himself down the next. He could hear footsteps on the levels above him as the security team left the hotel's upper accommodation floors and ran after him.

He heard the staccato shouts of commands over his earpiece. He tuned them out mentally – he was concentrating on one thing and one thing only. To find the mysterious waiter who had eluded the security that had been meticulously planned for the event.

Dan leapt down the last four treads of the staircase and propelled himself through an open fire exit door. He emerged in the alleyway to the rear of the conference centre and slid to a halt, panting, his heart hammering between his ribs.

To his left, a dead end – a brick wall, the rear of another building. Spinning to his right, the open end of the alleyway was ablaze with red and blue flashing lights. The silhouettes of two armed officers ran towards him.

'Where did he go?' demanded Dan, shielding his eyes against the bright lights of the emergency vehicles.

Dan spun round, his eyes frantically searching the surfaces of the buildings crowding in around them. As Browning's security team burst through the fire exit door and joined him, he heard one of them exclaim, 'There he is!'

Dan craned his neck and saw him – the waiter was clawing his way up the wall towards the roof, his jacket flapping in the breeze. Dan pushed his earpiece into place and activated the microphone. 'Where are those extra security guys?'

A voice filtered through the static. 'On their way.'

Dan peered up at the waiter as the man reached the top of the building.

He suddenly stopped in mid-air. A split second later the echo of a gunshot reverberated around the alleyway and the man scrabbled wildly at the air before plummeting towards the ground.

Dan turned away, but couldn't avoid hearing the sound of the body hitting the footpath below. He cringed, then looked. The body lay spread-eagled across the ground, blood pooling out from under the man's caved-in skull.

He glanced up at the roof opposite. A lone sniper stood, his rifle cradled casually across his folded arms. He saw Dan and nodded once.

***

Dan stood next to the waiter's body, blood leaking from the ragged exit wound and over the pot-holed tarmac of the alleyway.

Dan watched as the new security chief closed his eyes and tapped the radio antenna against his forehead. Finally he opened his eyes and spoke into the transmitter.

'Okay,' he said, breaking away from his thoughts. 'Seal the area and wait for the police and forensics.' He put the radio back on his belt clip and turned to Dan.

'You can go – you're no longer needed here.'

Dan frowned. 'Wait a minute, I'm here to help – aren't you at least going to wait and see what your surveillance cameras have picked up?' He pointed to the waiter's body. 'We need to find out who he was working for…'

The security chief lunged at him, grabbed his collar and shoved him against the wall of the building.

'This is my command,' he hissed, 'and you're nobody. Get out of my sight. You were meant to be here as an observer. Instead, I've got one person dead and my boss is in a critical condition. *My* team will handle this, not you!'

Dan pushed the man's grip off his jacket. 'Big mistake,' he snarled.

He turned his back on the man and walked down the alley, pulling his mobile phone from his pocket as he walked, scrolled through the contacts list until he found the name he wanted and hit the dial button. It went to voicemail.

He ended the call, stepped out into the main street and flagged down a black taxi, cursing under his breath.

Chapter 13

Paul Spiteri revved the engines of the multi-million dollar yacht as it broke through the waves of the small natural harbour. Squinting against the glare of the rising sun on the horizon, he smoked a cigarette, his lined face screwed up in concentration. He coughed gently and waved the nicotine-laden air out of the open window next to the controls.

The skipper cast his eyes over the coastline as the engines powered the craft away from the coastline and out to open water. Travelling parallel to the steep cliffs, Paul turned the wheel of the boat and gazed fondly at the familiar surroundings. Unlike the coastline further north, the area hadn't yet been discovered by mainstream tourists.

After collecting the boat from the Greek Islands for its new owner, Paul had called in for supplies at his home port of Marsaxxlokk before starting the mammoth task of taking the motor yacht through the Atlantic to New York. He smiled, already spending the payment in his mind, while he put the yacht through its paces and ran the final checks before heading towards the international marina at Vittoriosa.

Spiteri steered the motor yacht round a steep outcrop of rocks which jutted out from the cliff face, sheltering the villa above from view. As he swung the boat left and out towards his usual fishing ground, the cigarette fell from his mouth, while Spiteri, eyes wide open, gaped at the sight ahead.

A large black shape slowly sank beneath the surface two hundred metres from the yacht, churning the waves in its wake, and then disappeared under the water.

Spiteri guided the yacht a little closer, awed by the sight. He wiped the sweat from his eyes. As he drew closer, the enormous rocks above blocked the sunlight. Spiteri shivered. He craned his neck, looking up the length of the cliffs. Jagged openings appeared in the limestone rock, remnants of Neolithic and Bronze Age settlements which were rife along the Maltese coastline.

He strained his eyes as the yacht rocked in the waters. Leaning over the edge of the chrome railing which ran the length of the vessel, he peered into the dark depths, trying to spot the shape he'd seen.

Spiteri stepped back to the controls and slowed the engines, before he returned to the deck rail and looked up at the cliff face which towered over him. He thought he'd heard a shout. Leaning out of the wheelhouse, he peered upwards. There was no-one in sight. He killed the engines, and reached into his shirt pocket for another cigarette.

He leaned against the frame of the wheelhouse and squinted down at the churning waters, deep in thought.

The gunshot blew him backwards into the wheelhouse, the bullet exiting through his shoulder leaving a gaping wound. As he lay slumped on the floor, lungs blown apart from the force of the shot, he held his hand up in front of his face, shock and pain registering as he stared in horror at the blood covering his fingers.

A movement in the cliff face from one of the openings caught his attention and Spiteri's eyes wandered up at the cave mouth as a figure came into sight. It was a man, tall, and carrying a sniper's rifle, the glare from the rising sun glinting off the sight as the man peered down at him. Spiteri's eyes opened wide in fright. He tried to scream as the sniper took aim and fired a last fatal shot.

The sniper dropped the rifle, and crawled towards a fifty calibre gun positioned within the cave opening. He carefully aimed at the hull of the motor yacht. Squeezing the trigger, he fired at the fibreglass hull, below the water line.

Using the gun's sight, the sniper checked his handiwork. Sure enough, water was beginning to leak into the boat. As the weight of the water began to increase, the boat slowly began to sink out of sight, taking Spiteri's body with it.

Satisfied, the sniper pulled the weapon out of sight and disappeared.

***

The civil servant stepped to one side and allowed Dan into the room, quietly closing the door behind him.

Five men, all with grim faces, sat around an enormous wooden oval table which filled most of the room.

David turned in his chair and stood up to greet him. 'Good timing Dan. Take a seat anywhere you like. You've already met the Vice-Admiral. You also know Sheik Masoud Al-Shahiri and the Secretary of State for Defence's representative, Hugh Porchester.'

Dan acknowledged the men and took a seat facing the door.

David sat back down and continued. 'The gentleman to my right is Richard Fletcher, who has carried out studies for the Government in relation to energy security in the UK.'

Dan shook hands with Fletcher. 'What's the latest?'

David pointed to a large digital display at the end of the room. On it, a news channel's footage of the Ras Laffan port disaster played repeatedly, showing aerial footage from a helicopter hovering over the stricken LNG tanker wallowing across the burning jetty. 'This is.'

Dan glanced at the television report, then at the Sheik. 'Any thoughts about this message you received last night?'

The Sheik nodded miserably. 'It would seem my enemies really did not want me to strike a deal with your

Government, Mr Taylor.' He withdrew a handkerchief from his pocket and wiped his forehead.

'Do we know anything about the waiter?' asked Dan.

David nodded and passed a photograph across the table to him. 'Ibrahim Abbas. Born in Markazi Province, Iran. He moved here as a ten-year-old with his parents in 1978 when the Revolution began. Acquired British citizenship in 1992.'

Dan frowned. 'How the hell did he get caught up in this?'

'He's been working for the hotel for the past two years,' said David, reading from his notes. 'No criminal record, not even a parking fine.'

'Could he have been blackmailed?' suggested the Admiral.

'I do have a statement from his wife to say he was fond of playing cards,' agreed David. 'Maybe he had a cash incentive waved at him.'

'Perhaps that's why he was chosen,' mused Dan.

'What do you mean?'

'Well, the Iranians couldn't attend the gala themselves,' said Dan, 'so perhaps they sent a messenger?'

'That's a very strong claim to be making without any hard evidence,' said Porchester, holding up his finger in warning. 'We are certainly not going to jump to conclusions.'

'This could ruin me forever,' said the Sheik. 'My family's reputation...' He fell silent.

'With all due respect, Sheik,' said Porchester, 'I don't think we can assume that to be the case until we've investigated other possibilities.'

'It seems highly circumstantial,' said David. He turned to the Sheik. 'How long will supplies of LNG be interrupted by this accident?'

The Sheik shook his head. 'It depends on how long it will take to remove the tanker and ensure there are no pieces left in the seabed in the port area that could damage other ships.'

He sighed. 'In the meantime, our clients are going to start checking the wording of our export contracts very closely and will probably start charging us for late supply. There are already three LNG super-tankers waiting in the main breakwater to enter port – their owners will be talking to their insurers about our culpability in them losing money while they wait. We also have one fully-loaded tanker in port which has to be checked for damage. We were able to get one Q-Max tanker out of the port and on its way to the UK before the attack.'

'If I could interrupt,' said Fletcher, 'we've looked at weather projections for the next three months and the UK's current gas reserves are not going to withstand a prolonged delay to its supply chain. The demand on our ability to provide sufficient gas for industry and domestic use is going to be immense.'

David glanced across the table. 'How bad could it get, Richard?'

The other man looked at his hands and Dan heard him sigh before he answered. 'Based on what happened a few years ago when our supplies were diminished beyond our expectations, we can expect a significant loss of life – mostly in the aged population percentile and those deemed "at risk" by the medical profession. Existing hospitalised cases of pneumonia, that sort of thing. Also, if we factor in the probability of increases in cold and influenza cases due to the cold weather, we'd have to start expecting fatalities in the very young too.'

Dan shook his head. 'We take it for granted our homes are going to be warm every time we flick a switch,' he said. 'It doesn't seem possible that we're faced with such a crisis.'

'Rationing would have to start within days,' said Fletcher. 'We can't predict how long Ras Laffan is going to be out of action.'

Porchester signalled to the civil servant standing by the door. 'I'll have my department make some phone calls – we'll ask the Tunisians to release a tanker to us. At least that will buy us some time.'

He murmured instructions to the civil servant, who nodded once before hurrying from the room.

Dan leaned forward. 'We should get a team to look into the reports coming out of the preliminary investigations. I've only heard of ships this size collapsing in port when they're fully loaded with ore – I've never heard of an empty tanker just sinking, have you?' He turned to the Vice-Admiral, who shook his head.

'It does seem strange. I'll help you with that investigation – we can't rule out sabotage at the moment. We've currently got two destroyers travelling through the Atlantic. I'll send them to meet the Q-Max tanker – that should stop any attack at sea on those supplies.'

Dan nodded. 'This might not be a personal attack against the Sheik, but an attack on the United Kingdom's gas supply. If this isn't an accident, the perpetrators of such an attack will have put the UK in a very vulnerable position.'

Porchester blanched. 'Don't be preposterous! I can't go back to the Prime Minister and tell him that this country is under attack based on a ship sinking in port! The Sheik is right – this is a local problem, nothing to do with the UK.' He stood up. 'I'm very sorry about the whole thing, Sheik, I really am, but these are conspiracy theories, nothing more.' He turned to David. 'Send me a copy of the reports as soon as you get them. Then reconvene a meeting and we'll discuss what *really* happened and what you're going to do about it.'

Porchester stalked across the room and ripped open the door, slamming it behind him.

'Well,' said Dan. 'That was helpful.'

The Sheik shook his head. 'I am just glad our computer systems were upgraded eighteen months ago,' he murmured. 'If they hadn't, this disaster could have been a lot worse.'

Dan turned to face the man, and noticed the worry lines which creased his face. 'What upgrade?'

The Sheik smiled briefly. 'A British engineer approached us at an energy conference in Dubai. He had invented a computer programme which would sit within our existing controls system. In the event of an emergency, it would allow one system user in the main control room to run the entire facility.'

Dan frowned. 'How?'

'The software he designed automatically sourced data in the system which could pinpoint where a problem was occurring within seconds, then protect the facility by shutting valves and pipes around the problem area and isolate it.' The Sheik paused. 'Not only that,' he said, lowering his voice, 'he was also aware of our concerns regarding certain *viruses* that had appeared in the Middle East, software attacks on utilities companies and the like. His programme was designed to attack those viruses and dismantle them in real time – as the virus was trying to attack the system.' The Sheik glanced up at the news report repeating silently on the wall-mounted television, then back at Dan. 'His system saved our facility from being completely destroyed.'

Dan leaned back in his chair and looked at David, who was already pulling out his mobile phone. 'What was the engineer's name?'

***

'Grant Swift,' began the analyst. 'Born in Bristol, May 1974. Educated at Tudor House in Berkshire, gained exceptional grades and was accepted to Churchill College, Cambridge in 1992, where he studied computer programming and physics.'

The analyst paused and flicked to the next page in the brief. He cleared his throat and made the mistake of glancing up at Dan, who was glaring at him, drumming his fingers on the table.

'Ahem,' the analyst coughed, 'Mr Swift appears to have then accepted a job in the city with IBM where he stayed for eight years before leaving and setting up his own consultancy firm.'

The Sheik impatiently flicked his hand. 'Yes, yes – all of this I know. I had my own people check Mr Swift's credentials very thoroughly before we offered him a contract.' He shrugged and picked up his water glass.

The analyst blushed, glanced at David and battled on. 'For the first two years of his consultancy business, Mr Swift worked in secret with the Centre for the Protection of National Infrastructure.' He paused and raised an eyebrow as the sound of the Sheik choking on his water interrupted him.

'This we did not know,' said the Sheik, spluttering into a napkin.

David suppressed a smile and indicated that the analyst should continue.

'During that time, it is likely Mr Swift was assisting the CPNI with investigations into malware and Distributed Denial of Service attacks.'

'Wait,' said Dan, leaning forward. 'What?'

'Computer hacking and system infiltration attacks,' said the analyst. 'Preventing people breaking into organisations' computers and taking control.'

Dan leaned back in his seat. 'Well, at least we know where he got the idea to develop a system to protect computers from those sorts of things, *and* why he's been kidnapped, right?' He looked around the table, then at the analyst, who was glaring at him, his mouth silently opening and closing.

Dan grinned. 'Sorry – did I spoil it for you?'

Chapter 14

Malta

Hassan walked through the villa, his footsteps echoing through the living area as he strode among the rooms. The white walls reflected the winter sun streaming through partially opened windows and cast silhouettes on the tiled floors. A light breeze blew through the property, aided by slowly turning ceiling fans.

He breathed in the scent of jasmine. Towards the back of the house he could hear raised voices from the kitchen as lunch was prepared. He smiled, revelling in the atmosphere, and the fact his plans were slowly but surely falling into place.

He slowed as he turned into a wide hallway, crossed a decorative rug and approached the study. He adjusted the sweater draped casually across his shoulders over a navy blue polo shirt, and thrust his hands into the pockets of his beige trousers. He nodded to the bodyguard standing in front of the heavy wood-panelled door and waited while the man stood to one side, pushed open the door and respectfully stepped out of Hassan's way, his head bowed.

Hassan strode over to a desk which had been set beside patio doors. He reached out to touch a briefcase that had been placed on the desk. Picking it up, he felt the weight in his hands. He closed his eyes and remembered. *This is an investment.*

He glanced up at Mustapha, who waited patiently by the patio doors, gazing out across the barren landscape.

The second of the two bodyguards waited for Hassan's signal, then slid open the tinted glass-panelled patio door. Hassan closed his eyes, savouring the faint sea breeze that wafted in from the adjacent cliffs, and then lifted his face up to the sun at its zenith in the blue sky.

Lowering his chin, he opened his eyes and gazed at the barren landscape in front of him. The farm had long since ceased producing anything of use, with many of its outbuildings falling into disrepair from years of neglect. The stone walls, erected a century ago by skilled stonemasons, would in all likelihood remain long after Hassan had finished with the property.

He tested the weight of the briefcase in his hand and stepped out onto the flag-stoned terrace, pulling his sunglasses off his head and over his eyes in one fluid motion.

A pagoda provided shade over the area of the patio nearest the house, climbing plants left to entangle themselves up and over the wooden frame, providing natural shade from the noonday sun. A wrought iron round table and four chairs were placed under the shade. Two of the chairs were empty while their former occupants stood to the left of the shaded area, smoking cigarettes and talking animatedly between themselves.

The other two chairs were taken up by one man who sat in one, and languidly stretched his legs across to the other. He appeared to be watching the other two men converse, a lazy smile playing across his lips. As he heard Hassan approach he turned his head and looked up at his host.

'Everything okay?'

Hassan nodded, and placed the briefcase on the table. 'Your money is in there.'

The man smiled, turned to the two smokers and signalled them over. They nodded, ground out their cigarettes on the flagstones and walked towards him. 'You won't be insulted if we count it?'

Hassan shook his head. 'I'm an honourable man, Mr Ivanov, but no, I won't be insulted.'

He waited as Dmitri Ivanov swung the briefcase round, looked at the combination lock, glanced up at Hassan, smiled and flicked the briefcase open. 'If you're so honourable, Hassan, how is it you know my personal pin code?'

Hassan shrugged. 'I like to know who I'm dealing with.'

Ivanov shook his head and laughed. 'I guess I'll be changing my passwords.' He pushed the briefcase towards his two colleagues. 'You know what to do.'

The men pulled up chairs and began sifting through the bundles of American dollars, methodically stacking the one hundred dollar notes as they progressed through the case.

'Walk with me,' said Hassan and turned, pacing across the patio area and towards a short flight of steps.

Ivanov eased himself upright, took a sharp intake of breath as his knees clicked, and followed.

The two men left the confines of the house and its unkempt garden. Ivanov caught up with Hassan and the men walked in silence. They stopped near an outbuilding which, compared with the others, appeared to have been recently repaired.

'Were there any problems?'

Ivanov glanced at the new doors and locks, the metalwork shining in the sun. 'None. Your contact in the Iranian Navy diverted a frigate under the guise of investigating a reported sighting of an American vessel and we took control of the torpedoes from them at sea. It was a textbook manoeuvre.'

'How will he explain their disappearance?'

'Competently. He's been paid generously for his help – and my contacts will use his family to remind him of his obligations to you if required.'

Hassan nodded. 'There's no damage after passing through the Suez?'

Ivanov shook his head. 'None. We did as you commanded and followed a large Tunisian cargo ship to disguise our progress. We surfaced earlier and checked the hull – it's holding up well.'

Hassan smiled. 'The Israelis will be shocked to find they're not the only ones who can successfully manoeuvre through the Canal.'

'They usually have the support of the Egyptians when they do.'

Hassan waved his hand. 'No matter. It is done now.' He lifted his chin towards the building and handed the Kazakh a set of keys. 'Everything you and your men need is in there. The other supplies are in the cellar of the main villa.'

Ivanov nodded. 'How do we move it all?'

'There's a passageway from the cellar to the cove. A gift from the smugglers who used to roam these parts.'

'We'll start straight away.'

'It will probably take you a few nights to prepare everything.' Hassan turned to the man, and placed his hand on his shoulder and squeezed. 'I have to briefly return to England but I'll be back before you depart. It would be an honour for me to have you here as my guests until it's time for you to leave.'

The other man nodded. 'And it would be our honour to accept.'

'Good.' Hassan turned from the building and began walking through the parched grass back towards the house.

'Hassan?'

He stopped and turned, frowning. 'What?'

Ivanov stood where they'd been talking, tossing the keys in his hand. 'What's in it for you?'

Hassan cocked his head to one side, thinking. 'Satisfaction,' he finally said, then turned and began walking again, smiling as he heard the other man running to catch up.

'Satisfaction,' he murmured to himself, and raised his head to watch a hawk floating in the air currents above the cliffs.

Chapter 15

London

Dan rubbed his hand over his eyes, scowled as he felt the stubble on his face and sighed, leaning back in the leather swivel chair.

'Run it again.'

The woman next to him pushed her glasses up her nose, leaned forward and moused over the playback controls. 'How many times is this?'

'I lost count after we hit double figures.' He frowned. 'Is there another camera angle we can try – perhaps from the port side, rather than the jetty?'

The woman gathered up her long red hair, grabbed a pen from the desk and shoved it through the loose tendrils, sweeping her hair out of the way. That done, she began to scroll through the list of closed circuit cameras situated around the Ras Laffan facility.

'You realise I could be using my amazing analytical skills to help David, and you could do this yourself, don't you?'

'Four eyes are better than two Philippa,' said Dan. 'You rarely miss anything happening around here, so you're stuck with me.'

'Huh.' Philippa found the recording she was looking for and hit 'play'.

They stared in silence at the now familiar scene – the port lit up by arc lights, the LNG tanker moored alongside the jetty, its bulk silhouetted against the overhead lights behind it.

Dan drummed his fingers on the control desk as he watched, his eyes scanning the scene, hunting.

'What exactly are you looking for?' asked Philippa, stifling a yawn.

Dan held up a report in his hand, his attention to the recording unwavering. 'One of the engineers at the port said he saw the ship lift out of the water just before the initial explosion,' he said. 'To me, that sounds either like an explosive device fitted to the ship or jetty – or a torpedo.'

Philippa nodded and leaned closer to the screen, entranced. They cried out at the same time.

'Stop the recording!' Dan leaned forward and pointed to the screen, his finger resting under the image of the ship, the beginning of an explosion frozen in time.

Philippa rewound the image a few seconds and then began working through the recording one frame at a time.

'There!' Dan jabbed his finger at the water surrounding the ship, its black depths reflecting the port lights.

The analyst frowned. 'What am I looking at?'

Dan rubbed his finger along the water line in front of the ship. 'See how the water looks different here compared with the regular wave motion?'

Philippa nodded.

'Run it forward frame by frame up to the explosion. You'll see the point of impact,' Dan said.

Philippa did as he instructed and watched open-mouthed as Dan's finger traced the tracks of an underwater missile heading towards the ship. A fraction of a second later there was a minute pause, followed by a blinding white and yellow flash as the hull disintegrated.

She turned and stared at Dan. 'Holy crap.'

'Can you capture some images of that?' he asked.

'Sure. Do you want them printed or emailed?'

'Emailed – send them to the Vice-Admiral to see what he thinks. I reckon we're on the right track about a submarine being used, but I'd like his opinion.'

Philippa nodded, her fingers sweeping over the keyboard in front of her. 'Okay, that's done – what next?'

'Keep playing the recording,' said Dan. 'The transcript of the interview with the engineer says there was a second explosion a few moments later.'

They turned their attention back to the screen and watched in silence, neither of them aware they held their breath, anticipating the next strike. As the digital display counted off two minutes from the first explosion, a second blast illuminated the already burning jetty.

'There!' said Philippa. She paused the recording and pointed to the dark expanse of water. She sat back in her chair, a smile forming. 'Got you.'

Dan frowned, peering at the picture frozen on the screen. 'I think it's time the Sheik organised a dive team to take a closer look at that ship's hull.'

Philippa leaned forward and picked up the phone. 'Better still, I'll organise it,' she said. 'If there are any traces of explosives under there, I want them sent back here for analysis so we can see what we're up against.'

'Or who,' muttered Dan. He patted Philippa on the shoulder as he stood up. 'Good work.'

Philippa nodded and smiled, already giving orders to her team over the phone.

Chapter 16

Dan walked into the conference room, the lights automatically flickering on as he strode over to the table and dumped the pile of paperwork on the wooden surface.

Mitch followed, carrying a coffee in each hand, a rolled up map under one arm. He kicked the door shut behind him, handed one of the coffees to Dan, tossed the map onto the table and began to sift through the papers. 'Where do you want to start?'

Dan frowned as he flicked through a document. 'The Admiral made some phone calls – these are transcripts of calls made to the police over the past two years where people have reported anything suspicious which might be a threat to national security.' He took a slurp of coffee. 'We'll go through everything here. See if anything catches your attention and could link into what we know so far – anything that just seems *odd*. Go with your gut instinct.'

Mitch nodded. 'Okay.' He pulled out a chair, picked up a report and put his feet up on the desk as he began reading.

Dan paced around the conference table as he discarded one document and selected another, reading as he walked. His eyes quickly scanned one page then he flicked to the next.

The reports were a mixture of transcripts of calls that had been monitored and flagged by the security services as warranting attention, but no further immediate action, and phone calls from the public directly to the security services or police where suspicious activities were thought to have taken place. Many of the issues had already been investigated by either the police or security services but had been deemed to be of a non-urgent threat. Others remained flagged until a threat could be ascertained.

As the morning wore on, the pile of discarded transcripts grew larger and Dan felt the words merging into one another, swimming on the page. He glanced up at Mitch who had a similarly bored expression on his face. 'Any luck?'

'No, and I think I just read the same paragraph three times.'

Dan sighed and put down the document he was reading. He glanced at his watch. 'We're not going to do this properly if we don't have a break. Wasn't it your round for lunch?' He absently turned to the next page and scanned the first few lines.

'Mitch?' Dan looked over at his colleague who was sitting transfixed at the report he was reading. 'You okay?'

Mitch nodded slowly. 'Uh-huh.'

'What is it?'

A smile slowly spread across the other man's face. 'I think I've got something.' He put down the report he was reading and slid it across the table to Dan. 'What do you think?'

Dan picked it up. As his eyes skimmed the text, his heartbeat began to race. He looked up at Mitch and grinned. 'I think we're going to visit a museum. And you can buy lunch on the way.'

***

Omani Embassy, London

Hassan Nazari stopped writing and looked up at the sound of a loud knock on the door to his private office.

'Come,' he commanded, putting back the fountain pen into its gold case. He carefully blotted the page, glanced at the diplomatic seal across its heading, and slipped it into a plain white envelope which he then tucked under the desk blotter. As the door opened he folded his arms across the desk and waited, expectantly.

A tall man entered the room. Thin, his body not quite filling the pale grey suit jacket and trousers which he wore, his white shirt disguising a painfully concave chest. His face appeared etched with concentration, slight frown lines furrowing above his eyes.

As he approached the desk, Hassan could hear the man's rasping breath and shivered. To so many, that sound was the last noise they heard. As a courtesy, he stood up to greet his visitor. He stepped around the desk, put his hands on the arms of the taller man and gently squeezed.

'It's good to see you,' he lied. Although the man was useful, Hassan abhorred Fahd Baqir. Not only was he taller, he was pure evil – Hassan swore it leaked through the man's pores. 'Your lungs are not good today?'

The man shook his head, spluttered, and pulled a handkerchief from his jacket pocket. He coughed into it, and then glared at his host.

'This damn cold and damp weather Hassan,' he growled. 'Why on earth did you get me sent here?'

Hassan frowned. 'Because under the new accords, I'm only allowed into the country for a short stay each time. You, on the other hand, have been granted asylum – it's much easier for you to move around.'

He gestured to a seat opposite his desk and Baqir lowered himself into it, grimacing as he did so.

Hassan sat in his own chair and lifted an eyebrow.

'Rheumatism,' spat Baqir. 'The sooner I move to a warmer climate, the better.'

Hassan smiled benevolently. 'Not long now. Tell me,' he said easing forward, his smile disappearing, 'what progress have you made?'

Baqir sighed, a bronchial wheeze escaping his lips. 'It is very difficult to cite progress when you forbid me to use my most successful techniques.'

Hassan shook his head. 'That can't happen, Baqir. We discussed this at the beginning. If something goes wrong and he dies, we're lost. He's a civilian, not a soldier. Being interrogated for any length of time is going to stress his system, so we have to be selective in our approach.' He leaned back. 'So, what *have* you got?'

Baqir held up his hand, raised himself slowly from the chair and shuffled over to the door. He opened it, spoke briefly to someone waiting outside, and then closed the door.

As Baqir returned to the desk, Hassan noticed a battered briefcase in his hand. He pointed to it as the older man sat down and placed it on the desk between them.

'This is his?'

Baqir nodded. 'We found nothing of use in it.' He gestured to the locks and pushed it closer to Hassan. 'Open it. It's not locked. See for yourself.'

Hassan turned the case around to face him. He ran his fingers over the worn, cracked black leather, opened it and flicked through the contents, frowning. A paperback crime novel sat on top of a pile of documents. Hassan tossed the book to one side and began flicking through the paperwork. They appeared to be scopes of work, notes of client's requirements, and hastily scribbled notes on A4 pages torn from notepads and clipped together.

Hassan threw the pages onto his desk and pushed his fingers into the various pockets. He pulled out two ballpoint pens, a ruler and a faded business card. He peered over the lid at Baqir.

'We checked the lining as well – there was nothing,' said Baqir.

Hassan grunted, picked up the papers and threw them back in the case. He slammed the lid shut and pushed it back to Baqir. 'There were no computer files?'

Baqir shook his head. 'We waited until his wife left the house to report his disappearance and then conducted a search. We found nothing.'

'You were careful?'

'No-one saw us enter or leave and we disrupted as little as possible. The place was clean.'

Hassan steepled his fingers under his chin. 'So it's hidden somewhere safe, like a deposit box or something.'

'There is another, slightly more difficult possibility,' mused Baqir.

'What?'

Baqir tapped his head. 'It's in here.'

Hassan sighed and leaned back in his chair. There was just so much information to be extracted. Slowly. Carefully. He shook his head to clear the thought, and rubbed his hand over his eyes. There was no way he was prepared to let Baqir loose just yet – the man was too dangerous to unleash through impatience. 'Has he remembered anything yet?'

Baqir shook his head. 'Next time, we use our own people,' he growled. 'The imbeciles used so high a dosage of drugs, it could be a few days before anything comes back to him – and even then it could be sporadic.'

Hassan sighed. 'Make sure he's watched day and night – if he talks, I want to know what he said immediately.'

'I'm sure a little more persuasion would help him remember.'

'Wait, Baqir. Be patient. We have to be careful or we could lose him before he gives up his secrets.'

'We're running out of time.'

'I know full well what the implications are, so don't lecture me,' Hassan snapped. He fell silent, considering his options. He looked across at Baqir who was watching him expectantly. 'There may be another way to approach this problem,' he said.

A small smile played across Baqir's lips as he listened.

Chapter 17

Dan slewed the car on the loose gravel of the car park and brought the vehicle to a halt. As they walked towards the small office, Mitch handed Dan a copy of the transcript from the security services which he'd read that morning.

'They received the call six months ago. A chap here took a phone call from someone saying they were interested in the submarine – the local marine preservation society has been trying to raise funds to keep it in working order but is running out of money.' He stopped while they looked across the small harbour, a cold wind blowing off the sea.

A motley collection of vessels rocked in the choppy water, leftovers from the Navy's history, their hulls' fenders bumping against the quayside. Dan spotted a small cruiser, a patrol boat and, lashed with ropes next to that, the black hulk of an Oberon-class submarine.

Dan stuffed his hands into his pockets and tried to ignore the earache developing from the wind buffeting his body. 'What did the authorities do?'

Mitch shrugged. 'Traced the call to a mobile phone. The SIM card was purchased in Soho.' He began walking again. 'The usual problem though – the number hasn't been used since, so the SIM card was probably destroyed as soon as the call was made.'

Dan grunted. 'Who are we meeting today?'

'The guy who made the call to the security services. They've spoken to him and you've got a copy there of the transcript of that meeting. I figure it's worth having a chat with the curator again though, see if he can remember anything else he might not have mentioned at the time. You know how people get nervous chatting to investigators – they clam up and panic because they think they're in trouble.'

Dan nodded and led Mitch up the steps to the harbour office. He pushed open the rough weather-worn door and stepped into a surprisingly modern reception area. A polished reception desk blocked their path through to the museum, a sign proclaiming only visitors with the appropriate tickets would be granted admission through the turnstile and into the bowels of the exhibits.

The reception desk was unmanned, the piped voice of a documentary filtering through from the museum while the sounds of explosions and excited children's voices filled the air.

While Mitch walked up to the desk and rang a small brass bell, Dan took advantage of the wait and began to pace around the room, examining the various maritime memorabilia in tall glass display cases.

The sound of footsteps approaching along wooden floorboards caught his attention, in time to see a man walking towards them. Dan tucked the transcript into his jacket pocket and wandered back to the reception desk.

The man finished wiping his oil-covered hands on a dirty rag, then held out his hand to Dan.

'You must be the men from the Government,' he said, smiling as he shook hands with Mitch. 'I'm Doug Hastings, the curator of the museum. Come through here – I've got an office where we can talk in private.'

He turned and led the way to a small room leading off the reception area, pushed some paperwork to one side of the desk which took up most of the room and threw the oily rag onto it, then gestured to Dan and Mitch to sit in the two chairs opposite him.

'Right gentlemen, how can I help? You said on the phone it was about the report I made to the police last year?'

'That's right,' said Dan, leaning forward in his chair and resting his elbows on his knees. 'I'll apologise up front if we're repeating any of the questions you've already answered, but that's just the way with these things. Often there are different angles we need to explore and we can't afford to miss anything.'

Hastings nodded. 'That's okay, I understand. I'm just glad it's being taken seriously. There's always the worry that reporting something like this is wasting your time.'

Dan shook his head and smiled. 'It's never a waste of time. Why don't you tell us what happened?'

The curator leaned back in his chair. 'Back in September, the museum's Trust decided we had to do something to raise more funding.' He gestured around him. 'As you can see, we'd spent quite a bit of money on a refurbishment project which depleted the coffers, even with some help from some of the big national historical charities. It was a hard decision as it was something we'd kept on the backburner as one of our next projects, but we decided to sell our Oberon class submarine, *Oscar*. She's been in our wet dock for the last ten years and is getting the worse for wear – if we weren't going to get to her in the next two years, it'd be too late to do anything to stop the corrosion – so it was better to sell her on to another museum or private collector.'

'Private collector?' asked Mitch. 'People actually buy those things for themselves?'

Hastings nodded smiling. 'Think of it as big boys' toys,' he said. 'I know of one bloke who had a Sherman tank sitting in his back garden until the missus gave him an ultimatum.'

'How many enquiries did you have?' asked Dan, steering the conversation back on track.

'Nothing the first month – we took out some paid advertising in the usual trade press but with the economy being as it is, we received very little interest,' explained the curator. 'Then one of our younger volunteers suggested advertising it for sale online. Of course, we laughed at first, then realised he had a valid point – we'd reach a much bigger international market, and it helped drum up local interest too, you know – newspaper publicity, some of the collectors' magazines...'

'How long after offering the submarine for sale online did you get the call?'

'About three days. I got a message through the website first, two days after placing the advert, saying there was an interested buyer who wanted to ask some more questions and that it was probably easier to do so over the phone rather than emailing. It made sense to me so I sent a message back with our number here. I got the call the next morning just after we opened.'

'Do you still have a copy of the message?' asked Dan.

'I expect it's still in the online account,' said Hastings. 'I'll log on and print out a copy for you.'

'Thanks. And the number the buyer called –was that the main museum number?'

'No – my private office number. We didn't want our reception area having to deal with the calls on top of everything else they do on a daily basis.'

'I'll need a note of that number too, please,' said Dan. 'Would you mind signing some paperwork to enable us to do a search on that number so we can try to trace the caller?'

'Not at all.'

Dan pulled out a document from inside his jacket, wrote in the gaps and passed it across the desk to Hastings who quickly read it, signed it and passed it back.

'Thanks,' said Dan. 'Now, what did the caller say that made you report it as suspicious?'

Hastings paused for a moment. 'It started out innocently enough. He asked how old the submarine was, what condition it was in, how long we'd had it and what I'd suggest would need to be done to it. I explained what our plans were to preserve it and that we'd acquired it after it had been decommissioned.'

'At what point did you become suspicious?'

A thin smile played across the curator's lips. 'When the caller asked how much fuel it carried, what was left after it was decommissioned, and what it's range was. He seemed very disappointed when I told him it wasn't seaworthy and hung up pretty quickly.'

'Okay,' said Dan, 'that's great. Let's go back a few steps. What did the caller sound like? Did he have an accent, or something to make his voice recognisable if you heard it again?'

'He wasn't born here, that's for sure. His accent sounded foreign. Kind of gruff, as if he was a smoker.'

'Age?'

'Hard to tell with that voice. Perhaps late forties, early fifties?'

'Were there any specific words he had particular trouble with? Did he have a lisp, or roll his r's?'

Hastings shook his head. 'Not that I can remember, no.'

'What about background noise? Did you notice anything that might indicate where he was calling from?'

'No.'

'Okay.' Dan sat back in his chair, thinking, and stared at the surface of the desk. 'I think that's covered everything we need at the moment, Doug. Perhaps you could log into your account and print out that email for me before we leave?'

'Sure. No problem.' Hastings turned in his chair, pulled a keyboard towards him and logged into his computer. Minutes later, the printer next to it began whirring and spat out a single page, which the curator handed over the desk.

'There you go.'

Dan flicked the page round to face him and looked. It was a generic email account, but one which the analysts would be able to hack into in no time. He smiled, stood up, and extended his hand to Hastings.

'Thank you for your time,' he said, giving the other man a card. 'That's got our contact details on. If you think of anything else, perhaps you'd give us a call straight away.'

'Of course.'

'What eventually happened to the submarine?' asked Mitch as they were led out of the office and back through to the reception area.

Hastings smiled. 'One of the local millionaires decided to step in and help us. Turns out his father built Oberon class boats in Greenock and he couldn't bear the thought of one being sold for scrap or an overseas museum getting it. We'll wait until better weather in May before making a start. Give us a year or so, you can come back and see her.'

'We may well do that,' grinned Dan.

Chapter 18

Malta

Hassan glanced up from his work as a knock on his office door interrupted his thoughts.

Mustapha entered, his breath laboured as if he'd been running.

'Yes?' Hassan frowned.

'With respect sir, you need to come now,' said the bodyguard, his eyes lowered to the ground. 'There's a problem.'

Hassan pushed back his chair, stood, and reached for the jacket he'd slung over the back. Shrugging it over his shoulders, he began to follow Mustapha out of the room and down a naturally lit hallway through the villa. 'What is it?'

As they stepped outside, the bodyguard stopped and turned to Hassan.

'Mutiny, sir.'

Hassan managed to disguise his shocked intake of breath by clearing his throat. He gestured to Mustapha to lead the way, and the two men walked through the long grass and scrubby plants, across the property towards the cliffs. Hassan could hear the crash of the waves below, in between laboured breaths as he kept up with the long gait of his bodyguard.

As they crossed the wasted grass, six figures could be seen standing a little way from the cliff's edge. One man, of average height and slight build reminiscent of undernourishment as a child, stood slightly apart from the others, his arms folded across his chest, his shoulders sagging and his gaze solemnly contemplating his feet.

Hassan stopped a few metres from the group and let Mustapha continue while he quietly caught his breath and took stock of the situation. It didn't look promising. He strode over to Ivanov who stood facing the lone man, his fists clenched by his side, jaw set, glaring at the other man.

Hassan stood next the submarine captain. 'Explain,' he said quietly.

Ivanov breathed out, which seemed to expel some of the man's tension. 'He has changed his mind,' he replied softly.

'A little late.'

'Indeed.'

'The money?'

'Sent to his mother. Gone.'

'I see.' Hassan rubbed his chin and began to pace around the small group. A whiff of a nervous fart emanated from one of the men and Hassan wrinkled his nose in disgust, turning into the sea breeze to clear his nostrils.

'Ivanov, I was *clear* in my instructions for this crew, was I not?'

'You were, sir.'

Hassan nodded. 'I thought so.' He reached the man then looked away, out to sea. The mixed blues of the sky and water sparkled in the early morning sun. He turned and walked back to Ivanov. 'Where did you find him?'

'At the quayside at Valletta, trying to bribe someone to take him to Sicily.'

Hassan shook his head and fingered his moustache. 'You know,' he said, waggling his finger at Ivanov. 'I really cannot abide betrayal.' In two strides, he was in front of the would-be deserter, glaring at the young man. 'I take it personally.'

He stepped back and frowned as the man pissed himself, the liquid turning to a faint steam in the cool morning air. The other four crew members shuffled their feet awkwardly, and avoided meeting Hassan's gaze.

Hassan glanced over his shoulder at Ivanov. 'Can you do it with one less?'

The man in front of him whimpered.

'We'll give it our best shot.'

Hassan nodded. 'Good enough.' He turned to the remaining four crew members. 'When the Romans ruled this part of the world, they found a *very* effective way of dealing with failure, desertion and mutiny,' he said, beginning to pace around the group once more. 'They called it *decimation*. One hundred men under a centurion. One in every ten of those one hundred men beaten to death by nine of their colleagues. A very effective lesson I feel, even if we are a little short on resources.'

He turned back to the young man who was visibly shaking as he looked up from under a fringe of hair at Hassan, nervously licking his lips. Mustapha placed a hand on his shoulder, preventing him from running.

'Kill him,' said Hassan. 'Or die.'

The man let out a cry as his crew mates descended on him, their fists pummelling his kidneys, face and stomach. An audible crunch preceded an ear-splitting scream as the man's arm was stomped under a boot, before Ivanov pulled his men off the young man and hauled him to his feet. In one swift motion, the captain dragged the man to the edge of the cliff.

Hassan followed, making sure he kept well clear of the man's flailing limbs.

As they reached the edge, Ivanov looked over his shoulder at Hassan, an eyebrow raised.

Hassan nodded, his eyes gleaming.

'This is your own doing,' Ivanov snarled, then loosened his grip.

The man screamed as he was launched over the edge of the cliff, the sound echoing in the cry of the gulls wheeling overhead.

Hassan walked carefully to the cliff's edge, and watched the body spiral through the air before it bounced off the jagged rocks below, into the churning water.

The man's face and an arm appeared briefly as he thrashed in the angry surf, then a moment later he disappeared under the waves.

Hassan turned carefully and walked back to the four remaining crew members. Blood covered their knuckles and had splashed across their clothes, while their faces remained ashen with shock, their eyes wide.

Hassan waited until Ivanov and Mustapha had joined him and noted with relish the look of shock on their faces.

'There will be no more desertion, no more talk of mutiny,' said Hassan, his words barely audible over the waves crashing below. 'You were employed to do a job. Now get on with it,' he growled, and walked back towards the villa, pulling his jacket tighter around him against the cold morning breeze.

Chapter 19

London

Dan handed over a twenty pound note to the girl serving behind the bar, waited for his change, then handed a bottle of beer to Mitch. They clinked the bottles together and each man took a deep swallow of the European lager.

Resting his bottle on the worn wooden surface of the bar, Dan sighed. 'I can't help feeling that visit was a total waste of time.'

Mitch shrugged. 'Nature of the beast. Sometimes we're going to get lucky, sometimes we're not.'

Dan nodded, and glanced around the bar. It was deserted apart from himself and Mitch, the lunchtime rush over some hours before, the dark afternoon adding a gloom to the small room.

'You still seeing that journalist?' asked Mitch.

Dan shook his head. 'No.' He took a swig from his beer. 'That didn't work out.'

'So you just disappeared to the States.'

Dan shrugged. 'Well, look what coming back here got me – a whole lot of trouble I could really do without.'

'I'm surprised you came running when David called – it's not like you work for him.'

'He can be persuasive. Besides, it sounded like he needed my help, so here I am.'

'With the whole British Government ready to lynch you.' Mitch turned his beer bottle around on the bar. 'I have to admit, I didn't see that one coming.'

They looked up as the pub door opened, to see David hurrying through, running his hand through his hair, and holding a briefcase in his hand.

David closed the door behind him, gestured to Dan and Mitch to sit at a table away from the main bar area, then ordered a beer for himself before walking over and collapsing into the chair Dan pulled out for him. He gripped the armrests and stared at each man opposite him in turn.

'What I'm about to tell you doesn't get discussed outside this meeting until I say it can, you understand?'

Dan and Mitch both nodded their assent.

David paused, and then pulled his briefcase up onto the table. He unfastened the latches and opened the lid, before removing a sheet of paper.

Dan noticed the Ministry of Defence seal at the top of the front page and glanced at David, who ignored him and continued. 'Whatever questions you two have been asking today triggered an alert in the intelligence community's system. They've decided to share this information with us.'

He pushed the briefing paper towards Dan. 'Four days ago, the Indian Navy realised it had lost one of its submarines being taken to be decommissioned, after it passed an area of water currently being used for a joint naval exercise.'

'You mean it was sunk by accident?' asked Mitch.

David shook his head. 'No – not sunk. Lost. Gone. Vanished.'

'Shit,' said Dan. 'It took them four days to realise that?'

David nodded. 'The naval exercise dictated radio and sonar silence in the area. The Indians only found out when the Americans alerted them.'

Dan raised an eyebrow.

David shrugged. 'The Americans were taking part in the naval exercise in the Indian Ocean with the British and Australian fleets when they picked up the signal. They were cheating. Usually do. The game is to let them think the rest of us don't know it – and make sure we beat them anyway. Ask the Australians.'

Dan grinned, and waited for David to continue.

'The submarine was being crewed by six personnel recruited from Russia – contractors. Our analysts say they're originally from Kazakhstan – recruited into the Russian Navy during the eighties, but freelance now. Bear in mind this is a shit job. They're basically nursing an old second-hand diesel submarine to its graveyard.' David leaned back in his chair. 'The conditions on those old subs are dismal to begin with, so you can imagine what it'd be like in one on its last legs.'

'Where was it travelling to?' asked Dan.

David shook his head. 'The Indians won't tell us – which isn't surprising. No navy in the world would divulge where it decommissions its old fleet – it wouldn't want other countries trying to gain access to gather intelligence about the onboard systems.'

Dan leaned back in his chair, stared at the ceiling and rubbed at the stubble forming on his chin. 'So, they steal a submarine, strike a ship at Ras Laffan – then what?'

David put the briefing document to one side and pulled out another folder from the briefcase. He extracted a sheet of paper and laid it on the table in front of Dan and Mitch.

'Thirty-six hours ago, Israeli intelligence picked up a faint signal at these coordinates.'

Dan frowned, picked up the document, handed it to Mitch and looked at David.

'That's the Cairo end of the Suez Canal.'

Mitch whistled. 'Is that even *possible*?'

Dan nodded. 'Evidently so. The sub must've piggy-backed onto the wake of a large ship, stayed just under the surface, and escaped into the Mediterranean.'

David took the document from Mitch and put it back in the folder, which he slipped back into the briefcase, before putting the case on the floor between his feet.

'So, what do you want us to do?' asked Dan.

David sighed. 'Take a look at what we've got so far then tell me where you think we need to go next. Whatever we do, it has to be quick, effective, but subtle – we don't want to start a pitched battle if we can manage this covertly.'

He stood up, indicating their meeting was over. 'And if I haven't made the urgency of the situation clear enough for you, I'll remind you that we could have a rogue submarine on the loose...'

David broke off as the door burst open and a man stormed into the room, brushing a light dusting of snow off his shoulders. He glanced around the pub, saw the three men sitting in the corner and rushed over to the table, thrusting a note at David.

'You've got to see this,' he said. 'We just took a call from that maritime museum.'

David read the note quickly and passed it to Dan.

'My god,' he said. 'That's a stroke of luck.'

'What just happened?' demanded Mitch.

Dan held up the note. 'The museum curator just phoned. He was sitting at home watching the BBC news when a story came on about the UK and US wanting more sanctions against Iran. The BBC managed to get an interview with the current Iranian delegate holed up at the Omani embassy. Hastings swears blind the man they interviewed is the same man who called him about the *Oscar* six months ago.'

'Right,' said David. 'Back to the office. *Now*.'

***

'Hassan Nazari,' Philippa began. 'Started his career doing a stint in the Revolutionary Guards and then side-stepped into a minor Government role. Worked his way up into the diplomatic corps. First posting was in Jordan in 2001. After that he disappeared from view for fourteen months, and then reappeared in Tangiers in 2009.

'What does he actually do at the embassy?' asked Dan.

Philippa flicked through her notes. 'He's one of two Iranians allowed to enter the country to assist with consular activities – passports, family law issues such as divorce and marriages, et cetera,' she said. 'Since the British Government closed the Iranian embassy in 2010, any approved diplomats are only allowed into the UK for a short period of time before they have to leave again. It's supposed to make it difficult for them to establish any sort of covert relationship outside their embassy duties.'

'Okay, here's what I want you to do,' said David. 'Have a look the movement on his diplomatic passport – and those of anyone in his office. He's up to something, and I want to know what.'

Chapter 20

Hassan looked out at the grey snow-laden skies from his office window, his mind racing. His UK visa renewal application had stalled, with the British Government refusing to comment on whether the current arrangements which allowed him temporary visits into the country would be extended.

The Omanis, whose embassy he was currently restricted to, were being equally opaque about the situation.

He rubbed a hand over his eyes and turned back to the room after hearing a soft knock on the door.

'Come in,' he said.

He lowered himself into his chair as Fahd Baqir entered the room, closing the door behind him. As the other man sat down, Hassan considered his options once more, and found them to be limited.

'I just heard the news from the Omanis,' said Baqir. 'It would seem our plan to use your Maltese connections to enable you to circumvent the British visa conditions may be under threat?'

Hassan scowled. 'Not that it is any concern of yours.'

Baqir lowered his head. 'My apologies Hassan. I only seek your assurances we will not lose our advantage. I respectfully remind you that we must proceed within the next three days if we are to succeed with your plans.'

Hassan held up his hand. 'I know. And I appreciate your dedication to our cause. Do you have any progress to report?'

The other man leaned back in his chair. 'Not as much as I would like. The prisoner is still suffering from the after-effects of the drugs. It has required an extreme amount of... patience... just to ascertain he has been working on the English facility's computer systems.'

'That's good,' said Hassan. 'So now find out exactly what he's doing with them.'

Baqir sighed. 'Hassan, with respect, the man is not going to give up information like that without an element of persuasion.'

Hassan eased himself out of his chair and began to pace the carpet. He glanced at the office door to make sure it was closed before he spoke.

'You'd have to be careful,' he said quietly. 'Do not employ your usual heavy-handiness from the outset, understand?'

'Hassan – you either want fast results, or you don't.'

'Surely you have other... techniques... you can try before going down that path?'

Baqir shrugged. 'I suppose so – but fire is always an excellent motivator, as is electricity…' He stopped and smiled, noticing Hassan flinch. 'I didn't realise you were so squeamish, honoured friend.'

Hassan shook his head to clear the images in his head. 'I've seen the remains of your handiwork before, Baqir. I wouldn't want this man to die before we unlock the secrets his mind holds.'

'How is the submarine team progressing?' asked Baqir. 'You *need* this information before they reach their target, or everything you've set in motion will be in vain.'

Hassan frowned. 'I phoned the villa an hour ago. They'll finish putting supplies on board within the next thirty-six hours. I'm due to fly back this evening. They're currently doing the work of a sixty man crew remember, so it's taking a little longer than expected.'

'Especially since one of those crew members is now at the bottom of the sea,' said Baqir. His eyes gleamed as Hassan glared at him. 'And you have the audacity to imply *I* am evil.'

Hassan smiled. 'I had a good teacher,' he said.

Baqir inclined his head in acknowledgement, and watched as Hassan sat back down, steepling his fingers under his chin, deep in thought.

After a moment, Hassan raised his eyes to meet Baqir's gaze.

'Can you get that information out of him?'

The other man pushed his chair back and stood up. 'If you leave it to my judgement to determine the best techniques to obtain it, yes.'

Hassan closed his eyes. 'Then get back to the safe house,' he said, 'and begin.'

Chapter 21

David's face was grim as the team filed back into the conference room. He paced next to the head of the table, his brow knotted, while Dan and the others settled into their seats.

He bent down and shared a murmured conversation with Sheik Al-Shahiri as the last person entered the room and closed the door. The Sheik glanced at him, nodded once, and looked around the gathered team as David took his place at the head of the table and opened the meeting.

'Right, Philippa – what have your analysts managed to find out?' he asked.

Philippa pushed her glasses up her nose before handing out a one-page biography of Hassan Nazari. 'This is just a cheat sheet to help everyone familiarise themselves with our lead suspect,' she explained.

'We've been talking to the Border Agency section of the Home Office. It would appear that Nazari does have a limited diplomatic presence here in the UK. Using what records they have, we can ascertain that he spends four to five days per month here in the UK on embassy obligations, but he seems to have established a household in Malta on the north-east coast of the island for the remainder of his time in Europe, rather than fly all the way back to Tehran.'

Dan leaned forward, Hassan's biography in one hand. 'You said 'what records they have' – what does that mean?'

Philippa sighed and leaned back in her chair. 'The Border Agency only has computerised records for exit and entry dates using major airports,' she said. 'The Ministry of Defence has long been complaining about the fact the UK doesn't have effective border controls at smaller airfields around the country.'

'So Hassan could be a lot more active here in the UK than the official records suggest?' said David.

Philippa nodded. 'Unfortunately, yes.'

'How is he financing himself?' asked David. 'Can we pinpoint that his activities are being supported by the Iranian Government?'

Philippa shook her head and checked her notes before answering. 'Not yet. The Government funds he receives are in line with what we'd expect. Though, as a diplomat, he has to declare all non-Government funding too. This is where we found an anomaly which might help us. He appears to draw down large sums of money from a bank account in the name of a charity set up for earthquake victims. As you know, Iran has been prone to several destructive earthquakes over the years, and it seems the charity was established five years ago to provide temporary housing and other assistance to those affected. Hassan is one of the registered patrons.'

'How often are those withdrawals made?' asked Dan.

'We've got a couple of our forensic accountants onto it,' said Philippa. 'There have been two large withdrawals in the past three weeks – one in Iran itself, the other was arranged through an intermediary in Sicily.'

'Which is only a ferry trip from Malta,' said Dan.

'Have you found out where the money went?' asked the Sheik.

'No,' said Philippa. 'In both instances, they were cash withdrawals. Hassan seems to be able to avoid any money-laundering investigations by utilising the charity's funds.'

David leaned forward, and took a sip of coffee before turning to Dan.

'Okay, Taylor – what did you come up with?'

Dan cleared his throat before speaking. 'I caught up with Philippa once she'd established the Malta connection and I've spent the last hour going through online newspaper articles to see how much of a public presence Hassan keeps in Malta. Basically – none whatsoever. He's very private, almost elusive, so we then started to look for any activities which could be linked to his villa's location on the north-east coast.'

He handed out copies of a newspaper clipping to the team. 'This is a small article from a community newsletter published three months ago, warning locals not to approach the property as the track leading up to it had been subject to heavy rain over the autumn and there was a risk of landslides.'

'Establishing a no-go zone?' suggested David.

'Exactly,' said Dan. 'I kept hunting, and found a couple of paragraphs in another local paper about a yacht which hadn't shown up as planned at a marina late last week.'

He held up another newspaper article. 'The captain and the luxury yacht he skippered was reported missing two days ago – it wouldn't have caught my attention except it mentions the area where they disappeared is extremely deep water and the authorities don't expect to be able to salvage his boat.' He paused. 'It's a perfect location for hiding a submarine, and it's the coastline next to Hassan's villa. I want to get out there and take a look myself. See if there's anything the newspaper or the authorities missed.'

David turned back to the table in the centre of the room and inspected the articles laid out on the surface. He picked up his coffee and tapped the side of the cup, deep in thought.

'What aerial surveillance have we managed to establish?' he asked.

'At such short notice, very little,' said Dan, 'but Mitch has a team talking to the Americans and some of our European allies at the moment to try to get some satellite coverage as soon as possible.'

David nodded. 'Good. Tell him if he needs my input to let me know straight away.'

'Will do.' Dan sat back in his chair and drummed his fingers on the table briefly before continuing. 'I really want to get out there, David – take a look on the ground. There's only so much we're going to achieve from here.'

'It's also going to be the only place we're going to stand a chance of installing some recording devices,' added Philippa. 'There's absolutely no way the Omanis will let us install anything in Hassan's rooms at the embassy.'

'If you're going to be investigating this I want my own people involved,' said the Sheik, leaning forward on the table.

David frowned. 'I'd have to clear it with a higher authority,' he said. 'Who do you have in mind?'

'My daughter, Antonia,' said the Sheik.

'Your daughter?' said Dan. 'What experience does she have?' He turned to David. 'I won't have time to act as a babysitter,' he growled.

The Sheik leaned back in his chair. 'She excelled in computer programming at university – you're going to need someone to help guide you through our systems and help with the investigation into how they were hacked.'

'So she can work from here then,' said Dan, satisfied.

The Sheik shook his head. 'If you want my full cooperation, she goes with you.' He held up his hand to silence Dan, who had begun to argue. 'I want to be kept informed of your progress at all times,' he said. Turning to David, he shrugged his shoulders. 'He's still an unknown quantity to me,' he explained, nodding towards Dan.

'Dan's got a point though,' said David. 'He'll have enough to do without making sure your daughter remains safe.'

'Antonia is an excellent markswoman and has studied karate for several years. She's easily as resilient as her three older brothers. She is due to fly into Heathrow this afternoon from Doha. I can direct her to meet Taylor in Malta instead. I have to return to Ras Laffan tonight to inspect the salvage efforts,' the Sheik said, then pointed at Dan. 'Antonia goes with him.'

'Alright,' said David, ignoring Dan's glare. 'while we're waiting for the final reports out of Ras Laffan, we'll keep going with the submarine angle and find out what we can from Kent Police about Grant Swift,' said David.

He stood up and began to walk from the room. 'Get to Valletta,' he said to Dan. 'You've got forty-eight hours.'

Chapter 22

Malta

Dan plucked his kit bag off the luggage carousel, swung it over his shoulder and headed for the airport exit. As he weaved his way through the crowd from the cheap European flight that had landed behind his, he scanned people's faces and looked for the Sheik's daughter. The flow of human traffic filed through customs and out into an airy arrivals hall.

His attention was caught by a woman dressed in a white shirt and jeans, dark brown curly hair haloed around a coffee-coloured complex, with high cheekbones and liquid brown eyes. She was only a few centimetres shorter than Dan. She held up a placard with two words, *LOST CAUSE*.

Dan grinned as he approached her. 'Obviously David has told you all about me.'

She smiled. 'A little.'

He walked around the rope cordon to join her and extended his hand. 'Dan Taylor.'

She took his outstretched hand and shook it. 'Antonia Almasi.' She nodded over her shoulder at a sign on the wall. 'Welcome to Malta, as they say. Come on. I've got a car outside. We can make a start now if you like. Did they give you an address for the safe house we're going to use?'

Dan reached into his pocket, pulled out his phone and held it up. 'GPS. I'll drive,' he said, and followed her through the airport exit.

The glare from the later afternoon sun hit him as they left the building. He lowered his sunglasses over his eyes and moved his bag from hand to hand as he shrugged his jacket off his shoulders.

'I'm beginning to understand why so many English tourists escape here for winter.'

Antonia smiled. 'Not to mention the rest of northern Europe. It's a pretty spot here.' She looked to her left, checked for traffic, and stepped off the kerb. She turned towards a short-stay car park.

'How long have you been here?' asked Dan.

'I flew in late last night, as soon as I got the call,' she said over her shoulder.

'Been here before?'

She pushed her hair out of her eyes, a breeze whipping it over her shoulders. 'Twice. Only short visits though,' she added. She pointed at a small white two-door car. 'That's us.'

Dan waited while Antonia unlocked the vehicle then swung his kit bag onto the back seat. Walking round to the driver's side, he pulled open the door of the rental car. It creaked ominously on its hinges. He ignored it, dropped into the driver's seat then yelped as the hot leather burned through the material of his jeans.

He glared at Antonia as she grinned at him and laid a towel across her seat before climbing in and slamming the door shut. He started the engine and pushed the car into gear.

***

After parking a few streets away from the apartment which would serve as their base for the next two days, Dan and Antonia walked a circuitous route to make sure they hadn't been followed from the airport, before approaching the building. The winter sun began to dip on the horizon, bathing the sandstone brickwork of the apartment block in a pink light.

After climbing two flights of stone steps, Dan unlocked the apartment door and stepped inside, Antonia closing the door behind them.

Dumping his kit bag on the floor, Dan pulled out an anti-bugging device and began walking around the apartment, checking each of the rooms in turn.

Antonia walked over to one of the windows which pooled the late afternoon light into the living area and peered out at the narrow street below. She turned as Dan came back into the room.

'You don't trust anyone, do you?' she asked.

He glanced up and frowned. 'No.'

Antonia folded her arms across her chest and watched as Dan paced the apartment, the anti-bugging device in his hand.

'Is there anything I can do?' she asked.

Dan stopped, turned, and grinned at her. 'Can you cook?'

Antonia scowled and stomped out of the room.

***

Dan unzipped his kit bag, pulled out three rolls of paper and turned towards the table.

As he began to unravel the documents, Antonia picked up their plates and placed them in the sink, then leaned against it, watching as Dan laid out the reports and photographs.

'What are those?' she asked.

'Latest satellite imagery of Hassan's villa,' explained Dan. 'I've got a colleague back in London who's monitoring a satellite feed for activity. We need to know if anything changes from what we've got here.'

Next, he leaned down and pulled out a laptop from the kit bag, together with a series of cables and a small box-like structure, setting out the equipment on the table.

Antonia put down her wine glass and picked up the black plastic box, turning it in her hand. 'What's this – a scrambler or something?'

'Yeah – something,' said Dan, taking it from her and putting it back on the table.

'This is a safe house – your signal won't be tracked.'

Dan glanced at Antonia, then back to his work. 'It's not *my* safe house, so I don't know for sure I won't be tracked.' He began to connect the equipment together, started the laptop and frowned at Antonia. 'No offence, but look the other way while I type in the access codes.'

Antonia shrugged, picked up her wine glass and turned away. 'None taken.'

Dan smiled and typed in the twelve digit code. 'Yeah, right,' he murmured under his breath.

Within minutes, he'd set up a satellite feed between himself and London. The screen flickered briefly, and then Mitch appeared, clutching a jumbo-sized take-out cup of coffee.

'Come here,' said Dan, calling over his shoulder to Antonia. 'Let's get started.'

Introductions made, Antonia glanced at Mitch's image on the screen, then at Dan. 'All right,' she said, 'what have you got so far?'

Dan leaned over and picked up one of the aerial photographs. 'Okay, this is a broad sweep of the property, showing all the buildings. There's the main villa, a structure which appears to be used for storage, then this area here,' he said, tapping the photo with the base of his wine glass, 'is an open structure – just a roof, no walls – where they're probably keeping vehicles.'

Antonia took the photograph from him and stared at it. 'Do we know how many guards there are?'

Mitch nodded. 'Not many. Hassan has a driver, a cook and a house-keeper based at the villa. Then there're the two bodyguards he travels with at all times. Your lot at the Qatari embassy have told us that there's probably only another two or three men on the property who guard the perimeter.'

'That's not many,' said Antonia, frowning.

Dan shrugged. 'Doesn't need to be. The villa's bordered by the cliffs on two sides, so they'd only have to worry about patrolling a relatively small area.' He picked up his wine glass and took a sip.

'How often does Hassan leave the villa?'

Dan picked up a report, his eyes scanning a series of highlighted sections. 'Only to meet with some people in Valletta once a week – we think they're representatives of the Iranian Government. So far we haven't been able to get anyone into the building there to set up any sort of listening devices though.'

'I thought that was illegal in embassies?'

Mitch shook his head. 'They don't meet in an embassy – they're using a small three storey office block near the ferry terminal.'

Antonia pulled out a chair, sat down and took a sip of her wine before setting her glass on the table. 'So, what's the plan?'

Dan pulled out another chair and joined her, topping up their wine glasses before he spoke. 'We can't get close to Hassan in London – he's probably holed up at the Omani embassy,' he explained. 'We know he has a regular meeting on a Wednesday at a building here in Malta – in Valetta,' he added, pointing at the photograph. 'That's under heavy guard and is probably being used by the Iranian Government, so, like I said, we can't bug that place either. Which leaves,' he said, tossing a photograph across the table to Antonia, 'the villa. It's about four miles from here, and it's where our comms team picked up a phone call made by Hassan.'

'You're not going to try to break in and bug the house?' said Antonia, frowning.

Dan shook his head. 'No – too dangerous. I plan to use some small camouflaged directional microphones which will stick to the windows.' He bent down and pulled out a thin aluminium case from his kit bag and popped open the lid. Inside, a set of four fake hand-crafted cicadas sat nestled in a velvet base.

Antonia reached out to touch them. 'They're beautiful,' she murmured.

Dan pulled the case out of her reach. 'Our comms section chief is a keen fly-fisherman,' he explained. 'With any luck, these won't be noticed for a few days and we'll get the information we need.'

He put the case back into his kit bag and sifted through the photographs on the table in front of him. 'Has anything changed with the surveillance since these were taken Mitch?'

'No – but bear in mind we only have a two-hour window each time the satellite passes over.'

'How often does that happen?'

'At the moment, three times a day – we're piggy-backing onto an American satellite to help with the surveillance.'

'Okay. Then Antonia and I will go there tomorrow and recce the place as best we can.' He pointed to an area near the property. 'There's a hill or a rise about a mile away from the villa – we should be able to access that from this road here.' He stabbed the photograph with his finger and pushed it towards Antonia. 'I want to see what we're up against before we try anything.'

He scratched his chin. 'Mitch – I need you to fly out as soon as we're finished here. Once we've done the initial on-ground assessment tomorrow, I can go in under cover of darkness while Hassan is away from the property. You can track his movements on the satellite feed while I see what's in those outbuildings.'

Mitch nodded. 'Sounds good. I'll bring the comms equipment out with me. Antonia can go with you and act as your look-out.'

'Works for me,' said Antonia.

Dan began to collate the photographs and documents off the table. 'Okay. Mitch – we'll see you tomorrow. In the meantime, we'll get some sleep and then go to the marina where that yacht disappeared from.'

Mitch held up his hand in mock salute. 'Happy hunting.'

Chapter 23

'What's the name of the place we're heading for?' Dan pulled his sunglasses down over his eyes to protect them from the early morning glare.

'Vittoriosa marina,' said Antonia. 'If we ask a few questions we might be able to shed a bit of light.'

Dan nodded. 'Sounds good to me.'

'You used to live in Malta?' Antonia asked.

He shrugged. 'A while back – just passing through,' he said. He looked out the window. Two months' work four years ago seemed like a lifetime ago. And not the happiest of times.

Antonia noticed his reticence and let him brood. She steered the small car out of the car park and turned left, turned on the radio and beat her hands on the steering wheel in time with the music.

The car cruised easily down the main road to the southern end of the island. Dan watched the scenery passing by, remnants of medieval walls and buildings punctuating the mainly flat landscape while small walled fields lay barren and ploughed, ready for the spring.

Dan wound down his window, leaned his elbow on the door frame and turned to Antonia. 'Did David tell you much about this mission?'

She shook her head. 'Just to meet you at the airport, provide support when needed, and take you to the marina when you wanted to go.' She smiled. 'I took the liberty of phoning ahead to make sure someone would be there to talk to us.'

Dan nodded. 'Good thinking.' As the car turned off the highway and began to follow a narrow winding road, he told her about the missing yacht.

'Why is the yacht so important?' she asked, slowing as the car approached an old bus lumbering along the road.

'It might help explain some questions we have on a case we're working on,' Dan said. 'It's a long shot, but we're under pressure for answers so we're investigating everything.'

Antonia nodded, craned her head to the right then overtook the bus. The road dropped down into a pretty coastal town, the sea sparkling in the mid-morning sunlight.

She expertly steered the car into a narrow parking space next to a shop selling tourist souvenirs and switched off the engine. The quayside curved round the natural harbour on the opposite side of the road, the brightly painted fishing boats a blaze of colour next to the sandstone harbour wall.

'The marina is further down,' she pointed to a series of yacht masts in the near distance. 'We can start there.'

Dan climbed out of the car, stretched his legs and turned, taking in his surroundings. 'Okay, lead the way,' he said and followed Antonia as she crossed the road, weaving between an old mini-bus and two cars.

They walked side-by-side along the harbour wall, a light breeze whipping Antonia's long hair around her face. She pushed it out of the way and curled it round her neck with a practised flick of her wrist. She pointed out the quayside stores as they passed. 'This is one of the more popular tourist destinations on the island,' she explained, 'so there are a lot of bars and cafes along this stretch. Then the marina was completed and the place exploded for business.'

'It's a lot different from how I remember it,' said Dan, his eyes taking in his surroundings. His height was an advantage – he could peer over the traffic and see the row of shops and cafes stretching out along the gentle curve which followed the harbour wall.

'You've been here?' asked Antonia, surprised. 'When?'

Dan shrugged. 'A few years ago.' He pointed to a building on a corner which housed a stylish café on the ground floor and what appeared to be living space on the next two floors. 'That used to be quite an unsavoury bar.'

Antonia frowned. 'Yes, there were plenty of places along here once where the clientele – and the staff – could be a bit rough.'

Dan grinned. 'I know – I used to work there.'

'I'm sorry. I didn't mean it like that.' Antonia blushed.

Dan laughed as they passed the café. 'Don't worry about it – I wasn't exactly on my best behaviour in those days.'

'Ah,' said Antonia and looked away, smiling.

The row of fishing boats thinned out, and gave way to small private motor boats and yachts. Dan gave each a cursory glance, admiring engines on the back of some, and noticing that more than one yacht was in need of a fresh coat of paint. Various items of laundry strung along decks flapped in the breeze, while ropes clanged against masts. A man paused with a mop in his hand and gave a friendly wave, before turning his back and carrying on with his work.

As they reached the final curve of the harbour, the small marina came into view. Dan stared admiringly at a large motor cruiser moored alongside the wall, its freshly washed black and white bodywork gleaming in the morning sun, a dive deck surrounded by tan leather seats and a jet ski parked on the back.

'You like boats?' asked Antonia, amused by his gaze.

'I like the *idea* of boats,' Dan grinned. 'Not sure I want the work that comes with them.'

Antonia laughed and gestured at the cruiser. 'If you can afford that, you can afford the staff to go with it,' she said. 'Come on – the office is down here.'

The marina office was a small modern wooden building, with a covered deck area at the front with tables and chairs and a drinks vending machine next to the front door. An older man who sat with a newspaper spread out in front of him glanced up at them as they walked up the steps to the deck, nodded, and went back to his reading as they entered the office.

A cluster of small bells hanging from a piece of string on the door announced their arrival. A woman appeared from a back office, wiping her hands on a towel and smiling.

'Morning,' she said. 'How can I help?'

Antonia stuck out her hand. 'I'm Antonia Almasi,' she said. 'We spoke on the phone this morning I believe.'

'Ah yes,' said the woman. 'Sylvia Camelleri.'

Antonia introduced Dan and then pointed out to the marina. 'Did you know Paul Spiteri?'

Sylvia nodded. 'He was based here for the last two years,' she said. 'Before that I think he worked in Greece – I'm not sure. But always on the yachts – the clients trusted him.'

'Did he have regular customers or just take whatever work came up?' asked Dan.

Sylvia frowned, thinking. 'I know when he first came here, he didn't advertise – people just knew him by reputation. But then times got hard, people had to sell their toys and Paul started to take work where he could find it.'

'Was he trustworthy?' asked Antonia, and put her hand up to placate the woman. 'I mean, if times were hard, would he worry about who he worked for?'

Sylvia leaned on the counter and looked at the marina outside. 'You know, I'm not sure. I'd like to say yes, but,' she shrugged, 'if you need work and you need it badly enough, who knows?'

'What records do you keep for people who use the marina?' asked Dan.

Sylvia smiled, bent down and picked up a large book which she placed on the counter-top. 'This is our register,' she explained. 'Everyone who wants to stay has to provide identification, like a passport, and how long they'll be staying. Phone number, place of origin, that sort of thing.'

Dan glanced down at the register. 'Do you mind if I take a look?'

Sylvia shook her head and turned the register to face Dan.

He casually flicked through the pages, figuring that just because people provided details, it didn't mean they were correct, or were even checked in the first place.

'The yacht that disappeared,' prompted Antonia. 'Whose was it?'

Sylvia took the register back from Dan and traced her finger down the page. 'Here. Paul had brought it from Rhodes at the beginning of the week. He was supposed to be leaving yesterday for New York.'

Dan fished into his jeans pocket and pulled out a photocopy of the news report about the missing yacht. 'Apparently a film producer had bought the yacht after seeing it during filming in Rhodes,' he read, then folded up the page. 'I guess he'll be screaming at his insurers right now.' He leaned on the counter. 'What about family? Is anyone over here looking for answers?'

Sylvia shook her head. 'Paul was a loner. I remember we had a party at our house once and a few of us got pretty drunk. He sat on the terrace with Antony, my husband, and said that's why he loved crewing yachts for people – he got an adopted family every now and again.' She gazed sadly out the window. 'I don't think anyone's looking for him.'

'How good a sailor was he?' asked Antonia.

'Very good,' said Sylvia. 'Some people just think they are, but Paul had years of experience in some very tough conditions. Just disappearing into thin air off the coast here…' she frowned. 'Impossible.'

Chapter 24

'So, Daniel,' said Antonia, easing herself forward on her elbows and squinting at the house in the distance, 'what exactly is your plan?'

'It's not Daniel.'

She turned. 'What?'

Dan smiled. 'My name – it's not Daniel.' He lifted the binoculars and peered at the villa.

'So what is it?'

He sighed. 'It doesn't matter.'

Antonia grinned. 'Come on – tell. What embarrassing name did your parents give you?'

He groaned. 'It's on a need to know basis – and you don't.'

'I'll find out anyway.'

'Dante.'

Antonia put her hand over her mouth and tipped sideways into the grass, laughing.

'It's not that funny.'

'It is,' she wheezed. 'Oh my god – you should be selling artwork or something, not working for the British Government!' She broke off, coughing.

'Be careful you don't choke,' Dan growled, and put the binoculars to his eyes, ignoring the giggling next to him.

Antonia nudged Dan in the ribs. 'Give me the binoculars.'

'In a minute.'

'At least tell me what you see.'

Dan swung the binoculars to the right of the outbuildings, being careful not to raise his head and shoulders too high above the rocky outcrop in case someone spotted his silhouette against the ridgeline.

'Okay, there's a dirt road leading up an incline – that drops down to the villa. A set of wrought iron gates with a guard behind them. Looks like he's pacing backwards and forwards to stay awake at the moment. Must be the end of his shift.' He slowly swung the binoculars to his left. 'The outer perimeter has a concrete wall around it. Hang on.' Dan adjusted the binoculars. 'There's razor wire along the top of the wall.'

'Electrified?' asked Antonia, leaning forward on her elbows.

'No – can't see any transformers along the wire.'

'Good.'

Dan raised the binoculars slowly. 'Past the gates, there's a small outbuilding, single storey.'

Antonia shaded her eyes with her hand. 'I see it.'

'Looks like it's being used for storage,' said Dan. 'There're two guys standing outside it, smoking – maybe it's doubling up as accommodation too.'

'That would make sense,' agreed Antonia. 'Give me the binoculars.'

'In a minute.' He winced and moved his elbows, small sharp stones sticking to his skin. 'Further up the track you've got the main villa and a smaller outbuilding – by the looks of it, it's being used as a garage. I can see a small Jeep.'

Antonia banged her fist on the dirt in front of her. 'Enough.' She slapped Dan's arm. 'Hand them over.'

Dan took the binoculars from his eyes and held them out. As Antonia reached out for them, he snatched them back and grinned.

She punched his arm.

Dan stopped grinning and dropped the binoculars on the dirt in surprise. 'Where the hell did you learn to punch like that?' he hissed.

'I have an older brother,' Antonia smiled, picking up the binoculars and holding them to her eyes.

**

The rhythmic chirp of cicadas pierced the evening breeze as the team sat in their vehicle hidden behind a low wall on the farm track.

On his arrival from London that afternoon, Mitch had run through the telecommunications equipment with Dan, selecting the best kit for the job. He now handed earpieces and throat microphones to Dan and Antonia, then switched on a tablet computer, checked the comms channel was working, and nodded to Dan, his face illuminated by the screen's low glow.

'You're good to go.' He glanced over his shoulder. 'Are you sure you don't want me to come with you instead?'

Dan shook his head. 'I want you here as my eyes and ears,' he said. 'This is going to be tricky enough as it is.' He put the earpiece in place, and tapped the throat mike to check it. 'Is David watching this?'

'Yes I am,' a dismembered voice came over the comms channel. 'So don't fuck up.'

'I hear you.' Dan leaned forward and pointed at the image on the tablet computer in Mitch's hands. 'I'll go in here – the trees on the other side of the wall will give me a bit of cover to start with.'

Mitch nodded. 'As soon as Hassan leaves the property, I'll use the satellite feed from London to track his movements and give you a heads up when he's on his way back from Valletta.'

Dan grunted and checked his watch. 'Good – that should give me half an hour to get away from the property.' He turned in the passenger seat to face Antonia, who was twisted on the back seat, pulling a long-sleeved black sweater over her head. 'I need you to boost me up the wall so I can cut through the wire – think you can take my weight?'

She nodded. 'I'll be fine, don't worry. Where do you want me to wait for you?'

Dan took the tablet computer from Mitch and held it up so Antonia could see the live satellite image of the property. 'There's a ditch opposite the wall here. Get me over the wall then wait here. Don't move until one of us tells you to.'

'Copy that.' Antonia pulled a black woollen mask over her head.

'Hey, that's an improvement,' grinned Mitch, and then flinched as Antonia slapped him on the side of the head.

Dan scowled. 'Let's go.'

**

Dan and Antonia sprawled in a ditch opposite Hassan's property. Dan felt his heartbeat in his ears as he cupped his hand around the luminous face of his watch.

'How are we doing for time?' Antonia whispered.

Dan pulled his sleeve down over his watch, using a piece of electrical tape to tighten the cuff so the watch dial wouldn't give away his position once he was over the wall and enveloped in darkness.

'We're fine,' he murmured. 'Any moment...'

He broke off. They ducked simultaneously at the sound of a vehicle approaching the opposite side of the wrought iron gates to their right.

Dan peered over the edge of the ditch as the gates were opened by the guard on duty, then it turned and swept down the road away from them. Its rear lights flashed as it rounded a corner and disappeared from sight.

Dan held up a hand to Antonia until the sound of the car's powerful engine had completely faded.

They slowly raised their heads, peering over at the gates as the guard pushed them closed and looped a chain around them. Satisfied, he reached into the top pocket of his coat and pulled out a cigarette. A flame flared brightly, then disappeared, leaving the tell-tale pinpoint of a cigarette end glowing in the darkness.

'While the cat's away…,' murmured Antonia.

The guard turned away from them, and began to walk away along the inside length of the wall. Dan counted to ten in his head.

'Go!' he whispered.

Crouching low to the ground, they scurried across the rough track, hugging themselves to the concrete wall on the opposite side.

Silently, they listened for any movement on the other side of the wall.

Nothing.

Dan eased himself away from the wall, glanced down at Antonia and nodded, pulling a set of wire clippers from the pocket of his black trousers.

Antonia cupped her hands, bent down and braced her back against the wall.

Dan slipped his boot into her hands, steadying himself with a hand on her shoulder. He glanced up at the wall, then at Antonia and winked.

'Ready?' he whispered.

She nodded. 'Just don't take too long to cut that wire.'
She shuffled her feet, planting her boots firmly on the
ground. 'On my count…'

Dan launched himself at the wall, his momentum
boosted as Antonia straightened her legs, grimacing under
his weight, until she was standing upright. Dan then
stepped onto her shoulders, her back supported by the wall,
and quickly snipped through the wire. He dropped the wire
cutters to the ground and pulled apart the broken pieces of
wire. Placing his hands on the top of the concrete wall, he
heaved himself up onto its surface and kept low.

Antonia gasped and stumbled from the relief of
shedding his weight. Gaining her balance, she grabbed the
wire cutters from where they'd fallen into the long grass at
her feet, checked the road each way, then ran across the
track and threw herself into the ditch.

Turning, she looked up to see Dan lowering himself
over the other side of the wall. He glanced up, gave her a
brief wave, and dropped from view.

Antonia tapped her throat microphone. 'Tango One,
this is Tango Three. Confirm Tango Two is live, I repeat,
Tango Two is live.'

Chapter 25

Dan dropped to the ground, kneeling until his heartbeat slowed. He remained still, straining his ears.

No-one approached.

He slowly drew himself up to his full height, glanced down at the ground, then carefully placed his feet one after the other through the rough undergrowth.

Ducking under a low branch, he peered through the trees, getting his bearings.

'Okay, I can see your heat signature,' said Mitch over the radio.

Dan slowly made his way through the trees, keeping the driveway to his right within sight. He crouched behind the trunk of the last tree and peered out across the barren earth towards the larger of the two outbuildings.

On the ground, the structures looked more dilapidated than through the binoculars earlier that day, but one was in better condition and appeared to have had its walls recently rebuilt. Modern concrete blocks jostled for position with older limestone hand-hewn stone, weathered by time and the elements.

The roof of the structure was constructed from salvaged tin – rusty in some places, newly galvanised in others. A sturdy wooden door had been fixed to the front, and new bolts gleamed in the moonlight.

He glanced up at the night sky. Clouds scurried intermittently across the moon, providing better cover than the full moon.

He touched his throat mike. 'Where are those guards Mitch?'

The line crackled once, then Mitch's voice reached out through the static. 'Other side of the property. Hang on, I'll zoom in to your position.'

Dan waited, silently watching the building in front of him. It was only fifty metres away, but it was across exposed ground.

'Okay,' said Mitch. 'I've got two people inside that building, in the room to the far side of your position. You've got a clear approach.'

'Copy that. Waiting for cloud cover.'

Dan stood, watching the clouds scuttle across the night sky. A faint breeze blew salt air into his face and he took several deep breaths to calm his nerves, while he peered across the low ground ahead, looking for any rocks or obstacles which could trip him.

Then the moonlight waned.

Dan sprinted across the bare earth, his footsteps muffled by the dirt under his boots. In seconds, he threw himself against the stone wall and dropped into a crouch.

He waited, catching his breath, then reached into his pocket for the case of micro-transceivers.

'How are we doing, Mitch?' he murmured.

'All good. Guards in your building haven't moved – looks like they're playing cards. Two on patrol have reached the covered area east of your position. Estimate they'll be turning back towards you in five minutes.'

'Copy that.'

Dan opened the case and picked up one of the disguised micro-transceivers between his fingers. Returning the case to his pocket, he edged slowly round the back of the outbuilding until he was under the window of the room where the guards were playing cards.

He glanced up. Light shone through the glass, pooling onto the ground.

'Mitch – confirm there's no-one to my nine through to three o'clock position,' he murmured. 'I'm going to be very exposed here.'

A few seconds' silence preceded the other man's response.

'You're clear.'

Dan tapped his throat mike twice in confirmation. He pulled off the cover of the adhesive grips on the base of the cicada and slowly edged his body into an upright position next to the window frame. Breathing deeply to steady his hand, he turned to face the wall and slowly moved the tiny cicada-shaped gadget into position. His hand stopped at the edge of the wooden frame. If the guards saw any movement on the glass as he placed the transceiver, their mission would fail.

'Guards are turning back,' said Mitch. 'Estimate you've got fifteen minutes.'

Dan closed his eyes. Fifteen minutes, and he still had three more micro-transceivers to put into position.

A sudden roar from within the room made him jump. Then laughter and voices, as a good-natured argument ensued.

Now.

Dan reached across and carefully placed the cicada on the glass, then dropped into a crouch once more.

'Are you getting the signal?' he hissed into his throat mike.

'Copy that. Works perfectly,' said Mitch. 'Sounds like someone was trying to cheat.'

'Okay.' Dan lifted his sleeve, glanced at his watch then tapped his throat mike.

'Three more to go.'

***

Antonia grimaced and shifted her weight to alleviate the prickling sensation in her arms and legs. The temperature had dropped since sunset and a chill breeze whipped along the dirt track.

In her earpiece she could hear the exchange between Dan and Mitch, her heart beating in a shared adrenalin rush as Dan had sprinted towards the outbuilding.

She caught a movement out of the corner of her eye, and glanced up.

'Shit!' she murmured.

A guard had appeared to her left, walking along the *outside* of the perimeter wall.

'Mitch!' she hissed into her throat mike. 'What the hell? I've got a guard on the outside of the wall heading my way!'

Mitch swore at the other end of the comms link. 'Get your head down in that ditch and don't move!'

'Why didn't we know about an outer perimeter guard?' David's voice demanded over the link.

'Maybe something changed at the villa today,' said Mitch. 'Perhaps they're in lock-down?'

'And you didn't spot him?' asked David.

'I was busy watching Dan's back!' hissed Mitch.

Antonia whipped off her balaclava and pushed her nose into the dirt. If she was spotted, it'd be a hell of a lot harder to explain herself with a mask covering her face.

She stayed silent, listening to the voices in her ear.

'Antonia – do not engage,' said David. 'I repeat – do not engage. Not unless he finds you. Let him walk past.'

Antonia tapped her finger on the throat mike twice as an affirmative, not wanting to risk her voice carrying down the track towards the approaching guard.

She held her breath as the guard's footsteps drew closer. The beam of his flashlight swept each side of the dirt road, momentarily brightening the grass beside her, before sweeping across the road to the wall.

Her heart sank as the guard halted in front of her, and uttered a curse under his breath.

Antonia slowly raised her head.

The guard was shining his torch up the wall, craning his neck as he shone the light onto the broken wire at the top of the structure.

Antonia raised herself up into a crouching position, her fingers curling tightly around the handle of the wire clippers in her pocket. She drew them out, and tapped on her throat mike three times.

'Shit,' said Mitch. 'She's going to engage, David – she's got no choice.'

'Engage confirmed.' said David. 'Make it clean.'

Antonia launched herself up and across the track.

The guard turned, his left hand fumbling for his radio, his right hand tucked into his jacket, searching for his weapon, his jaw dropping open in surprise.

Antonia didn't hesitate. With a low snarl, she jumped on the guard's back and thrust the wire clippers into the side of his neck.

As he dropped to the ground, Antonia grabbed one of his legs and dragged him gasping into the ditch.

Blood started to gush from the wound, the guard's strangled breaths forcing blood out from between his lips.

She stared down at him dispassionately, grabbed a piece of the wire Dan had cut from the wall and wrapped it quickly around the guard's neck. Bracing her feet against the side of the ditch, she began to pull, until the barrel of a gun pressed hard against her temple.

'Stop, or I'll shoot,' said a voice, before her throat mike and ear piece were ripped off.

Antonia let the ends of the wire slip through her fingers. As the guard slumped forward on the ground, groaning, Antonia slowly raised her hands and turned, moments before the man's fist drove into her cheek, knocking her to the ground.

Chapter 26

Dan edged round the corner of the outbuilding, listening to the frantic exchange in his earpiece.

A loud expletive from Mitch ended the conversation.

'What the *fuck* is going on?' Dan hissed.

'Antonia's out of action,' explained David. 'We've just lost all comms contact with her.'

'Shit!' Dan glanced around the open expanse between the outbuilding and the villa. 'Mitch – I've still got three bugs to plant. What's the status of the guards?'

'Move now. The ground's clear but you've probably got seconds until word gets out about Antonia and the two guards in that building hightail it out of there.'

'Copy that,' said Dan, and sprinted towards the villa.

He slid across the last five metres of gravel and dirt, sliding to a standstill against the side of the house.

Hearing a shout from the outbuilding, he glanced up. The two guards had spilled out of the doorway, chattering excitedly into their radios.

He heard the splutter of an engine revving, and saw an open-top Jeep reversing out of the garage building. It spun in the loose gravel and then shot forwards down the driveway towards the front gate.

'Looks like they've found Antonia,' he murmured.

'Is she alive?' asked David.

'I don't know yet. I'll let you know.'

Dan pulled out the aluminium case and selected another cicada. Edging slowly along the wall, he approached another window, wooden blinds silhouetting the light from within.

He remained still, listening to the sound of voices through the open window above his head, straining to hear what was being said. A crash of metal confirmed his thoughts – he was outside the kitchen area.

He slowly made his way along the side of the house, pausing under each window, taking his time, planting one more of the micro-transceivers. As he moved, he kept a watchful eye on the yard, ready to drop to the ground if anyone appeared.

A few minutes later he heard the sound of the vehicle returning, the noise of its engine increasing as it sped towards the house.

He tentatively raised his head and peered around the side of the villa. His heart sank.

Antonia sat between two guards on the back seat of the vehicle, her arms pinned behind her back.

The driver skidded to a halt inside the gates. One of the guards jumped out and re-fastened the chain.

Dan watched as Antonia gazed around the compound. He ducked lower. He couldn't afford for her to see him now. He felt the anger rise as he recalled the red welt visible on her cheek.

The vehicle lurched forward. The guard finished securing the chain before he turned and walked in the direction the vehicle had taken.

Dan raised his head and watched as the vehicle pulled up outside the villa and Antonia was dragged from her seat. He could hear her protests carrying over the slight breeze which ruffled the grass at his feet, and then a slap and her protests died out.

Dan tapped his throat mike. 'I'm going in.'

'Negative, Dan. Get out of there. We need to organise a proper rescue mission,' snapped David.

'There's no time,' hissed Dan. 'God knows what those brutes will do to her. Once Hassan gets back here…'

'Dan, no – it's too risky.'

'She's one of us, David. I'm not leaving her behind.'

Dan ripped out his earpiece and removed the throat microphone. Crouching down, he quickly scraped a small hollow in the earth with his bare hands, dropped the comms equipment into it, and covered it up.

Satisfied, he crawled along the wall. At the end, he took a deep breath and peered around the corner.

A paved terraced area appeared uninhibited, the moonlight not yet having crested the house. A cool breeze whipped dried leaves around the legs of a cast iron table and its chairs, which stood haphazardly, recently abandoned.

Dan considered his options. His eyes caught movement near the west-facing wall from curtains, which billowed in the breeze that blew in across the patio and through the house.

Silently, he began to edge towards the patio doors. As he drew closer, he noticed the curtain was billowing out from a door which had been left slightly ajar. He paused, and craned his neck to peer through the first window. The curtains blew outwards in the breeze once more and Dan caught a glimpse of a study, with bookshelves along one length of wall, a desk at the end nearest to him, and a low coffee table surrounded by four armchairs. At the far end, he saw an open door, which he presumed led out into a hallway.

He turned and, glancing over his shoulder and seeing no-one, strode purposefully over to the open patio door, pushed the curtain to one side and entered the room, carefully sliding the last micro-transceiver onto the glass surface of the patio door as he passed.

***

The first thing that struck Dan was the smell. It was a mixture of spices, sweet tea and a lingering afterthought of cigars.

He stopped just inside the patio doors, pulled them closed behind him, shut the curtains and listened.

From somewhere in the depths of the villa, he could hear a rumble of male voices – two or three men talking excitedly.

Mindful that he had to find where Antonia had been taken, he walked over and crouched next to the desk.

Made from a deeply stained mahogany, the desk appeared to be several years old, with decorative carvings adorning its edges. Dan ran his fingers over the rich wood, feeling the workmanship under his touch.

He pulled on the iron handle of the topmost of four drawers, but it refused to move. He stepped back as he spotted a corner of a page sticking out from the bottom drawer, bent down, glanced at his short fingernails, and cursed under his breath.

After trying each of the drawers and finding them locked, he stood up and began carefully sifting through the papers arranged in tidy piles on the desk.

Dan looked up sharply as the voices grew louder, more aggressive. His heart stopped as he heard Antonia's voice laced with fear, pleading.

'Please, *no*.'

The sound of a slap pierced the air.

Dan dropped the pages from his hand, the notes fluttering over the desk surface as he cleared the room in long strides and peered through the open doorway. The passageway was deserted, so he craned his neck round the door frame to get his bearings. The voices were coming from his right, back towards the direction of the kitchen. To his left, a flight of stairs led upwards, curving round to the right and hiding the upper level from view.

Dan turned right, keeping close to the wall, and checked over his shoulder as he progressed quickly towards the voices. As he drew closer he could hear the conversation.

'Who are you working for?'

'I told you – no-one!'

'So why were you here? The road is clearly private property.'

Dan frowned. The accent was familiar, Middle Eastern.

'I was out for a walk. I got lost. I wanted to ask for directions.'

Dan winced as another slap emanated from the kitchen, and Antonia cried out. He reached down for his Sig Sauer.

He edged closer along the passageway towards the open kitchen door, now only a few steps away. He stopped, trying to think of a way to get Antonia out alive, wondering how much time he'd have from the first gunshot being fired.

Dan breathed out hard. Two voices. Probably more guards in the house somewhere.

He heard a metallic rattle from the kitchen, a belt being loosened.

'Maybe it's time we taught you what happens to strange women who attack our friends,' said one of the voices.

Decision time.

He shook his head. It could turn out to be the worst decision of his life. And the last. He raised his gun and stepped out.

'Let her go.'

The conversation stopped in mid-sentence and two men turned to face him.

Chapter 27

Dan quickly scanned the room and took in the situation. Two men, and Antonia. They had forced her to sit on one of the wooden kitchen chairs. Her eyes widened in shock as Dan appeared.

The larger of the two men stood behind her, pinning her arms by her sides, while his accomplice stood in front of her, his arm raised, his head turned to face Dan.

'Who the fuck are you?' he growled, straightening up, his hand automatically seeking the gun tucked under his shirt.

'Don't,' said Dan. 'I'll kill you and your friend here before you've even thought about whether to fire or not.'

The man laughed, lowered his hand slowly then held up both in a placating gesture. 'Calm down. This is private property. Your friend here,' he jerked his head at Antonia, 'was trespassing. So are you.'

'Apologies,' said Dan. 'Now let her go.'

The man standing behind Antonia smirked and stroked her face. Antonia jerked her head away, but the man tightened his grip on her arms. She whimpered in pain.

'Maybe we let you go and keep her,' the man snarled.

Dan kept his gun up and his focus on the first man. 'In your dreams,' he murmured. He edged through the door frame, glanced left and right. No-one else in the room.

The first man blinked once, then glanced back at his colleague and jerked his chin at Antonia. 'Let her go.'

Dan relaxed a split second too soon. Too late, he saw Antonia's eyes widen, then there was an explosion in his kidneys and his legs gave way as he crashed to the floor.

He lay curled on the floor, tears in his eyes from the excruciating pain, gasping to get his breath. He turned his head at a cackle above him, his attacker grinning down at him, holding a pool cue in his hand.

'Didn't expect that, did you?' said the man.

'What took you so long, Mustapha?' asked the first thug.

Dan's assailant shrugged. 'I wanted to make sure there was only one of him. And there is. Must be her boyfriend.'

'Doesn't explain what he's doing here,' said the other man as he bent down and picked up Dan's gun. 'Or what he's doing with this,' he added, turning it in his hand. He looked down at Dan and kicked him in the back.

Dan groaned, and guessed he'd be pissing blood for a couple of days – if they got out alive. 'Up yours,' he mumbled then turned, gasping, as he tried to ease the pain.

'Get him up,' ordered Mustapha.

The two thugs bent down and forced Dan to his knees.

'Who are you?' asked the third man. 'What are you doing here?'

'Trick or treat,' said Dan.

He saw the punch coming and braced himself. As the impact hit him, his head snapped to the left and he tasted blood. He grunted and let his head hang for a moment as he ran his tongue around his mouth counting teeth. One felt loose. *Still there though*.

He raised his head and glared at the guard who stood back, grinned at him, and then nodded at the two guards who pinned Dan's arms behind his back.

'Throw them both in the cellar, Ali, and shut the door. The boss can talk to them when he gets back. Then they'll understand pain,' he snarled, before he turned and strode from the room.

'No!' screamed Antonia as Ali lunged for her and, grabbing her wrist, forced her down the stone steps with his revolver to her temple.

***

Dan looked around at his surroundings as their captors closed the cellar door. A set of shelves caught his eye. He lunged for them as the room plunged into darkness and the sound of deadbolts being closed echoed around the subterranean chamber.

'What are you doing?' asked Antonia, her voice quivering.

'Hang on.' Dan reached along the shelves slowly. He was sure he'd seen something they could use, but he didn't want to knock it on the floor – he'd never find it again.

His fingers traced over the rough surface, touching dust, old cardboard packets. He sneezed, and as his hand moved with the involuntary reflex that shivered through his body, his fingers brushed the surface of what he'd been searching for. He grinned as he pulled it towards him, his heart beating.

Please let this work.

He turned the object in his hands, getting his bearings. Holding it vertically, he pushed the switch jutting out from the side of it, and held his breath.

The torch hesitantly flickered to life.

Dan slapped the side of it with the palm of his hand and willed the beam to keep steady. He swung the light to his left and right, getting his bearings, then caught a glimpse of Antonia staring at him.

'Let's find a way out,' he said.

Easing himself past discarded boxes strewn across the floor, he handed the torch to Antonia then placed his hands above his head and pushed at the cellar door.

It was fixed solid, with no movement under Dan's efforts. He cursed.

'It would've been too easy,' said Antonia, as she handed him the torch and watched him swing the beam around the cellar.

'I know, but if you don't check the obvious, you could be wasting time looking for alternatives,' he replied. He shone the torch into the gloom. Cobwebs hung from every one of the exposed beams. He shuddered as one brushed against his face. He swept his hand across his face, and felt an involuntary shiver down his spine.

'Are you scared of spiders?' whispered Antonia, the amusement in her voice evident.

'Only the big ones,' he hissed.

He pushed his way to the back of the cellar, climbing over empty crates and boxes. He swung the torchlight across the faint lettering on the outside of the various wooden cartons and frowned. A military-like stencil array of letters and numbers had been printed across the lids. He turned his head, trying to fathom the abbreviations and numbered sequences, then shook his head and moved across to a pile of empty cardboard boxes, Antonia following in his wake.

'What is it?' she asked, her gaze following the torchlight while she carefully followed Dan across the cellar floor.

'Supplies,' he murmured. 'Which means we're on the right track.'

'Right track?'

Dan stopped and shone the torch across the cellar to the far wall. 'When I was upstairs in Hassan's study, I saw an old map on the wall. It had lines leading away from the villa – I thought they were old footpaths or something, but now I'm wondering if they were tunnels.'

Antonia frowned. 'Tunnels? Leading where?'

Dan swung the torch light round the cavernous cellar until he found the empty packing crates. 'Those are military markings,' he explained. 'I'm not sure what they mean,' he shrugged, 'but put them together with the empty food boxes and I'm thinking this is where they're resupplying a stolen submarine. That's why we're really here. I couldn't tell you before. If we can find the entrance to a tunnel, I'm betting it leads to the cliffs and somehow they've got their supplies down to the submarine.'

Antonia nodded. 'Sounds good.' She looked up at him. 'Where do we start?'

Dan jerked his thumb over his shoulder. 'Back there. It's the outer wall, and if my sense of direction is right, it's the nearest to the coastline.'

He turned, kicked an empty box out of the way, and began to move towards the back of the cellar.

Antonia grabbed his arm. 'Dan!'

He stopped and turned.

Antonia looked around them, then up at Dan. 'If they put us down here with this stuff, then we're not meant to be getting out of here alive to tell anyone, are we?'

Dan stepped forward and pulled her to him. 'No, we're not.' He hugged her tightly then stepped back and held her arms. 'But we're going to find a way, okay?'

She nodded as Dan turned, kicked an empty box out of the way, grabbed her by the hand and led the way.

Upon reaching the wall, they began to run their fingers over it, trying to find an opening.

'We're running out of time,' hissed Antonia as she desperately clawed at the stones set into the ancient mortar.

'Keep looking – it's here somewhere.'

Antonia cursed as a fingernail tore, then slapped the wall in frustration, turned her back and leaned against it. 'This is ridiculous,' she said. 'It's not like there's going to be a hidden latch or anything. We're wasting…'

She broke off and gasped as the wall gave way under her weight, stumbling as she lost her balance.

Dan reached out, caught her arm and steadied her, a grin plastered across his face. 'You've broken it! I told you not to have that extra croissant for breakfast.'

She slapped his arm. 'You…!'

'Come on,' he urged. 'Beat me up later. We've got to get moving.'

He stooped and shone the torch through the gap in the wall. A sand-strewn rough path led away from the house, just as the map had indicated. He looked over his shoulder, took Antonia's hand, and squeezed.

'Ready?'

She nodded, then ducked through the gap in the wall and fell into step behind him.

After they'd gone a few paces, a faint rumbling sound stopped them in their tracks. Dan raised the torch and shone it back the way they'd came, his fears realised in its narrowing light.

The door back to the cellar was closing.

Antonia gasped, a stunned expression on her face as she realised they were now entombed beneath the villa.

Dan looked down at her, and then swung the torchlight along the passage. 'Guess we keep going.'

Chapter 28

Hassan Nazari stepped out the side door of the sandstone-clad building and into the shadows cast over the street by the Church of St Augustine. He glanced at his watch, shifted his briefcase from one hand to the other and forced himself to calm his breathing. His head twitched from left to right as he watched the pockets of tourists who lined the street, before he walked down the steps towards the waiting car.

His driver opened the back door of the glistening black sedan, waited until Hassan had settled himself into the cool interior, then swung the door shut, climbed into the front, and glanced in the mirror.

'It went well?'

Hassan nodded. 'As well as can be expected.' He loosened his tie, undid the top button of his shirt and sighed, then flicked his hand at the driver. 'Get moving. The sooner I get back to the villa to use a secure line, the better.'

The driver nodded, slipped the car into gear and pulled out smoothly into the traffic along Triq l'ifran. He buzzed his window up and switched on the air conditioning, instantly wiping out the smell of exhaust fumes which had threatened to permeate the vehicle.

Hassan stared out through the tinted glass, his mind racing. The truth was, it had meant to be a simple meeting of like-minded individuals. Instead, his masters had baulked at his plans, intimated it was a step too far, and reminded him of his status within their Government.

Except that it was too late to stop. He pursed his lips. Perhaps then, let it play out. Show them he was right, and reap their praise later.

He smiled, relaxing into the leather upholstery, and imagined the contrite looks on their faces. He looked out at the street then leaned forward. 'Why are we going so slowly? What is the delay?'

The driver shrugged, and glanced down a side street as the car shuffled past it in first gear, then looked at Hassan in his rear view mirror. 'Looks like they're preparing for a festival,' he said. 'Must be a holiday or something.' He pointed at a pair of workmen attaching red streamers between streetlights. 'It's going to take a while to get back.'

Hassan slumped in his seat and growled. He plucked his mobile phone from his shirt pocket and jabbed at the buttons in disgust, then held it up so the driver could see it in the mirror. 'And we have no reception.'

The driver shrugged. 'We'll be fine once we get onto the main road. Reception's always bad this side of Tas-Samra.'

'How long do you think it will take us?' Hassan asked, glancing through the front windscreen at the bus in front belching exhaust fumes.

'Half an hour, perhaps a bit less once we get out onto the main road.'

***

'Anything?' asked Firuz.

Ali shook his head and slammed down the phone. 'I've tried him from this phone and my mobile. He must be in an area where there's no reception.'

Firuz glanced at his watch. 'The meeting would have finished ten minutes ago. I don't want to do anything with those two until he gets back,' he glanced over his shoulder towards the cellar door, the four bolts gleaming new in the low light.

Ali noticeably shuddered. 'I wouldn't want to be around while he's dealing with them,' he said.

Firuz laughed. 'What? You getting soft?'

Ali shook his head. 'No, but he's meant to be as bad as Baqir if he's pissed off. I heard back home that…'

He broke off as Mutstapha entered the room, and then stood to one side to let him pass.

The man pointed at the phone. 'Have you contacted him?'

'There's no reception.'

'Keep trying.' The bodyguard stalked over to the floor-to-ceiling windows. In a few hours it would be dusk, and they would be on their way. 'We can't move out until we've dealt with them.' He turned and faced the two thugs. 'And I don't fancy their chances of leaving in a taxi, do you?'

***

Dan and Antonia made swift progress through the narrow passageway. It had been used recently – large stones had been pushed to each side of the path out of the way, while the path itself was pockmarked with scrapes and scratches where the contents of the various crates and boxes had been pushed or dragged along the surface.

Dan traced the markings with the torchlight, glancing up as they went to track their progress. He paused and wiped the sweat from his face with the hem of his t-shirt. 'Christ, it's hot down here.'

Antonia nodded. She removed her sweatshirt, tied it round her waist and ran her hands through her hair. 'The sooner we're out of here, the better,' she gasped, fanning her face with her hand. 'How far do you think we are from the cliffs?'

Dan glanced at his watch, factored in the fast pace he'd set them and thought about it. 'I reckon we must've travelled a mile at least,' he said. 'Maybe further.'

Antonia kept a watchful eye on their rear. 'How long do you think we have?' she asked.

'Not long. I can't imagine Hassan has left the island – it looked like he was travelling light,' he glanced over Antonia's shoulder into the darkness behind them. 'And this island isn't big enough for a long road trip.'

The passage curved round to the right, and they stopped suddenly. Dan glanced down at Antonia. 'Do you hear it?'

She nodded. A muffled *boom* sounded ahead of them. 'What *was* that?'

Dan shook his head, and put a finger to his lips. He gazed at his watch, counted the seconds, and then another *boom* permeated the air around them. He grinned.

'What is it?' asked Antonia, clutching his arm.

'The sea,' he said. 'It's the waves against the cliffs. Come on – we must be close.' He grabbed her hand and pulled her along behind him, setting a fast pace towards the sound.

He slowed as a breeze brushed against his face, the salty air filling his lungs. He carefully swung the torch beam left and right, not wishing to fall out of the passageway and down the cliff face. As they rounded a left-hand curve, he saw it.

An opening, with light from a rising moon shining through.

Dan switched off the torch and handed it to Antonia. 'Don't lose it,' he said, and hurried towards the gap in the rocks.

***

The car weaved around the war memorial, and picked up speed along Triq Sant' Anna.

Hassan frowned as they passed the American embassy. The car was swept up in the traffic pushing south-west through Floriana and became boxed in behind a bus which spewed dark clouds of exhaust in its wake. He picked up his phone, and noticed one bar of signal strength wavering hesitantly on the display. His eyebrows raised as a low *ping* signalled a series of missed calls. He frowned as he recognised the number of the villa, growled as the signal disappeared, and leaned forward.

'Hurry. I have a feeling there's a problem.'

The driver nodded, floored the accelerator and pulled out from behind the bus. Hassan was jerked backwards as the driver swung out into the opposite lane, a truck carrying watermelons bearing down on them. From his seat, he could see the bus passengers observing the manoeuvre, their mouths open in silent 'o's as they watched in disbelief.

He peered through the front windscreen and noticed the impassive demeanour of his driver reflected in the rear-view mirror. The man calmly continued to accelerate towards the truck, his hands steady on the wheel as he worked through the gears. Hassan held his breath as the truck loomed closer and closer before his driver suddenly swept to the left out of the way and slid in front of the bus, leaving a trail of dust in their wake.

Hassan breathed out as the truck blew past, its driver sounding the horn and gesticulating wildly out his window. Behind, the bus driver was following suit. Hassan ignored them all, and held up his phone, trying to improve the signal.

He glanced up and saw they were approaching the intersection onto the main highway. *Twenty minutes, maximum.*

'We just passed Tas-Samra,' said the driver. 'You should be getting a full signal any time now.'

On cue, the phone started ringing. Hassan punched the answer button and put it to his ear. He listened, cursed silently, and then spoke four words.

'Leave them for me.'

Chapter 29

Edging slowly towards the opening in the cliff face, Dan tested the ground before putting his weight on each foot as he made his way forward. As he drew closer, he saw that stone steps had been carved into the rock surface. Grasping hold of a jagged rock protruding from the cliff next to him, he carefully leaned out of the opening.

The wind caught his hair and he blinked as sea spray punched the cliff below and sent droplets flying into his face. He looked down and noticed the steps leading from the passageway to a narrow plateau below, sheltered from view by the cliffs as they curved around the plateau, creating a small cove.

As his eyes travelled along the plateau to the edge of the sea, his foot kicked something. He glanced down. *Bullet casings*.

He crouched down and picked up the brass cylinders. They were recently used. He looked up as Antonia came closer and peered over his shoulder.

'What have you got?'

'Evidence Hassan's been employing a sniper, I imagine,' said Dan grimly. As he stood to tuck the casings into the pocket of his jeans, he suddenly glanced up and pushed Antonia back into the passageway. She tumbled to the floor, cursing.

'What…?'

Dan turned. 'Sorry – no time for manners.' He shuffled back to the opening and edged slowly round it until he could peer out. Sure enough, there it was.

Silhouetted against the moon's reflection on the water's surface, he could see the outline of the top of a submarine conning tower as it slowly disappeared below the waves.

'Shit!' he exclaimed. 'We're too late!'

Antonia made her way over to where he stood and peered round his side. 'Was it the submarine?'

Dan nodded, leaning out over the edge. Below, the sea churned up debris jettisoned by the submarine crew before leaving. 'And now we *really* have to find a way out of here to warn the Vice-Admiral.'

He turned and glanced at the walls of the passageway. 'Start looking for another way out. There must be something. There were lines drawn all over that map in Hassan's study. Smugglers wouldn't have built a one-way system. They must've factored in an escape route somewhere.'

***

Hassan's hand was already on the door release as the sedan slid to a halt outside the villa. He didn't wait for the driver to open the door for him. As the engine died, he hurried out of the car and up the steps to the front door. The door swung open as he approached.

'What happened?' he said as he stormed past Firuz.

He turned at the sound of running footsteps as Ali and Mustapha entered the hallway from the direction of the study. 'What's going on?'

'We got a call on the radio from the guardhouse when Marik was late back from his patrol. Firuz went to investigate and found a woman dressed in combat fatigues,' said Ali, handing Dan's Sig Sauer to Hassan. 'She'd attacked Marik. We secured her and brought her back here for questioning. She said she was a tourist and had got lost,' he sneered.

Hassan held up the gun. 'And this?'

'A man broke into the house. Tried to rescue her, but Mustapha knocked him around a bit first.'

'Who are they?' Hassan checked the gun for ammunition, and sighted it along the hallway to the front door.

'He wasn't carrying any I.D. – nor was she,' said Firuz, 'so we got a photograph of them both just in case.' He handed his phone to Hassan, who glanced at the photos, his gaze lingering on the one of Antonia, then passed back the phone.

'Where are they?' asked Hassan as he started to walk along the hallway to the study.

'In the cellar.'

Hassan stopped and spun on his heel to face the man. 'What?'

Firuz took a step back. 'In – in the cellar,' he repeated, his eyes darting to where Ali and Mustapha were standing, doing their best to distance themselves from him.

Hassan tested the weight of the gun in his hand, then brought it up and shot Firuz in the chest.

The man slumped to the floor, dead, his blood oozing steadily across the tiled surface, the walls spattered with the remnants of his spine.

Hassan tucked the gun into his belt. He turned and glared at Ali and Mustapha, ignoring the ringing in his ears from the gunshot. 'You had better hope they are still in the cellar.'

***

Dan retraced their steps along the narrow passageway, running his hands over the cracked surface of the rock. Antonia swung the torch light left and right from the entrance in the cliffs, both of them aware if they didn't find an escape route in the rock, they'd have no choice but to climb down the steps etched into the cliff face and hope for a miracle.

Dan spun round to his left at a sound from the direction of the villa. *A gunshot*. Obscured by distance and the natural curvature of the passageway, the sound echoed along the cavern.

'We're in trouble,' he said. 'Keep looking – and hurry.'

The light from the torch became more erratic as Antonia swept it across the surface of the rock, searching for something – anything – which might lead to a way out.

'Here!' she called. 'Look at this!'

Dan ran over to where she pointed the torch light. A large floor-to-ceiling crack split the rock face, partly blocked by large stones which had worked loose and tumbled to the floor over the centuries.

'That'll do us,' said Dan. 'Put the torch on the floor and help me move these – quickly!'

As they pulled each stone out of the way, they threw them back in the direction of the villa in a desperate attempt to slow their pursuers, even for a few seconds.

The crack slowly revealed an opening. Dan picked up the torch and shone it through. A passageway led away from the cliffs, turning to the right and out of sight.

He handed the torch back to Antonia and began to ease himself through the gap. His large frame struggled with the tight fit. He breathed out, forcing his chest cavity to sink and pushed his body through the rocks, ignoring the jagged edges tearing into his shoulders and hips.

Suddenly, he was through. He peered back through the gap and beckoned to Antonia. 'Come on – you're smaller than me – it'll be easy,' he said.

Antonia nodded, glanced over her shoulder and passed the torch to Dan. Reaching up with both hands, she raised herself over the last of the fallen rocks and began to squeeze through the gap. She cursed under her breath as

she scraped an elbow and heard Dan chuckle under his
breath on the other side.

'I don't know what you said, but it transcended any
language barrier,' he said.

'Shut up and shine the torch so I can see where I'm
going!' she hissed.

She wriggled again, felt something give, and then
found herself on the other side of the rock fall. Dan
reached up and helped her down. He held her in a brief
hug.

'Okay?'

She nodded, looked down, then back in the direction of
the original passageway. 'I've lost my sweatshirt!'

A muffled shout emanated through the natural wall.

'No time,' murmured Dan. He handed her the torch and
pushed her in front of him. 'Run!'

**

Hassan held his breath as the cellar door was unbolted and
swung open. As Ali hit the light switch, Hassan strode
down the steps. No-one stood up to greet him. He turned
his head left and right, searching, and then began to make
his way through the strewn crates and packing boxes,
throwing them to one side as he made his way to the back
wall.

He pressed his hand against the brickwork and held his
breath as the entry to the passageway rolled open. He

glanced over his shoulder at Ali and Mustapha, then bellowed down the passageway.

'There's nowhere to run!' he screamed. 'When I find you, I will kill you!'

He slammed his fist against the stone walls of the passageway and then flicked his hand at the two bodyguards. 'Move – flush them out. If you don't find them, don't come back.'

He moved to let the two men pass, the light from their torches bouncing off the walls and ceiling of the passageway as they hurried away. Hassan stepped back into the cellar, closed the door and made his way up the cellar steps to the study. He looked around at the familiar surroundings. There was no room for error.

He returned to the front door and gestured to the driver standing next to the sedan, its engine ticking as it cooled from the recent journey. The driver nodded, leaned into the rear of the car and turned, holding Hassan's briefcase.

'Be ready to leave in ten minutes for the airport,' said Hassan. 'Phone ahead and have the aircraft ready.' He turned back to the house and hurried to the study.

Unlocking the desk, he ripped open each drawer in turn and flicked through the contents, throwing what was needed into the briefcase before shutting its lid. He paused in the centre of the room, nodded to himself, and then made his way out to the waiting car.

Chapter 30

Dan stared at the solid wall in front of him which blocked their way, and shook his head.

They'd been travelling hard for a while, Dan setting a brutal pace to outrun Hassan's guards.

Antonia glanced down at the torch, its white beam fading quickly to a sickly yellow. 'We need to find a way out soon.'

'It doesn't make sense,' said Dan. 'This has to lead somewhere.'

He moved closer to the wall, feeling his hands over the surface. It was constructed of large stones.

Man-made, not rock.

He held out his hand to Antonia. 'Give me the torch.'

He took it and shone it at the wall. The masonry was crumbling in places, the large hand-hewn limestone bricks held together by a thin layer of mortar. Dan ran his finger along the mortar, testing it for weak points.

A brick shifted, sending dust cascading to the stone floor. Dan glanced at Antonia. 'I think we have a way out – help me loosen these bricks.'

Antonia crawled forward and began using the tips of her fingers to loosen the mortar around the bricks. Dan started to tug at the stones. Slowly, one by one, the bricks began to shift.

Dan began to toss the bricks behind them as they worked.

'Where do you think this comes out?' asked Antonia.

He shook his head. 'I don't know – a cellar perhaps. We've travelled a few miles I think, but the air is cooler here, so we must be fairly close to the surface.'

They soon had the first bricks out of the way. Dan crouched down and shone the torch into the hole they'd created in the wall. A silt-like dirt blocked their way. Reaching forward, he touched the surface, which felt soft and worn down by the years.

'Wherever we are, it's very old,' he said. He straightened up and shone the torch around them. 'This wall's been here for a few hundred years.'

He bent down and used his fingers to scratch away the soil. Soon he was able to grab fistfuls of the dirt. Antonia stood up and began kicking the piles of soil out of their way.

'Here, help me,' said Dan. 'There's something solid here.'

Antonia crouched back down and he handed the torch to her, before reaching into the recess with both hands. He pushed away more of the powdery soil and detritus until he could get a firm grasp on the object. He pulled and felt it give a little. He adjusted his grip and pulled again.

With a surprised grunt, he fell backwards, the object in his hands.

Antonia stifled a scream.

In Dan's hands was a decayed skull, its eye sockets full of soil, its teeth locked in a macabre grin. He dropped it on the floor and rubbed his hands down the front of his jeans, then glanced across at Antonia.

'Are you okay?'

She nodded. 'Yes. It took me by surprise, that's all. I suppose we should have expected something like that.'

He nodded, stood, and peered through the hole. 'Shine the torch closer.'

Antonia bent down next to him. In the glow of the light, they could make out more bones lying in the dust. Scraps of clothing clung to decrepit joints. A smell of decay permeated the air, only slightly subdued by the intervening years.

Dan looked down and pointed. 'Look.'

A scrap of blue cloth fluttered gently on a skull to the left of the recess.

'There's an opening through there!' exclaimed Antonia.

'And a way out,' added Dan. 'Keep digging through.'

Within minutes, they'd wrenched out two more skeletons from the recess, piling the bones behind them on the dirt floor of the passageway.

Suddenly, Dan stopped and held up his hand. '*Shh*, listen.'

Antonia stopped and forced herself to breathe steadily, straining her ears. She glanced across at Dan. 'Music?'

Dan grinned. '*Church* music. We must be in the crypt.'

They reached into the recess and continued to scoop out dust and bones. Soon, the gap widened enough for Antonia to crawl through on her hands and knees. Dan handed her the torch.

'Don't leave me here too long.'

She nodded and began to crawl through the narrow space. She shuddered as she felt bones and cobwebs clinging to her hair as she progressed through the tunnel they'd carved out. She winced as she placed her hands among the dead piled up beneath her.

Suddenly the ground fell away.

With a muffled cry, she tumbled head first down a slope of skeletons piled on top of each other. The torch spun in the air above her before falling a few metres away from where she landed.

She lay still, mentally checking her body for signs of injury.

'Tell me you're okay.' Dan's voice echoed from behind the stone wall.

'I'm fine,' she called. 'Hang on.'

She scrambled across the floor to where the torch lay flickering. She picked it up. The light faltered. 'Hang in there,' she murmured. She turned, swinging the beam up towards the hole in the crypt wall.

'Can you see that?' she called.

The sounds of scrapes and muffled curses emitted from the recess.

'Yes.' Dan's head poked out from the recess. He blinked in the light. 'Next time, we make the hole bigger – and I go first,' he said.

Antonia grinned as he carefully made his way down the pile of skeletons. She hugged him as he reached the ground. 'We made it!'

Dan turned at a shout from behind the wall. 'Give me the torch,' he hissed, grabbing Antonia's hand.

He palmed his fingers across the beam of the torch, dulling it enough so he could still see to clamber back up to the gap in the crypt wall without giving their pursuers an excuse to catch them quicker.

He held the torch in one hand, pulling himself up so he could peer back into the hole, and strained to hear the voices. His heart pounded in his ears, and he willed himself to breathe easily to relax his heart muscles.

A sudden flash of light on the other side of the hole caught him by surprise and he looked away sharply.

'They're through here!' came a voice, echoing hollowly off the innards of the crypt. 'Quickly!

'*Shit*!' exclaimed Dan, letting go of his handhold and sliding back down towards Antonia. He grabbed her hand and pulled her through the crypt with him. 'Hurry!'

They stumbled over collapsed masonry and uneven cobblestones until they reached a narrow stone stairway leading upwards. Dan ducked under the low doorway leading out of the crypt and together, they raced up the staircase. As it curled around on itself, he looked up and saw they were entering the nave. Hushed voices whispered around him. As he searched for the source, he saw a small group of nuns busily scrubbing the flagstones of the church floor, the wet surface gleaming under lights suspended from the ceiling.

The sound of Dan and Antonia's footsteps reached them. Their conversations faded away as they each stopped working, their scrubbing brushes held up in mid-air as they looked up in shock at the two bedraggled figures standing in front of them.

Antonia self-consciously ran her fingers through her hair, pulling cobwebs out of her curls. Dan brushed mortar dust from his shoulders and smiled sheepishly at the nuns.

'Excuse us ladies – but which is the way out?'

One of the younger novices giggled, but her laughter was soon stifled as a larger, elder nun appeared, rushing between two rows of pews towards them, her footsteps sounding across the flagstone floors. And she didn't look happy.

As she closed in on Dan and Antonia, she thrust a scarf at Antonia. 'Cover yourself in the house of the Lord!' she cried.

Antonia looked down at her bare arms and shoulders, took the scarf and apologised profusely.

The nun turned to Dan, glowering. 'What is the meaning of this?' she demanded.

Dan put on his best charming smile. 'I'm sorry sister, but we're in a lot of trouble.'

The nun automatically glanced at Antonia, and then slapped Dan hard across the face.

'Ow!' Astounded, it took a second for Dan to realise the misunderstanding. Glancing at Antonia, who blushed, he turned back to the nun. 'No, not *that* sister!' He rubbed his face and turned and looked over his shoulder. They had possibly twenty, maybe thirty seconds before their pursuers caught up with them.

'Please, we're being chased by some people that will probably harm us if they catch us,' he quickly explained.

The nun peered around Dan towards the direction of the crypt, then up at him.

Dan looked over his shoulder at a sudden crashing sound from behind. He gently took the nun's hand in his. 'Please, which is the way out of here?'

The nun stared up at him. *Good grief,* she thought. *Those eyes. If I was twenty years younger!* She shook her head to clear the image, made a mental note to carry out penance for her thoughts and pointed to their left. 'The main entrance is through there,' she said. 'But,' she added, grabbing Antonia's arm as she started to move, 'there's a second entrance through the side over there,' she pointed. 'It leads into a busy street – you'll be able to, perhaps, get lost?'

Dan pulled the nun into a bear hug. 'Thank you!' he said, let her go and grinned at her blushing face.

A giggle from the novices brought her swiftly back into action and Dan could hear her berating them as he and Antonia ran towards the exit.

Approaching the heavy wooden doors, he heard a shout from behind them. Glancing over his shoulder, he spotted Hassan's men pushing past the nuns who had stood up and formed a temporary barrier between them and their pursuers. Dan turned and pushed the door open.

Bright streetlights blinded them both for an instant and they shielded their eyes with their hands, before scurrying down the shallow steps which led from the church door to the footpath.

Dan took in their surroundings. True to the nun's word, the street was packed with buses, pedestrians and cars. The cacophony of noise assaulted his ear drums as he frantically searched for a taxi, or something he could use to aid their escape. He stepped back sharply as a moped cut along the footpath, seeking a shortcut through the traffic. A carnival atmosphere permeated the town, with people stringing up red lanterns and balloons and calling out to each other across the street.

Dan pulled Antonia along, pushing against the tide of people. He looked over his shoulder, and saw a taxi turn into the street a few hundred metres away. He waved his hand in the air to get its attention, when another taxi cut in front of it and pulled to the kerb. Dan pushed Antonia towards it and opened the back door for her.

'Get in, quickly!' he said and jumped into the back seat next to her. 'Drive!' he called to the driver. 'Just go!'

He felt his head rock back as the taxi pulled away from the kerb, a bus driver sounding a horn as the taxi swerved into his lane, narrowly missing the larger vehicle's fender.

Dan leaned forward to speak to the driver. 'Take us to the British embassy please.' He rested his head on the back of the seat and closed his eyes.

Antonia squeezed his hand. He opened his eyes and looked across at her.

She smiled. 'We're safe.'

Chapter 31

Dan pulled Antonia to him and whispered in her ear.

'Giggle as if I've said something funny then listen carefully,' he murmured.

Antonia raised her hand to her mouth and laughed, doing her best to look coy in the driver's rear-view mirror.

'Okay, good,' whispered Dan, a smile plastered across his face. 'In a minute, lean back over to your side of the car and put your hand onto the door lever. When we get to the next junction, wait for my signal – I'll squeeze your knee – then open the door and jump out. Run round the back of the vehicle and follow me as fast as you can.'

Antonia looked at him and frowned. She tilted her head to the side. *Why?*

Dan pulled her closer. 'The driver keeps checking his mirrors and his speed is erratic. I reckon we're being followed and he's making sure they don't lose us.'

Antonia glanced at him, nodded once then slid across the seat. She rested her elbow on the armrest of the car door and appeared to look nonchalantly out the window at the passing streets.

Dan scanned the narrow roads and alleyways off the main street. The footpaths were crowded, late night shoppers, tourists and market traders vying for space in the narrow streets. He glanced up as he felt the vehicle slow. The car was approaching a junction, a 'stop' sign visible at the end of the street. He forced himself to breathe slowly, through his nostrils, desperately trying to keep calm. They had one chance.

The vehicle edged slowly forward, two other vehicles in front of it.

Now.

Dan squeezed Antonia's knee and pulled the lever on the car door towards him. The door flew open and he launched himself from his seat and out of the vehicle. He ran across the road, veered around a bus that braked suddenly in front of him, and leapt up the kerb onto the uneven footpath. He quickly looked to his left and right, saw an opening into an alleyway and bolted down it. He could hear Antonia's footsteps behind him.

'You okay?' he yelled over his shoulder.

'Yes!'

Dan could sense the walls of the buildings closing in on him. Uneven paving stones jostled for space under his feet and he could feel the slight incline. Wrought-iron balconies overlooked the narrow cobbled alleyway, washing and potted plants decorating the cast ironwork.

Studded wooden doors led through to the houses' courtyards. As he ran past, Dan glanced through and noticed small gardens, fountains, chicken pens. He slid around a corner, knocking over an pot full of plants. Soil and terracotta shards scattered across the cobblestones in his wake.

He reached a small crossroads and stopped to catch his breath. Antonia caught up with him and leaned against him, panting.

'Which direction?' she asked, looking over her shoulder. 'They'll be looking for us.'

Dan glanced up at the moonlit sky, a narrow sliver of light showing between the roofs of the houses around them. He looked to the left and spotted another narrow street leading upwards and further away from the main road.

'This way – let's put some distance between us and try to gain some height to get our bearings,' he said.

He began to run, keeping to the sides of the narrow street and in the shadows of the streetlights hanging from the surrounding houses. Antonia followed closely at his heels. They ran carefully, trying to silence their footsteps on the cobbled street surface.

Dan passed a door to another courtyard and stopped. Antonia fell against him, stopping suddenly.

'What?' she hissed.

The door stood slightly open on its hinges. Dan took her hand. 'Through here – come on.'

He pushed open the door and pulled Antonia through after him. Once they were both safely in the courtyard, he turned and carefully pushed the door back into the frame. They stood, panting, trying to catch their breath.

Suddenly Dan held up his hand and put a finger to his lips to silence Antonia. *Footsteps.*

And they were coming closer.

Dan pushed Antonia behind him and peered through the crack between the door and the frame. He could see the curve of the alleyway along which they had run, but his view was partly obscured by a large red and white flag hanging low from the balcony of a patriotic resident. He listened as the footsteps grew closer, and then spotted three men as they rounded the corner. He held his breath as they stopped and looked around them. There seemed to be a discussion about which way to go. The shorter of the three, a stocky dark-haired man with a scar over his nose and cheek, pointed up the alleyway and they began running in Dan's direction.

He slowly pulled away from his view of the alleyway and pulled Antonia into the shadows with him as the men's footsteps grew closer. They had slowed their gait, looking for signs of their prey's progress. Dan strained his ears as the men passed the courtyard. He could hear them further up the alleyway. Pulling Antonia close to him, he slowly moved back towards the wooden door and opened it slightly. He could hear voices to his right, the direction the three men had run. He waited for a few seconds then peered round the wooden frame. In the dusk, he could make out the figures of their pursuers.

'Come on,' he whispered, 'quickly and quietly.'

They edged through the narrow gap and turned left, running as hard as they could. As they turned the corner, Dan looked over his shoulder – and saw the taller of their pursuers looking straight at him. There was a moment's hesitation, and then they were in pursuit.

Dan pushed Antonia in front of him. 'Go, go!' he urged as a shout from the three men echoed off the walls of the closely-packed buildings around them.

Dan overtook Antonia and grabbed her hand. 'Keep up!' he urged. 'Here!'

He slid round the next corner, ducked under a lantern hanging from the side of a house, and turned down another street. He didn't dare look behind them. He could feel his lungs burning from the effort and adrenaline.

Antonia suddenly gasped.

Dan looked down at her, worried she might have twisted her ankle. Instead, she was pointing up at the streetlamps.

'Look!' she breathed.

The lanterns were going out one by one up the alleyway, giving the narrow street the impression of a building corridor as the lights fluttered out in sequence.

'What's going on?' said Dan, 'is it a trap?'

Antonia shook her head. 'I don't know.' She continued to match Dan's pace along the street. 'Hang on,' she said. 'It must be a feast day for a saint or something!'

'What?'

'If it's a feast day here, all the street lights are switched off for a few hours for a candlelit parade.'

Dan turned a sharp right and slowed to a jog. The streets were now completely dark, lit only by a waning moon. He noticed the first of the candles in the windows of the houses they passed.

'This could work,' he said. 'Let's find that parade!'

Chapter 32

As Dan led Antonia down the gentle slope of the darkened street, they could hear the noise of the festival drawing closer. Music, cheering and whistles carried over the tightly packed buildings of the narrow streets.

Dan pulled Antonia through a stone archway. It led to a sheer drop overlooking the wide main street below. Cautiously, he leaned out, grasping the stone wall for support. The head of the procession rounded the corner below.

'Come on, hurry,' he said.

They glanced back out through the archway. They could hear their pursuers' footsteps growing closer. They turned right, keeping close to the centre of the alleyway which, unlit by streetlamps and far from the shallow light emitted from window-framed candles, was now dark.

They turned right again and reached the end of the narrow cobble-stoned streets. A high stone wall with a towering arch led through to the main street, onto which people poured from their houses to join the procession as it passed.

Dan could see Antonia was exhausted.

'Come on, a bit further and we'll be able to walk for a little while,' he urged. He pulled her through the archway. 'Put on your best tourist smile.'

He headed for the middle of the procession, grinning at those around him as he pulled Antonia through after him into the throng. Within seconds they had been swallowed up by the crowd and were towed along with the current.

Dan pushed through the people apologetically, not wanting to cause a fuss that could be seen by their pursuers, and they broke through to the far side of the procession. As they passed a café, the tables decorated with candles, Dan grabbed a couple of the longer tapers and handed one to Antonia.

'Follow the direction of the crowd and hold this above your head,' he explained. 'It'll keep your face in shadow.'

Antonia nodded and followed his example.

Dan held on tight to her hand. If they were separated here, he'd never find her among the throng of people who now lined the street. He risked a glance over the heads of the people next to them and spotted their pursuers entering the street through the arch. The smaller of the three scratched his head in frustration, while the taller one stood with his hands on his hips, scanning the crowd. The third appeared to be holding a mobile phone to his ear.

Dan averted his eyes and watched where the crowd was leading them. The line of people appeared to be walking towards the harbour. He thought quickly. Time to put some *real* distance between them and their pursuers.

As the crowd snaked around an undulating bend, he bent down to Antonia and murmured into her ear. 'When we get to the harbour, we'll make a break for it the first chance we get.'

'Okay. Over the water?'

He nodded. 'Exactly my thoughts. Keep your eyes open for a candidate.'

She nodded, her lips pursed.

The crowd slowed approaching the harbour as the street narrowed along the quayside.

Dan and Antonia worked their way to the edge of the water. Dan began to scan the brightly coloured fishing boats moored along the wall. Some fishermen and their families sat in the boats, watching the procession, waving to friends as they spotted them in the crowd. A man raised a wine glass at a small group near the edge of the crowd, shouted, and then laughed as they called back to him.

Dan nudged Antonia in the ribs. 'This looks hopeful.'

She looked to where he pointed. A few enterprising fishermen had placed small blackboards in their boats, advertising themselves as water taxis for the evening.

Dan led her down some steep stone steps carved into the quay wall and approached the nearest boat.

'We're late for a dinner date over there,' he pointed. 'How fast is your boat?'

The fisherman grinned. 'Fast enough,' he said, already loosening ropes from the cast iron mooring rings in the quay wall. 'Jump in.'

Dan took Antonia's candle from her and threw both onto the ground, stamping out the flames. Holding her arm to steady her, he lowered her into the boat before climbing down to join her.

He pushed her to the far end. 'Crouch down there,' he murmured. He looked at his watch theatrically as he sat down beside her, his back turned to the street above.

The fisherman chuckled. 'Don't panic – we'll be there in a few minutes.'

Dan grinned at him. 'Sounds good. Give it all you've got – I'm starving.'

The man laughed, gunned the engine and deftly steered the boat away from the quayside. Antonia looked over Dan's shoulder as the boat edged its way into the harbour waters. Her eyes opened wide.

'Dan, look!'

He glanced back over his shoulder. The three thugs were pushing their way through the crowd, trying to get to the water taxis.

The fisherman looked over the tiller to where they were staring. 'Trouble?'

Dan looked at him and nodded. 'Big trouble.'

The man grinned. 'We'd better take the scenic route then. Hold on,' he said, and opened the throttle.

Dan felt the wind ruffle his hair as the boat picked up speed and bounced across the small waves in the harbour.

'Do you know where you want to really go?' shouted the fisherman over the roar of the engine.

'Sicily would be good,' mused Dan, 'but better make it Sliema.'

Dan felt the boat swing to the left and push forwards. Antonia turned to him and frowned. He grinned and glanced over his shoulder. There were too many people on the quayside – too many witnesses – for their pursuers to take out their guns and start shooting at him as they made their escape. He could make out the silhouettes of all three as they stood at the edge of the procession.

Chapter 33

After paying the owner of the boat, Dan led Antonia
through a maze of streets until he found a public telephone.

He picked up the phone, punched in a series of
numbers, cited a six-digit code and waited to be
transferred. He turned round in the small phone booth to
face the street. Antonia paced back and forth on the
footpath, her arms crossed, a frown creasing her brow. She
looked up, saw him watching her, and quizzically raised an
eyebrow.

Dan raised his hand. 'This won't take long, I promise.
Just keep a look-out for any trouble.'

She nodded and kept pacing.

He held the phone tighter as a voice came on the line.
'Hello?'

The voice was female, upper class. 'This is the England
Club. How can I help?'

Dan smiled. 'Anyone for tennis?'

'Thank you. Transferring you now.'

He heard a series of clicks on the line, and then the voice returned. 'Okay, Dan, you're now secure and through to the ops team. Go ahead.'

'David, we've got some serious problems.' Dan quickly told David what he'd discovered. 'We've been compromised here though. They'll be on the look-out for us. How quickly can you get us off the island?'

'Hold fire, Dan – we're going to need some hard evidence before I can go to the Prime Minister with this. Did you manage to get anything from Hassan's villa?'

'Negative – his study was clean. He's too careful to leave anything lying around. It was only luck I spotted the map with the tunnel marked on it. We picked up cartridges which look like fifty calibre. Possibly the same ones used to sink that luxury yacht.'

'It's not enough, Dan. You'll need to go back.'

Dan blinked. 'What?'

'Go back and get me something I can use. Hard evidence – I need proof it *is* the Iranians – or if not them, where the threat's coming from. *I* believe you saw the submarine, but others won't. They'll expect evidence to back up a claim like that.'

Dan leaned against the wall adjacent to the phone booth and closed his eyes. David was right. 'I'll need somewhere else to stay while we work this out. The apartment might have been compromised. We can't go back there.'

'We've located a house you can use – it's on the edge of what used to be a Royal Marines base at Ghajn Tuffieha. Call this number,' he rattled off a local number, 'and he'll organise a pick-up point for the key and a vehicle for you. He knows you're on your way and has made sure there are enough provisions to last a couple of days. Mitch has been frantic the past three hours trying to locate you – I'll tell him to meet you there.'

'Okay, thanks – I'll be in touch when we've got what you need.'

'Don't hang about, Dan. If you're right about the submarine, we've got to move fast on this. I'll brief the Vice-Admiral and have his team listen out for any signal activity in the Mediterranean.'

Dan hung up the phone and turned, grasping Antonia by the arm.

'Come on,' he said. 'Time to go.'

***

With the car parked behind a low wall, Dan stood on the edge of the road and looked across at the entrance to the disused Royal Marines barracks and firing range. A hotel had been built a mile away, but the old road running through the facility remained. A metal five-bar gate blocked the entrance, with a padlocked chain looped around the top of it the only deterrent. A sign for the local Scout association flapped in the breeze on a piece of string.

Dan turned to Antonia. 'Ready to step back in time?'

She smiled. 'This should be interesting.'

Dan helped Antonia climb over the gate and onto the cracked concrete road on the other side.

Weeds broke the surface of the old road, pushing up the concrete in places leaving it cracked and broken, turning to a white powdery dust over the years. Some of the old buildings remained. Dan stepped through long grass over to one of them and poked his head through a windowless opening. As his eyes adjusted to the gloom, he spotted an old screen hanging from the ceiling and a few chairs scattered about on the floor. He realised it must have been the camp's cinema.

Returning to the track, he glanced about and saw Antonia a few metres in front of him, her hands on her hips while she surveyed the landscape. She turned back to him.

'Where exactly are you taking me?'

He grinned and pointed along the road which curved upwards and over to the right, towards a small hill at the end of the old camp towards the firing ranges. A two-storey square block of a house stood on the tip of the hill, its faded whitewashed walls gleaming in the bright moonlight.

'There.'

He caught up with Antonia and they walked in silence side-by-side as the road began to rise on the incline, their boots scuffing up dust trails behind them. The clicking of cicadas in the long grass and weeds filled the air.

As they drew closer to the house the road surface broke up completely, leaving a threadbare track up the remainder of the hill. The sound of the sea against the cliffs below reached them as they drew closer to the house.

As the track curved to the right, the house came into view. Faded white walls obscured by ivy and shrubs left to grow wild had fallen apart in places from neglect, while among a tangle of prickly pear bushes, a tumbledown chicken coop leaned precariously to one side, its sides open, the chickens long gone.

Dan stepped to one side of the track, crouched down and carefully pulled a prickly pear bush to one side, revealing a capped drainage pipe.

He placed his hands either side of the wire mesh and pulled hard. The mesh gave a little, but the rust around its edges held fast. Dan gave it another hard tug and the mesh broke free. He set it aside, reached inside and felt along the top of the drain until his fingers found a metal surface.

He glanced over his shoulder. Antonia had her back to him, her arms folded as she gazed out across the cliffs towards the hotel complex in the distance. He turned back to the drainage pipe, wrapped his fingers around the metallic surface and pulled the gun away from its bindings, deftly tucking it under his shirt.

He reached in further, until his finger brushed against a smaller metal object. Grinning, he pulled it out and replaced the wire mesh cover.

'What have you got there?' asked Antonia, turning towards him.

He held open his palm and showed her.

'Front door key,' he said. 'You didn't expect me to break in, did you?'

***

Dan played absentmindedly with the cylindrical casings on the table, slowly rolling them backwards and forwards, backwards and forwards. He jumped as Antonia leaned over and placed her palm firmly on the casings and stopped their movement.

'Enough,' she said. 'You're driving me crazy.'

Dan grunted. 'We have to find out if that submarine is still there, or if it isn't – who the crew is.' He stood up, pushing the wooden chair to one side, and strode over to the open windows. He closed his eyes and listened to the cicadas. A rumble of thunder carried across the wind. 'There has to be a way to find out,' he murmured.

Lightning arched across the sky, nebulous grey clouds tumbling over each other as a second clap of thunder echoed around the small bay.

Dan moved to the back porch of the house, and leaned against one of the hardwood pillars supporting the tin roof as he stared out to sea.

The rain began to hammer on the roof, large drops splashing onto the tin, sporadic at first. Suddenly the heavens opened and a torrent fell across the bay, the noise an ear-splitting cacophony on the tin roof.

He could smell the ozone in the air and jumped as a double-forked lightning bolt streaked across the water in front of him, sending purple and white light flashing out in all directions.

'Here,' said Mitch, interrupting his thoughts. 'Beer.'

Dan turned and took the cold bottle from the other man. 'Cheers.'

He stepped back across the deck, nearer the house. As much as he enjoyed storms, he was getting wet from the water splashing out of the gutters onto the ground below.

Mitch pulled out a chair from under the small wooden table in the dining area and dragged it towards the open door. He sat down, contemplating his drink and watching the lightning show, lost in thought.

Antonia turned from the stove as Dan approached her, a wooden spoon in one hand and her glass of wine in the other. She watched him then waved the spoon at him as she spoke.

'I know what you're thinking. You need to be very careful,' she said. 'The cliffs will be guarded by Hassan's guards, and there are no dive sites nearby – the seas are treacherous.'

She turned, thrust the wooden spoon in the bubbling sauce and stirred it aggressively.

Dan frowned. There had to be a way. 'What about abseiling?'

Antonia stopped stirring, turned and laughed. 'Not there. Only a madman would climb those cliffs.' She turned back to the stove.

Dan picked up his glass and looked at Mitch as he watched the enveloping storm, then smiled to himself.

Chapter 34

Dan braked gently and turned the hire car off the highway.
As he left the main road, stones and gravel began to drift in
the vehicle's wake, sending up a dust cloud which tracked
their progress along the narrow road.

'Given your last successful attempt, what have you got
planned this time?' asked Mitch as he slouched in the
passenger seat, his arm hanging out the window.

'I could have left you in London,' said Dan.

'No you couldn't – you can't cope without me. You
know that,' replied Mitch, pulling his arm in and running
his hand through his hair. 'Did you piss blood this morning
or what?'

Dan glanced at Antonia in the mirror then scowled.
'None of your business.'

'Ha.'

Antonia leaned forward, her hands on each of the front
seats. 'You realise you two argue like an old married
couple?'

Dan glanced at Mitch. 'He started it.'

Antonia raised an eyebrow and fell back into the upholstery of the rear seats, her arms crossed over her chest. 'You're impossible.'

Dan grinned, changed down a gear as the vehicle began to climb the gradual ascent up a hill, then wrenched the car to the left-hand side of the road as an enormous cloud of dust appeared on the ridge line, heading towards them.

Mitch quickly wound up his window. 'What's going on?'

Dan shook his head. 'I think we're about to find out.'

They watched as two fire trucks crested the rise of the hill and bore down on them, dirty and black with ash. Dan glanced up at the open windows of the crew cab of the first truck, and noticed the smudged faces of the fire crew inside.

'That doesn't look good,' he murmured.

The second truck blasted down the hill past them, rocking the car in its wake, then silence returned to the hillside.

They then noticed the wisp of black smoke rising above the incline.

'Oh no,' said Dan. 'It can't be.'

He jerked the car into gear and floored the accelerator. The wheels spun briefly on the loose gravel of the track, and then they were at the crest of the hill. Dan cut the engine and they climbed out.

'Now *that's* how you hide evidence,' said Mitch.

Dan leaned against the car door, shaking his head in disbelief at the scene below.

The charred remnants of the villa smouldered in the morning breeze. A wisp of smoke rose from the centre of the ruins then faltered as the wind snuffed it out.

The outer walls of the building remained upright in places, a lone chimney leaning precariously against the eastern flank of the structure. The roof had completely collapsed, a solitary oak beam pointing up at the sky in defiance.

Dan turned and kicked the car in frustration. Mitch shook his head.

Antonia stood at the crest of the hill, her hands on her hips, her mouth set in a fine line. She turned slowly and faced Dan. 'Well – we might as well see if there's anything left,' she said.

He nodded. 'Let's go.'

He eased the car down the hill, carefully avoiding the numerous potholes and ruts carved deeper by the fire trucks, the car rocking sideways as he swerved around the bigger holes. As he approached the perimeter wall, he noticed the fire service had left the steel gates open. He drove through, and up to the charred remains of the building.

As they climbed out of the vehicle, the stench of burnt plastic, wood and acrid smoke burnt their sinuses.

Dan coughed involuntarily and turned to face Antonia and Mitch. 'Be careful,' he said. 'Don't take any risks.

These walls could still collapse, so tread carefully and don't walk under anything, okay?'

They nodded.

Dan turned to face the ruins, and pointed in front of him. 'This is where the front door would have been.' He glanced to his left. 'I'm going to take a look down there where the study used to be.'

He turned to the others. 'Look for anything that might tie Hassan to the submarine or gives us an idea who he's working for.'

They split up, walking the perimeter of the ruin, looking for a safe way in. Dan strode over the scorched grass and down a small dip, following the length of the walls until he reached the ash-covered flagstones of the patio. In his mind's eye, he could picture the patio doors leading into Hassan's study.

He carefully stepped through the sodden ash, his nose wrinkling at the smell of charred wood and plastics, and walked forward until he was standing in the middle of what had been the study.

He looked to his right and saw the burnt remains of the desk. Moving towards it, he carefully climbed over a collapsed roof beam, its surface still lukewarm despite the recent drenching by the fire hoses.

Dan bent down, pulled the first drawer of the desk open and began to sift through the contents. Flakes of blackened paper disintegrated at his touch, colours and words obliterated by the intensity of the fire.

He cursed, threw the drawer to the floor and wrenched the next from the desk. He looked up, shook his head at the sheer destruction of the building and concluded an accelerant such as petrol had been poured through the rooms before the fire was lit to achieve such an effective result.

He discarded the last of the desk drawers and stomped back across the remains of the study, along the hallway to what would have been the kitchen, and found Mitch at the top of the cellar steps.

'Anything?'

Mitch shook his head, smuts of ash covering his face. 'Nothing – I went as far as I could before the roof had totally collapsed, but any crates or boxes are gone. There's nothing left, and definitely no way through to the tunnel entrance.'

Dan nodded and turned. He gazed out at the disused fields, the breeze ruffling his hair. His eyes fell to the horizon, and watched a lone hawk floating in the air currents at the cliff's edge.

He turned back to Mitch. 'Guess we'll have to find another way then.'

They left the kitchen and went in search of Antonia. They found her crouched on the floor of the living room, a broken photo frame in her hands, the picture charred and blackened in her fingers.

'Any luck?' asked Dan.

Antonia eased herself up, tossed the photo frame aside and shook her head, looking at the damaged photograph. 'Nothing. What do we do?'

'We climb,' said Dan.

***

Dan and Mitch walked carefully to the edge of the cliff, small stones and dirt cascading over the side as they approached. Antonia leaned against the car, keeping one eye on their progress and the other on the track leading from the villa to the main road.

Dan lowered himself to the ground and crawled forward on his elbows until he was peering over the edge of the cliff. Mitch joined him.

'Do you see anything?'

Dan shook his head, his eyes scanning the churning waters below. 'The old diesel-electric submarines had to snorkel to run the diesel generators to recharge their batteries and get fresh air,' he said. 'Chances are, they'd have taken the opportunity to dump any rubbish.'

Mitch squinted into the water. 'We're not going to see anything from up here.'

Dan peered carefully over the cliff. 'I reckon if you abseil down to the leading edge of the plateau, you'd be able to crawl across and down to where the waves are coming in,' he said, pointing out the route as he spoke. 'If anything's going to wash up, it's going to get caught in that rip.'

A tight chuckle emanated from Mitch.

Dan glanced over at him. 'What?'

Mitch looked down to where Dan had pointed. 'I'm not going down there!'

Dan blinked. 'What do you mean? Of course you are – that's why you're here.'

Mitch laughed, edged away from the cliff and stood up, then folded his arms across his chest and shook his head. 'No way. What do you think I am – a madman?'

Dan stood up, glanced over Mitch's shoulder and caught Antonia watching them, an amused smile spreading across her face.

She held up her hands. *Well?*

Dan looked down at the boiling sea below, the waves crashing ferociously against the base of the cliffs, churning the water as they retreated for another assault. He sighed.

'Okay, *I'll* go.'

Chapter 35

Crawling out from under the car, Mitch backed against the passenger door, bent his knees against the strain and held the red and black rope tight between his gloved hands.

Dan glanced up at him. 'Don't let go.'

Mitch grinned, the sea and sky reflected in his sunglasses. 'I've strapped the rope to the axle and I'll belay it out so you can concentrate on getting down there in one piece. You'll be fine, as long as I don't sneeze.'

After an initial recce, the two men discovered the uneven cliff face would mean Dan would have to climb down, rather than abseil. The limestone surface undulated and curved along the coastline, fractured in places from the constant battering by the sea.

Dan glanced down, the wind ruffling his hair, and tested the new footholds against his weight and nodded to himself.

Not a bad start.

He lowered himself over the edge of the steep incline. As he kicked with his boots for a foothold, small stones and gravel gave way, tumbling down the face of the cliff.

Looking down, he concentrated on where his feet worked at the surface, kicking the soil to make a dent big enough to edge his toes into. He avoided the view down to the rocks below.

He let go of the rope with one hand and began to feel the rock face for a handhold, something to get him started on the way down. His fingers scratched at the rough surface, soil sticking to limestone rock held tentatively in place by ambitious tree roots. He eased himself into place, checked the rope was still fastened tightly to the harness around his waist then began the slow abseil down the cliff.

He disappeared over the edge and became more aware of the wind buffeting the coastline. As he let go with one hand, a sudden gust threatened to drag him away from his footholds. He clawed at the surface seeking out handholds and pulled himself into the stone and dirt to lessen the effect of the wind. Slowly, step by step, he eased himself down the sheer drop. The waves crashed against the rocks below, the sound fading then returning with the effect of the wind.

As he crept lower, a fine spray of water blew across his body as the waves below smashed against the rocks. He blinked behind his sunglasses as salt water stung his eyes. He balanced one foot on a protruding, rounded, weathered rock while he shifted his weight and kicked his boot into the rock face.

Before he could continue his steady descent, the soil around the rock cracked and disintegrated. Dan's biceps bulged as he dug his fingers into the soil. He desperately scrabbled for a handhold, glancing at the vicious rocks below, the grey-blue surf angry and boiling.

Dan's feet kicked the surface of the rock face, seeking sanctuary, something to step onto to stop his momentum. He grunted as his body slammed into the rock face then he shot out a hand to grasp onto a gnarly old tree root sticking out from the rough surface.

It held.

Dan lowered his face to the back of his hands, panting. He raised his eyes upwards and saw Mitch peering down, shaking his head.

Dan looked down between his feet. He was so close. He breathed out slowly. His knee joints were on fire from the effort and his fingernails were bleeding, huge blisters erupting on the palms of his hands.

He lowered his left foot, feeling his way for the next toe-hold. A few loose stones fell away.

A sudden squawk pierced the air. Dan lost his footing again as a seagull launched itself from the ledge below, flapping and screeching as it flew to safety. Dan yelled and instinctively let go with one hand to protect his face. The sudden movement threw Mitch off balance and Dan felt himself begin to drop with a sickening lurch.

The rope suddenly jerked and grew taut. Dan was slammed against the side of the cliff face, his shoulder hitting the rock. He cried out in pain and shock – then instinct kicked back in. He reached out, grabbed the nearest hand-hold he could find and held on tight. The momentum of the rope slowed and Dan pulled himself closer to the rock face, panting hard.

A shout came from the top of the cliff. 'You okay?'

'*Fucking* birds!'

'You're okay. Good to hear.' A pause. 'In your own time then.'

Dan shook his head in disbelief. As he edged further down towards the foot of the cliffs, cold spray from the rolling sea began to splash his body. He peered over his shoulder. Once his eyes grew accustomed to the pattern of the surf as it smashed against the rocks before plunging back into the sea, he began to see anomalies against the water's colour.

Debris.

He took a deep breath and began lowering himself once more. He ignored the burning sensation in his shoulders, not wishing to face the climb back up without finding some sort of confirmation for his theory.

The roar of the thrashing sea assaulted his senses, the ceaseless pounding of water on the rocks below hypnotic in its intensity. Dan concentrated on placing one foot carefully below the other, working his hands down the rope, kicking at the cliff face and wedging his toes into small nooks in the rock as he descended.

A sharp cold sensation brought him out of his reverie – he was at the bottom of the cliff, his legs already ankle-deep in the swirling surf. Looking around, he searched among the debris being pummelled against the rocks for a clue, and crawled further into the cold water, balancing on a rock ledge which ran under the water's surface. Debris littered the waves, sloshing against his body with the vicious tidal current.

He gasped as a large wave engulfed him. Hanging tightly onto the rope, he held his breath as the wave washed over him and away. Shaking his head to clear the water from his hair and eyes, he turned his head left and right, searching for something, *anything*, which might provide a clue to the submarine's crew or its ultimate destination.

He gripped the rope with one hand, thrusting the other through the cold water, sifting through galley scraps and waterlogged food packaging. As another torrent of water struck the rocks beside him, he looked across the surface and saw a bundle of rags, borne by the waves, slowly being driven his way.

Dan looked along the rock face, calculating the ebb and flow of the water, then lurched for the collection of coloured material. As his fingers touched its surface, he frowned.

It felt solid, rather than something discarded by a submarine, jettisoned through its torpedo tubes.

He dragged the bundle closer, feeling its weight as another wave rushed towards the cliff face, rolling the collection of rags in its wake.

At first, Dan's mind refused to comprehend what he was looking at. Where there should have been a face were only two empty eye sockets, a small crab clinging to the scraps of skin hanging out of one orifice. The nose had been eaten away, or broken against the rocks. The skull was flat along one side, caved in by heavy blows, while the soft skin of the lips and ears had already been eaten away by fish.

Dan yelled, and let go of the body.

He slipped off the rock he was balancing on under the water and plunged into the icy depths.

His heart racing, he resurfaced, his right hand flailing in the water until he located the safety line. Wrapping his fingers around it, he pulled himself to the surface, aided by Mitch hauling the rope back up the cliff face, until he clambered back onto his rock perch, shivering – both from cold and shock.

He glanced up at the sound of a yell from the top of the cliff and raised his hand.

I'm okay.

He waited until his breathing was back under control.

'Didn't see that coming,' he muttered, and then coughed up a mouthful of sea water.

He retched, and spat over the side of the rock, then began to search the water for the body.

His eyes soon found it – the waves were keeping it trapped at the base of the limestone cliff to his right.

He took a deep breath. 'Alright,' he said. 'Let's find out who you were.'

He carefully tied the rope around his waist, gave it two quick pulls, gave Mitch a thumbs up, then slowly lowered himself back into the churning water.

He clambered along the rock face, digging his fingers into the rough surface as he crept closer and closer to the body as it rose and fell with the motion of the waves. Edging closer, he reached out with one hand until his fingers touched the denim material of the jeans covering the lower half of the body. Looping his fingers through a leather belt around the cadaver's waist, he pulled the body closer.

Ignoring the shredded remnants of its face, Dan began to search the body and clothing. He reached into the front pockets of the denim jeans, and pulled out the remains of a document. The papers fell apart in his hand, pulped by the salt water. Dan threw the scraps into the waves in disgust.

Tightening his grip on the cliff face, ignoring the burning sensation in his shoulders, Dan hauled the body over in the water. As the body rolled, he saw movement in the water next to it. A square object, coloured, escaped the back pocket of the corpse's jeans and began to float away.

'Shit!' Dan exclaimed, and pushed the body out of the way.

His eyes frantically searched the water for a flash of colour, anything which would indicate where the object had escaped.

Then he saw it. A cigarette packet, floating only two metres to his right. It bobbed up and down annoyingly, teasing him as it survived wave after wave, its blue and white packaging catching the sunlight as it turned in the water.

Dan frowned. The colour scheme of the packet was tantalisingly familiar, but he couldn't remember where he'd seen it.

He glanced up at the rope, then at the surf as it lunged towards the cliff face once again. He'd have to time it carefully. Letting go of the rope at the wrong moment and being swept out to sea was not an option he wanted to consider.

He held his breath as the next wave shot towards him. As he felt it sweeping over his body and away, he let go of the rope with one hand and used the momentum of the receding tide to edge closer to the cigarette packet. His fingers clawed through the water, desperately trying to reach the object, before he roared with the strain on his other hand and returned his grip to the rope.

Just in time.

Another wave crashed against the cliff face, sucking the air from his lungs. As the wave receded, he spluttered to the surface and immediately thrashed towards the cigarette packet. His fingers grazed the surface of it, but it slipped away under the weight of his hand.

'Fuck!'

He glanced over his shoulder and saw the next onslaught heading his way. He filled his lungs with air and held tightly on to the rope, his eyes screwed shut as another blast of cold water enveloped his body.

Coughing as the water receded again, he felt himself starting to shiver uncontrollably and knew this would be his last chance.

He launched himself at the cigarette packet, scooping handfuls of water towards him in an attempt to bring the packet closer. When he was sure he would get a good grip on the debris, he lunged at it. For a fleeting moment, he felt the rope loosen in his left hand before his fingers tightened their grip, and his right hand clutched the cigarette packet.

He put it between his teeth and sought out the safety of the rope, as another wave smashed over his head and into the rocks.

He waited until the surf retreated then began the long agonising haul back up the rope. It began to rise with him, Mitch having felt the new sensation in the rope and realised that Dan was on his way back up.

Dan used his legs to power himself up the cliff face, his hands and arms exhausted from the climb down and the treacherous minutes in the surf. As he neared the top, he saw Mitch peering over the edge at him as he pulled the rope easily through his hands, a grin on his face.

Dan hauled himself over the cliff edge, crawled a few metres then collapsed. He spat out the cigarette packet and lay on the ground, panting.

Mitch wandered over and peered down at him, his shadow over Dan's face.

'You know,' he said, kicking at the cigarette packet next to Dan's head, 'most people find just one at a time works, rather than the whole packet.'

Dan grinned, his eyes closed, feeling the sun warming his body.

'I ran out of nicotine patches.'

Chapter 36

'Take her up, let's have a look.' Ivanov held his nose and blew gently, equalising the pressure in his ears as the submarine began to rise slowly through the waves.

As the boat neared the surface, Ilya slowed the ascent to keep the conning tower under the water, while Ivanov pulled up the periscope and peered through. Rain lashed the lens as he turned it slowly through a rotation, getting his bearings and searching the darkened horizon.

Another five degrees to the right and he had his target. The cruise ship leapt into view, a towering floating city, lights blazing from portholes and strung from wires along its decks as it made its way out of the Mediterranean.

Ivanov blinked as a large wave engulfed the periscope, even though he was still safely dry several metres under the surface and then cursed at the natural reaction.

He stepped back from the periscope and gestured to his weapons specialist, Alexei. 'Come and take a look.'

Alexei moved away from the bulkhead he'd been leaning against and stepped up to the periscope. He glanced through, nodded, and took a step back. 'We'll be fine.'

'The timing's important,' said Ivanov. 'Too soon and we're trapped. Too late and there's a risk of being located.'

Alexei beckoned the captain over to a small chart table, and sat down in one of the chairs fixed to the floor. 'They're twenty-one nautical miles off Gibraltar at the moment,' he said, tracing his finger along a line he'd pencilled in on the chart. 'When they reach this point *here*,' he added, stabbing his finger on the map, 'that's our point of no return.'

Ivanov leaned over the map. 'So, we'll steer round them, overtake them and attack.'

'I'd prefer to be in position before then. With this old thing, I can't guarantee we'll get a direct hit,' said Alexei. 'Look what happened last time.'

Ivanov nodded. 'Agreed.' He turned to Ilya. 'Get us down again, and into position. Keep us under five knots – this thing rattles like a can full of stones. I don't want to get this far and have to abort the mission because we've been heard by someone's navy patrol.'

***

Captain Brad Martin scanned the crowd, his brown eyes dark with exasperation. He nodded, giving the small group of passengers standing around him the impression he was enthralled in their conversation, until he finally located the first officer standing at the bar. He scowled as the first officer grinned and tipped his glass in Brad's direction in mock salute.

Brad looked down, made a polite excuse to the large lady draped in a bright kaftan standing next to him, gently peeled her hand off his arm, and smiled apologetically before striding across the ship's ballroom. As he walked, he straightened his tie and breathed a sigh of relief at his luck in escaping the next instalment of the woman's ghastly stories.

The first officer, Jim Stokes, grinned as Brad approached him. 'Gotta love these get-togethers, sir – that's what keeps them coming back for more.' He winked and took a sip of the remaining soft drink splashing the bottom of a crystal tumbler in his hand.

Brad groaned. 'My god – when can we escape back up to the bridge? Soon isn't it?'

He accepted a glass of lemonade from a waiter and turned to lean against the bar next to Stokes. The cruise ship had left Rhodes two days ago, called into Barcelona overnight and was now approaching the Gibraltar Strait before turning north towards Southampton. Two weeks of winter sunshine for the guests, two weeks of non-stop activity and customer service for the crew. Brad rubbed his jaw, noticing how much it ached after all the smiling he'd had to do at the evening's Captain's Dinner.

'It's only once a week, Captain,' laughed Stokes. 'Stop brooding.'

Brad smiled, acknowledging the jibe. 'I know, I know – I'd just much prefer to be upstairs right now.'

Suddenly, the ship lurched and the two men grabbed the brass railing running along the wood-panelled bar to steady themselves.

Brad glanced at Stokes who had spilt his drink down his jacket and was now staring back at Brad, his face white.

'W-what the hell was that?' he stammered.

Brad shook his head. 'I don't know, but I…' He broke off as the ship yawed to its port side.

A terrible groaning sound of steel under stress shuddered through the cruise ship. Screams pierced the ballroom as passengers tried to move out of the way of tumbling furniture. Brad jumped at a crash from behind the bar as liquor bottles fell from their shelves to the floor. He turned to Jim.

'Get to the bridge – now!' he commanded, running as best he could along the canted floor of the ballroom towards the exit.

As he reached the door, he stumbled against the wall, steadied himself then reached for the emergency radio. 'Send out a distress message with our coordinates immediately!' he said.

'Sir!' the communications officer on the other end hit a series of buttons. 'Confirmed sent, sir.'

'Patch me through to the main speaker system!' Brad ordered.

'Go ahead sir.'

Brad took a deep breath to steady his voice. 'Ladies and gentlemen,' he began. 'This is your Captain speaking. The ship appears to have been struck by something in the water and we're currently looking into the situation. Your safety is our priority. Please begin to make your way carefully to the lifeboat stations. Remember your practice drills. Our crew will help you. Thank you.'

He hung up the radio and turned, placing a hand on the wall to keep his balance, staying clear of the stream of people hurrying from the ballroom towards the lifeboats. The ship now listed at a precarious angle. Picking up the radio again, he barked an order and was soon through to the engine room. 'Report.'

'We've got a bloody great hole in the hull sir!'

Brad frowned as he listened to the panicked voice at the other end. 'How long have we got?'

'I'd say twenty minutes – maximum,' replied the engineer. 'We've got fires spreading through the lower levels, and we're taking on water.' He paused. Brad could hear someone shouting in the background before the engineer returned to the phone. 'Captain? When you send out the distress message, tell them we've been hit by a torpedo.'

Brad's eyes flickered as he processed the news, going over the information in his head. 'A *torpedo*?'

'Yes sir. Looking at the information here, it appears to have struck the stern. We need to evacuate immediately.'

Brad's face paled. *We'll never get everybody out.* 'Abandon ship,' he said. 'Immediately. Tell the lifeboat crews to steer away from the stern.'

He replaced the radio and began to stumble back through the ballroom towards a long passageway which ran the length of the cruise ship. As he passed along the passageway, he opened doors to check for stragglers, and called out to his crew to help older or injured passengers as they herded them towards the exits. 'Go, go!' he urged.

He glanced down as the opening chords of a Rolling Stones song permeated the air, and pulled his mobile phone from his pocket. 'Yes?'

'Where the bloody hell are you?' asked Jim Stokes. 'We're watching the evacuation from here but I can't see you.'

'I'm in the north-south passageway, deck two,' explained Brad. 'Helping staff check all the rooms are empty.'

'Have you spoken to the engine room?'

'Yes – I've ordered them to evacuate. Smith seems to think we've been hit by a torpedo.'

There was an astonished silence at the other end before Stokes spoke. 'Really?'

'Well I guess we'll find out if we get off of this thing in one piece. How are you doing up there?'

'It's bedlam,' said Stokes, 'but all the lifeboats are being deployed without a problem and the crew are doing a

floor by floor search above and below you to check off all
the passengers against the manifest. Text book evacuation
at the moment.'

Brad smiled, despite the seriousness of the situation.
The first officer's calm voice soothed him – all the training
the crew underwent was now being proven in dire
circumstances.

'Good. I've probably got another hundred metres to
check here then I'll make my way up to the lifeboats. You
should do the same.'

'Will do.'

Brad hung up and tucked the phone into his shirt
pocket, buttoning it safely inside. As he left the
passageway and began to climb the outer stairs, he opened
a door out onto the deck and peered out to sea. He took a
moment to glance over the side of the ship. The sea was
churning, rain lashing the sides of the cruise liner as it
rocked and swayed.

He hurried down a steel staircase, in time to see a
woman trip on the wet surface of the canted deck. She
cried out as she began to slide towards the rail, unable to
grip on to anything to stop herself.

Brad lurched forward, reached out and grabbed hold of
her arm to stop her sliding further. Pulling her upright, he
steered her along the slippery deck. She glanced up at him,
terror in her eyes.

'It's all right,' he said reassuringly, 'it's just like the
drill you did earlier this week.'

She nodded and, letting go of his hand, accepted the help of another crew member who guided her into the lifeboat.

He turned to the crew next to him. 'You too – go.'

He pushed a steward into the lifeboat, and stood back as the vessel swung away from the cruise ship and into the waves, before raising his gaze to the dark horizon. The water was impenetrable, not a single ship in sight. In the distance he could see lights along the Gibraltar coastline. He calculated the distance and shook his head in frustration. It would be nearly an hour before anyone reached them.

Brad turned, his eyes wide, as the ship's hull let out a deep groan. He felt the whole vessel shudder as a vibration ran through the structure and echoed through the lifeboat cables.

He pulled his phone from his pocket. 'Stokes – get out of there *now*. No hanging around. We're out of time.'

***

Dmitri Ivanov stood next to Alexei, his heart racing.

For the last twenty minutes they'd monitored the communications channels, listening to the reports from the cruise ship becoming more desperate.

He glanced at his watch. 'That's enough time. Let's finish it.'

Alexei moved across to the weapons controls. 'Are you sure, Dmitri?'

Ivanov nodded. 'We have to be sure. At the moment, our task is only half complete.'

Alexei shrugged and turned back to the controls.

'Ilya,' said Ivanov, 'make sure you get us away from here the moment Alexei releases the torpedo. I want us out of the area before the rescue ships arrive.'

'Yes sir.'

Alexei programmed in the coordinates of the stricken cruise ship, and then turned to Ivanov.

'Ready on your command.'

Ivanov leaned over to switch off the communications channel, cutting off the frantic voices from the cruise ship, and then turned to Alexei.

'Fire.'

Chapter 37

London

Dan pulled out a leather-topped bar stool and sat down heavily, exhausted from the morning's activities and the flight back from the Mediterranean. He leaned an elbow on the polished wooden surface and turned to glance at a muted television hanging from a bracket in the wall to the left of him. He checked the score, shook his head at the deficit Man United would have to make up in fifteen minutes, and beckoned to the barman.

'What beers have you got on tap?'

The barman glanced up the length of the bar. 'Stella, San Miguel, Heineken, Guinness...'

'Make it a Guinness, thanks.'

Dan watched the barman wander off and pick up a clean pint glass, then fished in his pocket for some money. He caught a movement out of the corner of his eye and looked up to see Antonia standing beside him, her handbag swinging from side-to-side.

'Buy me a drink?'

Dan cocked his head to one side. 'I didn't think you'd be allowed to drink in public?'

She smiled. 'What do you mean – my job, or your interpretation of what religion I might belong to?'

He grinned. 'You got me. I'm not usually so narrow-minded.'

Antonia arched her eyebrow. 'I'll bear that in mind.'

'What would you like to drink?'

The barman returned and set Dan's Guinness on a coaster in front of him. Antonia caught his eye. 'Make it another of those please – but a small one.'

Dan stood up and pulled out another bar stool for Antonia. She thanked him, set her bag on the floor then settled herself in her seat.

Dan watched, transfixed. It was the first time he'd really had a chance to look at her features close up. Her hair was recently washed, the dark curls tumbling down her back, setting off her dark skin. She wore a black dress which caressed her body and reached down to her calves, a simple silver-hewn watch on her left wrist.

He realised he knew nothing about her, and wanted to learn more. His reverie was broken by the sound of Antonia's laughter. He blinked and looked at her.

'You didn't hear a single word I said, did you?' she smiled.

'Yes. Sorry, yes – fine.' He noticed the barman patiently waiting next to them. 'Sorry – could I start a tab?' He glanced at Antonia, who nodded. 'I think we're going to be here for a while.'

He waited until the barman had moved to the other end of the bar then turned back to Antonia and pointed at her drink. 'Have you ever tried this stuff before?'

She shook her head.

'It's an acquired taste for some people,' he said. 'My grandfather started me on it when I was three.'

Antonia took a sip of the Guinness and delicately wiped the froth off her top lip with her finger.

Dan smiled at the gesture. 'So, how are you settling in over here?'

'I'm okay. It's a bit different from what I'm used to.'

'Cold?'

She shrugged. 'It gets cold in Qatar too. I guess I didn't expect it to be quite so, *grey*.'

Dan laughed. 'That's only London, remember.' He paused. 'Perhaps, maybe once this is all over, I could show you some of the prettier parts of England, if you like?'

Antonia smiled. 'I'd like that.' She reached out and put her hand on his.

He glanced up, struck by her beauty.

'What are you thinking?' she asked.

He smiled. 'That you scrub up pretty well for someone who was crawling through skeletons not too long ago.'

She grinned. 'Well,' she said, casting an appraising eye down his figure. 'You're not so bad yourself. I do believe this is the first time I've seen you not wearing desert boots.'

Dan tipped his chin in the direction of the barman. 'He was a bit funny about footwear. I thought I'd play it safe.'

Antonia laughed and took a sip of her drink. She pointed her finger at him as she placed the glass on the bar. 'You are a very funny man, Mr Taylor.' She squeezed his hand. 'But sometimes when I look at you, there's a sadness.'

Dan turned his hand over and caressed her palm. Her fingers were long, slender, with short fingernails painted a pale pink.

'Have you eaten?'

'Not yet.'

'I've heard the restaurant here has a great menu.'

She squeezed his hand. 'Then we had better check to make sure they're not lying.'

Dan grinned, drained his pint and stood up, offering Antonia his arm. 'Come on then. I don't know about you but, after the last few days, I'm starving.'

She grinned, picked up her bag, and allowed him to lead her from the bar into the restaurant area.

***

Their waiter had chosen a table tucked away at the back of the restaurant, next to French windows which overlooked a landscaped courtyard with small lights flickering among the ferns and shrubs. Dan sat down facing the room after seating Antonia, and watched with amusement as she edged her chair around the table until she was almost sitting next to him.

'I can't sit with my back to a room either,' she explained.

'I'd look out for you,' Dan murmured.

'I know,' she said, looking into his eyes. 'But we stand a better chance if there are two of us looking out for each other.'

Dan reached over, pulled her towards him and kissed her. 'Works for me,' he said as he pulled back, smiling.

'Good,' she said, and looked up as the waiter approached to take their order.

Once he disappeared towards the kitchen, Antonia turned back to Dan. 'So,' she said, turning the stem of the wine glass in her hand. 'Is London home for you?'

Dan took a sip of his wine, savoured the flavours around his mouth then swallowed and smiled. 'No – I stay wherever David puts me if I'm working for him.' He paused, and leaned forward on the table. 'I have a house in Oxfordshire – a couple of hours or so from here on a good day. It's my Dad's old house.'

Antonia put an elbow on the table and cupped her chin in her hand, her head cocked to one side. 'He is no longer alive?'

Dan shook his head. 'No – he passed away a couple of years ago.'

Antonia reached out and placed her hand on the back of Dan's. 'I understand. My mother died a few years ago. I still miss her.'

Dan turned his hand, laced his fingers through Antonia's and squeezed gently. 'What about your father?'

She laughed. 'He's usually busy with his business ventures. I rarely see him but he is a very clever man, so I forgive him. What about your mother?'

Dan shook his head. 'I really don't remember her. She died when I was about three years old.'

Antonia tilted her head, questioning.

Dan shrugged. 'A skiing accident – a freak accident by all accounts. Apparently she was really rather good.'

Antonia nodded then glanced up as the waiter approached with their entrees.

They waited until he had finished topping up their wine, then watched as he disappeared towards another table of patrons before they glanced at each other, grinned, and delved into the food in front of them.

'Here,' said Antonia, 'You have to try this – it's amazing.' She placed a forkful of food in Dan's mouth and watched as he ate, a smile playing across her lips.

'That's good,' he agreed. 'See what you think of this.'

Antonia plucked a forkful of his entrée into her mouth and closed her eyes. 'Mm, wonderful,' she smiled, 'but bad for the hips.'

Dan glanced down. 'Can't see any problems there,' he said and laughed as Antonia punched him playfully on the arm.

'You never said what your father did,' said Antonia.

Dan shrugged, swallowed a mouthful of food and picked up his wine glass. 'He was a geologist, although a bit of an adventurer too. He used to disappear for months on end all around the world doing tests and studies for mining companies.'

Antonia frowned. 'That must have been boring for you being stuck at home.'

Dan smiled. 'Boarding school for me for a while – although once I was old enough, I used to go with him during school holidays to some pretty amazing places, so it wasn't all bad.'

'So how did you end up doing this?'

Dan put down his fork, and swallowed hard.

'Dan? Are you okay?' Antonia reached out and gently touched his forearm.

'Yes – sorry.' He smiled and took a sip of wine. 'It still catches me out.'

He reached out for her hand and briefly told her about joining the Army, his tour in Iraq working with a bomb disposal team, and the explosive device which had killed half his friends and left him with scars – both physical and psychological. Then being contacted by his old Army captain, David.

'So now you keep England safe,' said Antonia.

Dan smiled. 'Well, I'd like to think the whole of Britain,' he said.

Antonia drew away as the waiter approached and cleared their plates.

'What about you?' asked Dan after their main courses had been set down in front of them. 'How did you get into all this?'

Antonia shrugged as she enthusiastically cut through her steak. 'By accident really,' she said. 'I was at university studying computer programming and had a gap in my final year subjects so I signed up for a political sciences course. Before the semester finished, one of the Government departments approached me with a job offer. I thought it would provide me with stability and a steady income.'

Dan laughed. 'The last few days must've been quite a shock for you then.'

Antonia smiled as she raised her wine glass to her lips then put it down again. 'It was better than being stuck in the office,' she said, and grinned.

Over their three-course meal, Dan found himself wanting to spend more time with Antonia. As they exchanged stories and experiences he realised he'd been spending far too much time on his own and wondered if it was time to permanently return home to England.

The waiter returned to refill their wine glasses. 'Would you like another sir?' the waiter enquired, holding up the empty bottle.

Dan shook his head and turned to Antonia. 'Coffee?'

'No,' she said. 'I've got a better idea.'

***

The lift doors opened and Dan led Antonia along the plush carpeted hallway. As they slowed and stood facing each other outside her room, he let go of her hand and caressed her bare arm, feeling her shiver under his touch. He glanced down at her, their eyes holding.

'What are you thinking?' he whispered.

'Don't leave me,' she said, and leaned into his chest.

Dan buried his face in her hair and inhaled deeply. He closed his eyes, aware he was about to break every professional rule he'd ever set himself. *Don't get involved.*

He ran his hands down her back, feeling her spine through the thin dress then settled on her hips, pulling her to him.

Too late.

She gasped as she felt him, pulled away to look in his eyes, then nodded and dragged him into the room with her. As the door closed behind them, she began to tear at the buttons of his shirt, pulling it over his broad shoulders and down his arms.

He wrapped his fingers in her hair, pulled her head back and began tracing his lips down her neck, along her collarbone. She shivered under his touch and groaned, then sank her teeth into his shoulder, nibbling the skin as she ran her fingers over his nipples.

Dan groaned, pulled back and slipped his fingers under the thin straps of her dress. His eyes met hers, their breathing heavy.

'Your father will kill me,' he murmured.

She shook her head. 'Deniable ops,' she smiled, and leaned forward to kiss the scars laced across his chest.

'Jesus,' he whispered, closing his eyes. 'Turn around.'

She did so, and he pulled down the zip on her dress, hard. He turned her around to face him as the dress fell to the floor, exposing her breasts and a lace black g-string.

He grinned. 'If I'd known you were wearing that in Malta…'

'…we'd be in a hell of a lot more trouble,' she said, pulling him to her, and kissing him deeply.

He lifted her up and, as she wrapped her legs around him, carried her over to the bed. Laying her down, he tangled his fingers in her hair as she began to loosen his belt, her breathing shallow now, desperate.

'Here, I'll help,' he said, and inched out of his jeans.

She leaned up on her elbows, her eyes blazing as he turned to her, and then she reached out for him, pulling him down onto her, guiding him inside.

As their bodies began to move together, he buried his face in her hair and closed his eyes. 'You realise this breaks every single operational rule ever invented?' he murmured.

'So shoot me.'

***

Dan's eyes slowly opened and took in the room around him. A grey dawn broke through the heavy curtains, the sound of sleet beating against the window shifting with the gusts of wind howling through the city.

He glanced down at Antonia's head resting on his chest, and stroked her hair. She stirred and peered up at him, tracing her fingers over the pockmarked scars which covered his skin.

'You okay?' he said.

'Mm,' she murmured, and smiled. 'What time is it?'

Dan moved his arm out from underneath her and held up his watch to the light, squinting through bleary eyes. 'Seven. We're going to have to get moving.'

Antonia growled. 'Sometimes I hate this job. Pity we can't stay here.' She looked up at him slyly as her hands began to move down his chest and across his abdomen.

He laughed and caught her hand before she went too far. 'Later.'

She stopped, and raised herself up on her elbows, her dark curls cascading over her shoulders.

Dan caught his breath. 'Do you realise how beautiful you are?'

Antonia smiled, then leaned down and kissed him. As she broke away, she noticed he was frowning. 'What's wrong?'

He shook his head. 'Nothing. I was wondering what the chances were of persuading you to stay here once all this is over.'

She laughed throatily, pushed back the sheets and straddled him. 'I think that's a possibility.'

He groaned as she started moving. 'And I think we're going to be late…'

Chapter 38

London

The murmur of voices around the conference table grew quiet as Dan and Antonia entered the room.

Dan closed the door behind him, nodded at Mitch who was in conversation with Philippa, then strode over to the table and pulled out a chair opposite Antonia. He winked at her as he sat down then looked up as David began to address the team, pacing the length of the room as he spoke.

'Right people, it's been a busy forty-eight hours, so let's have a quick overview of what's happened so far and see if we can draw any conclusions,' he said. 'Bear in mind I'm due at the Prime Minister's office in three hours, so you'd better have some results. Dan – you first.'

Dan nodded, and proceeded to bring the team up to speed on what he, Mitch and Antonia had uncovered in Malta. He stood up and walked over to a small table in the corner, picked up the clear plastic evidence bags that stood on the surface and brought them back to the conference table. Passing them round, he explained where the contents had been found.

'So to finish up,' he said. 'We've got a cigarette packet with a partial text print in a foreign language that looks a bit like Arabic – I'm not sure – and some food packaging. We've got a bit more text on that, but,' he glanced over at Philippa and handed her the bags, 'I could use one of your linguistics experts to confirm what language it is.'

Philippa nodded and took the bags. 'I'll get these processed now. With any luck, we'll have a positive identification for you within the next thirty minutes.'

David nodded, and Philippa hurriedly left the room. 'Right – what's the outcome of the reports from the Ras Laffan attack? Antonia – you're our programming expert, so why don't you get us started?'

Antonia nodded, stood up and walked around the table, handing each person a report. 'You can read this afterwards, but I'll give you the overview,' she began. 'That way, we can get moving on this straight away.'

She sat down in her chair, pulled it closer to the conference table, and opened the report. 'The team began by dumping the memory of each of the operators' computers so we could capture the system time, network connections made, any files opened and a note of logged-in users. For each computer, they also took a hard drive image which your analysts will need if they want to do any further work on this. They then identified any user

accounts which looked like they'd been compromised.'
She turned a page, and flicked her hair over her shoulder.
'The next thing they did was interview each of the
operators – the people who are using the system on a day-
to-day basis. All of them have access to emails so the team
began by asking if they'd received any unusual emails over
the past three months.'

'Why?' asked Dan.

'The easiest way for a hacker to infiltrate a system is to
send an email to a recipient,' explained Antonia. 'The
email contains a hyperlink, and when the recipient opens
the link, the hacker gets in. All the user sees is an error
message which says the page being looked for can't be
found – the user simply shrugs, closes down the window,
deletes the email and carries on working. The user doesn't
even realise someone has broken into the system.'

'Surely at a facility like that, they're going to have
firewalls and stuff to capture any rogue messages?' asked
Mitch.

Antonia nodded. 'Yes, they do – but the hacker posed
as Grant Swift, who was the lead engineer on the
programme upgrade project, and sent an email explaining a
new update was available. More than one controls engineer
clicked on the hyperlink contained within that message.'
She looked at the people gathered round the table. 'Those
engineers would have received an error message on their
screen and just closed their internet browser. Unknown to
them, that's all it took for the hacker to infiltrate the
system.'

She turned the page and scanned her notes. 'Once the hacker was into the email system, he was able to access every single email address for the facility. The next step was to try to take control of the system. To do that, the hacker used an email address of an engineer who had recently retired, and sent a message which supposedly included his contact details. The hacker included a hyperlink to a website that didn't exist, which of course most engineers opened to see what their colleague was now doing. Again, by clicking on the hyperlink, they triggered an error message. By doing this, the hacker could simply gain access to each individual's computer then key-stroke log everything the system was doing and find out how the facility was run.'

'How long had this been going on before the facility was attacked?' asked Dan.

Antonia flipped through the report. 'Based on interviews and the forensic evidence, the team over in Qatar reckon about six months prior to the attack.'

'Something like that has to take up an enormous amount of computer power,' said David. 'How on earth did they achieve that?'

'Easy – zombie computers.'

Dan leaned forward. '*Zombie* computers?'

Antonia nodded. 'It's a way of giving the hacker more processing power – and it protects his identity because he simply implements the same trick of sending a spam email to several computers. Not just in Qatar, but *worldwide*. By distributing the malware across several zombie computers, then utilising those computers to launch his attack, the hacker is able to reduce the risk of his own identity being uncovered…'

Antonia broke off as the conference room door swung open and Philippa strode into the room.

'Got it,' she announced. She walked up to David with the two evidence bags, put them on the table and pointed to the first one. 'Right, the cigarette packet's been matched to an Iranian brand of tobacco,' she said, 'and your food packet is also originally from Persia.'

'Could've been imported,' suggested Mitch.

Philippa shook her head. 'Trust me – if you were in Malta, you'd be smoking a Western brand, not these. In the words of our Farsi language expert downstairs, he'd rather smoke old shoe leather.'

'So someone on the submarine has stockpiled a supply of cigarettes,' mused Dan.

'And his mum packed some snacks for him by the look of it,' added Mitch, raising a small round of laughter from the other team members.

David held up his hand. 'Okay, settle down,' he said. 'We're running out of time – I need more...'

He looked up as the conference room door opened and an analyst hurried over to him. David's face paled as he read the message.

'In the early hours of this morning, a cruise ship was attacked off the coast of Gibraltar,' he read, his hand shaking. 'Reports indicate an estimated fifty-seven people remain unaccounted for, including eight crew members.'

A shocked silence filled the room.

'Attacked?' prompted Dan.

David nodded. 'Communications from the ship prior to it sinking indicate the Captain believed the vessel was hit by a torpedo.'

The room filled with a cacophony of voices as the assembled analysts all began speaking at once.

Dan pushed his empty coffee cup to one side and began sifting through the documents strewn across the table. The voices washed over him, his mind working. His thoughts were interrupted by a polite cough from the far end of the table. He looked up to find David staring intently at him.

'What are you thinking?' asked David.

Dan leaned back into his chair. 'Late last week an LNG tanker sinks at Ras Laffan in Qatar. That's only a short while after the submarine is lost. Any exports of LNG are going to be on hold until they can get the ship unloaded and salvaged. We've a missing yacht off the north coast of Malta and find evidence of a submarine there. We have to assume Hassan is now going after the UK's gas supplies.'

'Why on earth would Hassan have the submarine attack a cruise ship?' said Philippa. 'That doesn't make any sense.'

David held up the report. 'It does when you consider the rescue and salvage effort is now blocking the entire Strait of Gibraltar to heavy shipping traffic,' he explained. 'Including the emergency supply of LNG the British Government secured from the Tunisians.'

'Hang on,' said Mitch, putting up a hand. 'Slow down – I thought the UK produced its own gas still? Why are we so dependent on importing it?'

Richard Fletcher turned to the others in the room. 'If I may,' he said, and turned on an overhead projector. A series of graphs illuminated a screen on the far wall. 'The UK's gas reserves peaked in 2009 and have been in decline ever since. We went from being a gas producer, even exporting reserves offshore, to being a gas importer within a few years. The UK *has* been re-developing old gas fields for the past few years – some of these fields were previously abandoned because the gas was too difficult to reach. Lately, we've been implementing new technologies to reach it, especially as the price of gas currently supports deep water exploration like this.'

The analyst paused. 'We're still reliant on imports at times like these when we have a harsh winter and demand for gas is high across the whole of northern Europe. Our own gas production is currently supported by imports from Norway and the Netherlands via pipelines under the North Sea and English Channel, as well as what we buy from Qatar.'

'That's the liquefied gas which is pumped on shore at the Isle of Grain and Milford Haven, right?' asked Dan.

'Correct.'

'After the United Nations imposed more and more sanctions on Iran, encouraged by us and the Americans, it has to be said, the Iranians started sabre-rattling,' David interrupted. 'They're due to complete work on the final stage of the next trans-Persian pipeline in the next few months, supplying gas to some European countries.'

'I wouldn't imagine with the sort of sanctions currently in place they'd be allowed to trade with Europe?' asked Mitch.

David shook his head. 'Not Western Europe – *Eastern* Europe. They tend to be a bit more liberal about who their trading partners are. Especially with the price of Russian-supplied gas and the problems getting it out of Russia every time one of its neighbours throws a tantrum and disrupts supply.'

'So the Iranians could be trying to expand their client base?' said Mitch. 'Is that what you're suggesting?'

David nodded. 'If you consider the pounding the European economies have been dealt over the past few years, you can see why. Even France and Germany are talking to them on the quiet. They're struggling to get their economies into a budget surplus, so they're less fussy about how they meet energy demands. If the rest of the problems regarding Iran's nuclear programme are put to one side, they're actually quite a lucrative supplier. Iran is pushing quite heavily for export contracts considering it's only a matter of years before Israel's fledgling gas fields are up to full capacity and the North American shale gas industry floods the market. Given that the Iranians are becoming desperate to sell gas to wider Europe to offset the problems caused by UN sanctions, they could be getting more aggressive about their strategies.'

Fletcher shook his head. 'It's not enough for us to go on record and speak to the Iranian ambassador to accuse his country of attacking us.' He switched off the overhead projector and sat down.

David sighed. 'Well we can't just ignore it – we're in the middle of winter and all the forecasts are predicting this year's cold season will be as harsh, if not worse, than in 2010. The UK's gas supplies were seriously strained then. If we choose to ignore this threat, what happens then?'

Dan scratched his chin. 'Iran has enough allies to supply it with illegal weapons. Makes you wonder why they'd want an old beat-up submarine headed for the scrap heap.'

Mitch nodded. 'Has to be they want to avoid drawing attention to themselves. I can't think what their intentions are though. I mean, if they were going to suddenly attack us, I don't think they'd worry about what the world thinks of them – they'd just do it, and with their own gear.'

Dan ran all the scenarios through his head. He sat up straight as a thought occurred to him. 'What if Hassan is working on his own, without his Government's knowledge?'

'Why?' asked David.

'Power. Greed. Perhaps he's trying to work his way up through the Government to gain the attention of the mullahs,' Dan suggested. 'Maybe he thinks if he can pull off something like this, and force the UK to cancel the sanctions against Iran so we have to buy gas from them, he'll force the current president out, or get elected into office.'

'Which would help explain why he's had to steal a submarine.'

'Why kidnap Grant though?' asked Philippa.

'Maybe once the submarine is in place, Hassan will contact the UK Government with an ultimatum,' said Mitch. 'Start buying gas from his organisation, or else…'

'… he'll destroy the Isle of Grain facility like he tried at Ras Laffan,' finished Dan. 'With Grant out of the way, there'll be no system in place to prevent a hacker from making sure he causes as much destruction as possible.'

David stood up. 'Okay, finding Grant Swift has just become our number one priority,' he said. 'Philippa – speak to Kent Police, and get all the details they've got on his disappearance to date. Dan – do whatever you have to do to find him. The clock's ticking.'

Chapter 39

'Let's start with a view twenty-four hours before his vehicle was found abandoned,' said Dan. 'I want to see if his kidnappers had the sense to recce the area first. It was a bold move seizing him where they did, so they must've been absolutely certain they wouldn't be disturbed.'

He pushed his seat back and glanced around the room. Monitor screens filled the walls, feeding live images from various closed-circuit television cameras positioned on various roads around the country.

The camera operator nodded, typed in a series of commands and the screens in front of them flickered to life.

'The best I can give you is a camera positioned at the beginning of the exit ramp,' he said, pointing to the screen, 'so you'll see the back of vehicles as they leave the motorway at that junction.' He pointed to another screen. 'This camera is in the underpass below the motorway –

opposite the junction the exit ramp joins. It should give you a good cross-section.'

'Okay, let's try it,' said Dan, leaning forward in his seat. 'Keep the tape moving and stop it each time a vehicle appears – we'll capture an image of each to try to read the licence plates.'

The other man nodded and began to play the two recordings. Each time a car exited the junction and passed under the motorway under the cameras' watchful eyes, the computer took a photograph of the vehicle and a close-up of its licence plate and printed them out, a date and time stamp etched in the lower right-hand corner of each. Dan began to collect the photographs and spread them out on a table next to the camera operator.

After an hour of running through the recordings, Dan had a collection of ten vehicles.

'At least that shows us it's a quiet stretch of road,' said Dan.

'Certainly at that time of night,' agreed the operator. 'I took a look at it during daylight hours before you arrived – it seems to be busier during the school run than at any other time.'

'What about the road accident that night?'

The camera operator looked sideways at him. 'Nothing – when the emergency services arrived on the scene, both drivers of the vehicles involved had disappeared. General thinking is that it was staged to make sure Grant Swift took an alternative route.'

Dan frowned, and then pointed at the image on the screen. 'Is that it?' he asked. 'Are there any other angles?'

The operator shook his head. 'There's usually another camera at the other end of the underpass but it was broken two weeks ago and we haven't managed to get any of our contractors out to repair it yet.'

Dan grunted. 'What a coincidence.' He sighed and sat down. 'Okay, let's look at what happened when our project engineer disappeared.'

He chewed his bottom lip as the camera technician typed a string of instructions into his computer. The camera feeds then jumped to two hours before Grant's car had been found abandoned. The operator glanced over his shoulder at Dan.

'Okay. Play it. Not so fast this time though – we don't know the exact time he was taken.'

Twenty minutes later, Dan could feel the onset of eye strain after staring at the screens, hardly moving. He rubbed one eye, blinked and felt his heart lurch.

'Stop there – go back,' he said, standing up.

The operator rewound both recordings.

Grant Swift's silver Mercedes swept down the exit ramp, its tail-lights flaring as he slowed towards the junction. A grey van suddenly lurched into view, its brake lights flickering, before the vehicle slammed into the back of the Mercedes, pushing it over the junction. Then Grant turned his car across the junction and out of the camera's view.

Dan's head snapped to the next screen, the camera in the underpass picking up Grant's car, the grey van in its wake. The Mercedes disappeared under the camera, with Grant's face visible through the windscreen as he alternated between looking in his rear-view mirror to make sure the van followed him, and the road in front. As he passed out of view, the van behind his Mercedes slowed momentarily then slipped under the camera.

Dan slammed his hand down on the desk in frustration, making the camera operator jump.

'They're wearing baseball caps,' growled Dan. 'They *knew* the camera would pick up their faces.' He turned to the operator. 'What time was that?'

'Seven thirty-two.'

Dan frowned. 'Back up the tape – let's see it again.'

The two men watched silently as the recording replayed. Dan tapped a finger on his bottom lip, frowning. As the van disappeared from view a second time, he walked over to the table and began to sift through the photos which spilled across its surface.

'There wasn't a van earlier,' said the operator.

'I know,' replied Dan. 'That's what's bothering me. They knew the camera would pick up their faces, so they were familiar with the layout.'

He picked up each photo in turn, peering at the vehicles as they passed under each camera. His heart skipped a beat when he looked at the twelfth photograph taken from the first camera. He looked over at the camera operator, who was still staring at the grey van on the screen.

'Read out the licence plate on that van.'

The operator recited it, then turned and frowned at Dan. 'Why is that important?'

Dan held up the photograph. 'Because twenty-four hours before, it was on this.'

In the frozen image, a white sedan had exited the slip road from the motorway, crossed the junction and turned towards the underpass, passing directly under the second camera.

And the man in the passenger seat was staring up at the lens.

***

Dan laid out the road map over the desk and flattened it with his palms. Turning to the others, he explained what the cameras had picked up.

'What we need to do next is use the CCTV systems leading away from that underpass, together with the ANPR until we spot the van again, then track it to its final destination.'

'What's the ANPR?' asked Antonia, leaning across the table.

Dan managed to avoid looking down her shirt. 'It's the automatic number plate recognition system which the police use,' he said. 'The intelligence services monitor it, and it can link into the country's CCTV network so we can track vehicles.'

Antonia shook her head in wonder. 'I'd heard the UK had more CCTV cameras than any other country, but I'd never believed it until now.'

Mitch pulled the photograph of the white sedan across the desk towards him. 'Do we know anything about this one yet?'

'Philippa's running a scan of his face through her computers. Hopefully he has a previous conviction or something,' said Dan.

David put a flash drive into a laptop and began to replay the CCTV recording. He glanced at Dan. 'What else did you manage to get?'

'A feed into the system's intranet so we can piggy-back it and follow the two routes,' said Dan. 'They've given us access rights for twenty-four hours, so we need to get a move on.'

David nodded and stood to one side, letting Dan stab the commands into the laptop. When he hit the 'enter' key, the intranet page appeared on the screen.

'Okay, here we go,' said Dan. 'I'll enter in the van's licence plate number and the last CCTV camera location at the underpass. The ANPR should do the rest.'

'How does this work?' asked Antonia.

'Each time a camera picks up the van's licence plate, it'll alert the ANPR. That way, we can track the van – hopefully to its final destination.' He broke off as the first activation appeared on the screen. 'Here we go.'

After twenty minutes, the team had plotted a route through north Kent, along the M25 and onto the M4.

The van exited the motorway, setting off alerts as it travelled north-west through Reading.

Antonia moved across the room to stand next to Dan, peering over his shoulder at the laptop screen. 'What happens if the CCTV cameras don't cover this area?'

Mitch laughed. 'Trust me – it's very unlikely in that area.'

Dan raised an eyebrow.

'Hey,' shrugged Mitch, 'I should know – I went to school there.'

Chapter 40

Baqir wiped his hands on a stained towel, the soft material caressing his rough hands. Scraping a corner of the cloth under his fingernails to remove the blood, he glanced at the man slumped in the wooden chair in front of him.

He dropped the towel and scalpel onto a workbench, stepped over to the figure and slapped Grant's face until his eyes flickered, then opened, fear and pain etched across his face.

'You have done well,' wheezed Baqir. 'But we are not finished here yet.'

He let Grant's head fall, turned and walked up the stone steps leading out of the cellar. He knocked once on the wooden door and waited as the bolts were drawn back, nodded at the guard then walked down the hallway and out the front door of the farm house.

He squinted in the bright morning sunlight which reflected off the new layer of snow that had fallen during the night, and breathed deeply to clear the smell of shit and burning flesh from his nostrils.

He began to cough, a deep wracking vibration which shook his body, then spat phlegm into the pristine white powder. Cursing, he turned back to the house in search of Hassan.

He found him in the front room, pacing back and forth on the already worn carpet. The man looked up as Baqir entered, his face pale.

'Anything?'

Baqir smiled. The cellar was evidently not as sound-proof as he'd thought and it was as well they'd leased a property in a remote location. 'They are in the final stages of implementing his anti-virus software,' he said. 'It's not yet complete, but I shall find out if they can finish it without him.'

Hassan nodded. 'How much longer do you need with him?'

Baqir smiled. 'Not long. He's done well to hold out this far, although I think that's due to his natural stubbornness than to any formal interrogation training.'

He coughed again, and lowered himself into a threadbare armchair. 'You are returning to London?'

'I have to. It's too risky for me to stay here.'

'Why this particular gas facility, Hassan?' asked Baqir. 'Why not Milford Haven or one of the others?'

The other man smiled. 'For all the same reasons the UK Government expanded the Grain facility,' he said, pointing to a map of the British Isles spread out over a coffee table. A series of blue lines weaved their way across the counties of Britain. Hassan traced the web-like lines with his hand. 'Their National Transmission System provides gas to homes and industry all over the UK depending on demand,' he explained. 'Using this, they can send it anywhere. Grain connects straight into it. Naturally, it's also the first source of all power to London.'

Baqir frowned. 'But if you destroy Grain, they'll still be able to draw on supplies through their other facilities.'

Hassan held up a finger and smiled. 'Not now their gas supplies from Qatar have been disrupted,' he said. 'True, they'd normally be able to obtain supplies from Europe through the Bacton-Zebrugge connector pipe under the English Channel or from America by ship. However, we're in the middle of the harshest winter Europe has recorded in one hundred years. Countries such as the United States, the Netherlands or Germany are not in a position to help the UK without disrupting their own supplies.'

Hassan took a pen from his jacket pocket and circled the area which housed the gas facility. 'Finally,' he said, stepping back and replacing the pen, 'they have an enormous amount of gas stored here. All we have to do is take over their systems and start a chain reaction.' He smiled. 'Simply chemistry and physics will do the rest.'

'And once their supply chain is broken, you can offer to divert gas from your new Persian-Kazakh pipeline,' said Baqir.

Hassan smiled. 'It will be a very lucrative business venture for the Republic.'

Baqir joined Hassan, his eyes searching the map. 'It's very risky expecting the submarine to travel undetected through the English Channel.'

The other man nodded. 'They know the risks. However, it will also work to our advantage. The English Channel is one of the busiest shipping lanes in the world,' he said. 'What better way to mask their approach than shadowing the existing shipping traffic until they reach their destination?'

Baqir stroked his beard, his brown eyes flickering as he traced the route in his mind. He let his hand fall to his side and looked at Hassan.

'I do believe it will work,' he murmured. 'They might actually be able to do this.'

Hassan smiled, picked up his briefcase and headed for his car. 'I have every faith in them.'

***

'Shit!' exclaimed Dan. 'Where'd it go?'

Philippa scrolled through the data on the screen, her finger tracing the van's progress on the road map beside her. Sometime after leaving the border of Berkshire, the kidnapper's van exited a major road and turned into the Buckinghamshire countryside.

'Nothing,' she said, 'but I've run a search on major routes covering a ten mile radius from that last camera – they're holed up somewhere in this area.' She sketched a rough circle on the map.

Picking up a photograph of the van's passenger, Dan tapped it with his thumb. 'Okay, here's what I want you to do,' he said. 'It's a long shot, but circulate this to all rental agents in that area. The kidnappers have obviously spent time planning this, so they've probably rented a property where they're not going to be disturbed.'

'Got it,' said Philippa and took the photo from him, then glanced at her watch. 'Can't imagine any of these people are going to appreciate having to stay late at work this afternoon,' she grinned, and left the room.

Dan turned to Mitch. 'Contact any petrol stations in the area – if I'm wrong about the rental property, we'll find some CCTV images of the van at a garage and pick up their trail again.'

'Copy that.' Mitch picked up the road map, pulled up a chair to the computer and began searching for phone numbers.

'What can I do?' asked Antonia.

Dan smiled. 'Use your charm to help me convince David to rustle up some aerial surveillance at short notice,' he said. 'If we find the property, we'll need to carry out reconnaissance before the sun goes down in two hours.'

***

After convincing David to arrange the surveillance, Dan spent a frustrating half an hour helping Philippa's team as they worked through the list of rental agents in the area the van had disappeared, until a junior analyst slapped his phone down, shouted once and high-fived the man next to him.

'That had better be our agent,' said Philippa, glaring over her glasses at the analyst.

The man grinned, stood up and walked over to her, a notebook in his hand.

'I can go one better,' he said. 'Prescott and Durcher, an agency in High Wycombe, rented a farmhouse five miles out of town to our suspect two weeks ago.' He flipped to the next page. 'The man provided references and arranged to pay up front for a six-month lease.'

'Is the agent sure it's our suspect?' asked Dan, his knuckles white as he gripped the edge of the table.

The analyst smiled. 'Yes – even better, after the agency was broken into eight months ago, it installed security cameras. The cameras run continuously to capture everybody who enters its offices. The agency is arranging to email us an image showing our suspect right now.'

Dan slapped the surface of the table. 'Give me the address,' he said. 'Mitch, Philippa – start organising a surveillance team to get out there *now*. It's remote, so be careful. We can't afford to lose him when we're this close.'

***

Dan turned when he heard a knock on the door. Philippa walked in, carrying four rolls of paper under her arm and balancing a tray of coffee refills in her hand.

'These are the plans of the house and surrounding land,' she said, laying each document on the table and unrolling them. 'The building dates from 1870 so we spoke with the local historical society which sent through copies of the original plans from its archives. The next set of plans,' she continued, pulling the first set aside, 'are from the local Council – the owner of the house carried out some renovations about fifteen years ago and says downstairs is significantly different from the original layout.' She paused. 'He did also mention he'd appreciate it if you didn't cause *too* much damage to the property – he's not sure his insurance will cover it.'

She glared at Dan, who tried to maintain an innocent look and shrugged his shoulders. She shook her head, then leaned forward and pulled out the last two documents.

'Finally, this is an aerial photograph of the area taken late this afternoon. We've also obtained a topographical map here which you might find useful,' she said. 'The building's surrounded by woodland and is approached by a single vehicle dirt track. It should provide enough places to disguise your approach to the house.'

As she left the room, Dan pulled the aerial photograph closer to him, together with the accompanying report from the team of analysts. 'They've got a positive identification on the van in this picture,' he said to Mitch as the other man walked around the table to join him. He stabbed a finger on the driveway in the photo, the road surface blanketed by snow with two deep scars running through it, churned up by the vehicle.

'It matches the one in the CCTV footage?'

'Yeah – the angle of this photograph meant it could be enlarged so the analysts could get a partial read of the licence plate.'

Mitch picked up the report and began flicking through it, stifling a yawn as he reached for one of the coffee refills. 'One of our tactical teams has been watching the place since nine this evening – they've only seen two suspects so far. One guy exited the building to walk to and from a shed nearby and came back with what looked like a car battery. The other's only been spotted through the kitchen window.'

Dan pulled the house plans across the table. 'Might explain why the van hasn't moved for a few hours.' He tapped his finger on the plans. 'The kitchen has an exit into a back yard – the only other exit is the front door.'

'What about the renovations?'

'Looks like the owner pulled down a wall between the kitchen and dining room. The living room is separate. The front door opens into a hallway – stairs leading up on the right, living room to the left, with the kitchen and dining area at the back.'

'There must be a cellar or something in a place as old as this,' said Mitch, pulling the original plans towards him. 'Look – under the main staircase – there's another set of stairs leading downwards. Look at the thickness of the walls – they'd be near soundproof.'

'It seems to cover the whole footprint of the upper levels,' said Dan.

'Perfect place to hide a missing genius,' suggested David.

'True.' Dan traced his finger over the plans. 'Three bedrooms upstairs, and a bathroom. Easy.'

'Who's going in with us?' asked Mitch.

'We sent in a six-man team to carry out a reconnaissance – they're already on site so you'll be meeting up with them,' said David. 'They've familiarised themselves with the layout and have a feel for the place. We haven't time to organise another team and bring it up to speed on the situation so it'll just be the eight of you.'

'I'm coming too,' said Antonia, striding round the table and interrupting them. 'There's no way you're leaving me out of this.'

'No.' Dan shook his head.

'But you need all the help you can get,' Antonia protested.

David glanced at Dan and Mitch before speaking. 'He's not questioning your skills, Antonia – we can't possibly have a non-UK citizen running around the countryside with a weapon of any sort. We've got too many people watching us, waiting for us to screw up. If you want to help,' he said softening his tone, 'why not go with the medical team. They might be grateful for an extra pair of hands if this goes tits up.'

Antonia crossed her arms in front of her. 'I still say it's a waste of my skills.'

'Acknowledged.'

Dan raised his eyebrow at David, and then continued. 'Okay, let's get a move on.' He glanced at his watch. 'It's quarter to one now so we should be on site within two hours. Me and Mitch will go and get geared up.'

'Right,' said David. 'I'll phone the team and tell them you're on your way. I'll get our medevac team mobilised to meet you there.'

As he opened the door, he turned and looked back at Dan and Mitch. 'Just remember – if anything goes wrong, you'll be held accountable. If you rescue Swift, it's all good. If you shoot the wrong guy, you'll be facing murder charges.'

Chapter 41

Dan shivered, the cold gradually seeping through the front of his black clothing and into his skin. He cricked the muscles in his neck and re-focused his rifle sight.

The eight-man team sprawled out silently across the snow in a line along a shallow ditch, lying prone, facing forward, their rifles pointing at the red brick farm house in front of them. Clouds passed silently across the waxing moon, casting shadows among the trees and surrounding fields.

It had taken over an hour to reach their positions. Walking in through the surrounding woodland, the men had fanned out across a fifty metre line, stepping carefully, using a heel-toe movement through the undergrowth to reduce noise and conceal their approach using the trees and shadows.

Since establishing their forward position half an hour before, they'd seen no activity within the building. No lights shone in the front windows – a brief scout around the premises by one of the team located the living room at the side of the building, a television screen throwing light around the edges of the curtains in an otherwise dark enclosed space.

The van traced through the country's CCTV network was parked off to one side of the building – fresh snow covering its windscreen, roof and windows proving the kidnappers hadn't moved from their hideout within the past eight hours.

A quiet sniff emanated from the end of the line of men. Dan glanced at his watch. Quarter to four in the morning. He flexed his fingers on the rifle, the thin gloves providing little warmth to his hands.

He breathed out, his breath sucked away by the respirator built into the gas mask covering his face, which with the black helmet covering his head gave his appearance an alien likeness as he peered through the eye sockets using the night vision cameras built into the helmet.

He put his finger to the earphone in his right ear as it hissed to life.

Extraction in T minus three minutes.

His heart rate began to increase, the adrenalin pumping through his body. He tugged at the scarf around his neck and pushed it down into his collar, to give better protection from the breach which would be used to get through the thick oak doors of the farm house. He fingered the Sig Sauer which he'd strapped to his right leg, checking it was secure.

The cold forgotten, he stretched his leg muscles, arched his back and began to replay the plan in his mind. He checked the safety on his rifle one final time. *Off.*

All along the line the men flexed as one, listening to the countdown reverberating in their heads.

Three… Two… One!

Six men rose, wraith-like, from the ground. Crouching down, keeping their body shapes as small as possible, they scattered to their allocated attack positions – two to the rear, two to the front and one man on each diagonal, covering the windows on two sides. Two remained in their original prone positions, ready to act as snipers if any of the kidnappers escaped the building.

Dan and Mitch ran silently across the snow, their boots crunching softly into the crystallised surface, their steady breathing loud in their ears through the respirators compared with the silence the snowfall had created. Ducking under the level of the window sills, they pushed quietly past shrubs and edged around the farm house until they reached the rear of the building.

Dan crouched down facing the back door while Mitch provided cover to his rear. He reached out and touched the door handle.

Locked.

He reached into a zippered pocket on the front of his vest, pulled out a length of detonator cord and fixed it to the surface of the door. Next, he attached a shock tube initiator, checked his watch, then tapped Mitch on the shoulder and gestured for him to move back.

In his earpiece, he waited until the team at the front door confirmed they were ready and then began the short countdown.

'On my count – three, two, *one*!' He activated the initiator.

A split second later there was a short sharp *crack* as the door splintered inwards, a wisp of smoke emanating from the new opening. A similar blast from the front of the building echoed in the trees.

They were in.

'Remember, watch for weapons, not movement,' ordered Dan into his throat microphone.

He pulled out a stun grenade, flicked the pin and tossed it into the opening. He turned his face away from the blast, which rocked the farm house's kitchen and blew glass out of the window panes. Then, crouching low, rifle pointed in front of him, he entered the darkened building.

Smoke swirling in front of him, Dan crouched and checked through his rifle sight for movement. The kitchen area comprised a large stone sink to the right of the back door, gas oven and hob and fitted cupboards.

Dan walked over to the hob and oven, and checked the dials. *Off.*

A large central breakfast bar filled the remaining space. One of three stools lay on its side on the tiled floor, with no sign of its previous occupant.

To the left, Dan saw a small dining table, four chairs and the remnants of a Chinese takeaway spread across the table's stained surface. Standing up, he glanced in the sink. *Three plates.*

Silently, he pointed them out to Mitch, who nodded. Quietly, they made their way across the room, their breath echoing in their masks' respirators. As Dan approached a doorway leading through to the building's central passageway, his earpiece crackled to life.

'Team leader, this is Team Two – we've entered the front door. Rooms to our left and right are clear. Propose to climb the stairs. Over.'

'Okay,' said Dan. 'We'll continue down here. Out.' He turned to Mitch. 'Ready to check the basement?'

'Copy that,' Mitch nodded, Dan's silhouette reflected in the eye sockets of his goggles.

Dan lifted his rifle to his shoulder and edged closer to the closed door under the staircase, his heart beating rapidly. He noted the hinges would mean the door would swing out away from him. He grunted in satisfaction, and reached out his hand towards the handle.

A piercing scream came from the cellar, nearly turning Dan's insides to liquid.

'What the *fuck* was that?' hissed Mitch, his voice wavering over the radio.

'I think we just found our project engineer,' said Dan, unable to disguise the shaking in his own voice. 'No time to waste. Team Two, we're going in.'

'Copy that.'

'Got a flash bang, Mitch?'

'Ready.'

'On three.'

Dan counted in his head, wrenched open the basement door and stepped to one side.

Mitch leaned past him, tossed a stun grenade through the opening and moved out of the way as Dan pulled the door shut.

A loud *crack* filled the space, a cloud of dust billowed out from under the door, and then he wrenched it open and swung his rifle into the void. A dim light coursed up the narrow flight of steps. Dan switched off his night vision and located another button on the side of his helmet. Two torches sparked to life above his eyes, illuminating the staircase with a bright glare, pinpointed to Dan's direct line of vision.

He walked slowly down the steps, his rifle sight sweeping the floor below. As he reached the corner of the staircase, a figure lurched into view on his hands and knees, coughing and retching.

Stunned by the flash bang grenade, the man turned to face Dan and began to raise a gun.

'Put your weapon down!' yelled Dan.

The man leaned against the wall of the staircase, shook his head once and released the safety.

Dan fired once, low, hitting the man in the chest.

The man cried out, dropping his gun, and fell, his body slipping down the steps.

Dan bent down, pulled off his gloves and felt the man's neck for a pulse. *Nothing.*

'Shit,' he muttered. Standing up, he pulled on his gloves, glanced over his shoulder at Mitch, then began to descend the steps once more.

Dan glanced over his shoulder and held up a hand behind his back, slowing Mitch's descent. Reaching the final tread, he turned and surveyed the room layout. It was plain, some eight metres square, with exposed beams and little in the way of furnishings.

As he stepped down onto the basement floor, he almost tripped over a figure lying prone on the stone floor.

The man wore faded brown suit trousers, his jacket thrown over the back of a nearby wooden chair, while the sleeves of his pale blue shirt were rolled up to his elbows. He wore suede loafers, the heels and toes of one shoe badly scuffed as if he suffered a limp. He was also out cold from the force of the stun grenade which had landed near him.

Dan slowly approached the man in the brown suit. At his feet, a car battery stood on the stone floor, wires protruding from its connectors. As he drew nearer and moved his head to look past the figure in front of him, Dan's eyes followed the wires trailing across the floor.

His heart lurched.

A man hung from one of the exposed beams, his arms roped across the beam, his shirt ripped open, exposing large red welts. The car battery had been wired to his bare toes which dangled above the floor. Blood dripped from his mouth, a purple bruise developing across one swollen eye while the other remained closed, tears coursing down his cheeks.

As Dan watched, the man stirred and his eyes opened wide in terror at the masked figure now in front of him.

'Help me!' said Dan and hurried towards the man hanging from the beam.

Mitch ran down the stairs, pulled out a knife and began sawing through the ropes which bound the man, while Dan disconnected the clips from Grant's toes, coiled the wires and threw them to one side.

After gently lowering the engineer from the beam, Dan glanced around the basement, located Grant's shoes, then grabbed the man's ankles to steady the trembling in his legs and tugged the shoes onto his feet.

'Grant. Listen to me. We're going to get you out of here.'

The man began to shake, his hands trembling while a tic developed below his left eye socket.

'He's going into shock,' said Mitch. 'We need to move fast.'

The man suddenly lurched towards Dan, grabbed hold of his Kevlar vest and started to tear at the mask on his face, yelling.

'Get me out of here!' He began to push past Dan, who grabbed him roughly by the shoulders, spun him round and slapped him across the face, hard.

'Focus!' he hissed. He held up his hand. 'We're going to get you out of here but you have to do what I say, okay?'

Grant nodded, miserably.

Dan pushed the man towards Mitch, who reached out, caught Grant by the arm and steadied him. Dan looked over his shoulder at the man he'd knocked to the ground, who was easing himself into a seated position, holding his head. 'Do you know his name?' he asked Grant.

The engineer blinked and took a deep shaking breath before answering. 'I heard the others call him Baqir.'

'Okay. Good,' Dan glanced at Mitch. 'Let's get out of here.'

Mitch nodded, relaxed his grip on his rifle, and took Grant by his arm. 'Come on,' he said, 'let's go.'

Dan watched as Mitch dragged the man up the stairs away from the room which had been his prison. He glanced around the room, at the stinking bucket in the far corner, the stained mattress on the floor and the thin blankets strewn across it. He turned, kicked an empty water bottle and an instant meal pot out of his way and turned to Baqir, who was recovering from the stun grenade.

The man inched his way up into a sitting position, then turned and stared at Dan, grinning malevolently, exposing blackened rotten teeth. His ragged breath caught in his throat and he hacked uncontrollably before he spat on the floor.

Dan grimaced behind his mask, and began to pace towards the man, keeping his rifle trained on the torturer. 'Stay still,' he ordered.

The man cackled, shifted his position on the floor and held something up to the light.

Too late, Dan realised what he was looking at. The clips which had been attached to Grant's feet.

The man held the wires to each side of his head and kicked out with his right foot, knocking the car battery onto its side, the connection made.

Dan closed his eyes and turned his body away as the man's body writhed on the concrete floor from the force of the electric shock, a high-pitched scream escaping his lips.

Dan felt his stomach lurch, ripped off his mask and vomited over the floor. The air stank of burning flesh, assaulting his nostrils. He buried his nose into the sleeve of his jacket and concentrated on breathing through his mouth until he was certain he wasn't going to be sick again, then wiped his eyes and replaced his mask.

He blinked and looked away from Baqir's body, then turned towards the door at a voice in his earpiece.

'You okay?' said Mitch from the doorway at the top of the stairs.

'Yeah.'

'We need to get a move on.'

'Coming.' Dan repositioned his rifle and ran up the staircase.

Mitch stood at the top, one hand on his rifle, his finger on the trigger, the other hand on Grant's shoulder, steadying him. He cocked his head to one side, his expression hidden behind his mask.

'What happened?'

Dan shook his head. 'Later.'

Mitch nodded, glanced into the passageway and began to pull Grant towards the front door while Dan covered their retreat from the rear.

A sudden movement at the top of the stairs preceded a shout in their earpieces.

'We've got a runner!'

Dan and Mitch turned as one, pushing Grant down onto the floor behind them, their rifles pointed up the stairs.

A man dressed in black jeans and a blue sweatshirt launched himself down the top three steps, steadied his speed and stopped, glaring at the men below, sweat pouring from his brow.

As his pulse steadied, Dan levelled his rifle at the man.

'Stop right there!' he yelled. 'Do *not* move!'

The man froze in position for a split second, and then began to run down the remaining stairs. As he reached halfway, his hands fumbled an object out of a pocket of the sweatshirt.

Without a second's hesitation, Dan fired once – a clear shot to the man's chest, sending blood and tissue up the faded wallpaper.

The man tumbled, lost his footing and slid down the last three steps into a crumpled heap. As the man slumped to the floor, Dan's eyes opened wide behind his goggles. A small cylinder tumbled to the floor, its metal casing bouncing on the hard surface of the floor tiles.

'Grenade!' he yelled, and pushed Mitch and Grant sideways through an open doorway into the living room. Throwing himself in after the other men and covering his ears, he closed his eyes.

The blast shook the foundations of the building, blowing apart the wall they were hiding behind. Plaster fell in chunks from the ceiling, while in the passageway the wooden staircase splintered, sending its deadly shrapnel in every direction. Fire started to lick at the remaining furnishings, flames beginning to take hold of the building.

Dan groggily lifted his head, his ears ringing, his rifle still in his hand. He lifted a section of plasterboard off his body, rolled over and heaved himself to his feet. He peered out through the doorway, blinked, and edged carefully into the passageway, his rifle raised, Mitch following.

Dan glanced up the staircase, the topmost treads hanging precariously from the landing above. 'Team Two! You up there?' he called through his throat microphone then coughed as plaster dust hit the back of his throat.

A muffled retort echoed through the static, before a voice crackled in his ear.

'Was that you making all that noise, Taylor?'

'Sort of,' he spluttered. 'You're going to have to find another exit. Stairs are on fire. Move fast.'

'Copy that.'

Dan looked over his shoulder at Mitch. 'You okay?'

Mitch nodded, glanced at his shoulders and calmly dusted plaster dust from them. 'Yeah – go.'

Dan pulled Grant from the floor, the man covering his mouth and nose with his hands. He pushed him after Mitch, who grabbed the engineer by the shoulder and started to drag him from the burning building.

Glancing up at the ceiling through his blackened mask, Dan shook his head and began to force his way through the smoke-filled hallway towards the open front door. Daylight began to break through the fog around him, while the flames were getting hotter, closer, the house beginning to fall apart around them.

'Team Two – are you out? Are you out?' he shouted.

'Affirmative – we're making our way through an upstairs window.'

'See you on the outside,' said Dan, and began to run after the shadows of Mitch and Grant.

As he stepped out of the building, Dan noticed the morning sun beginning to crest the horizon. He walked carefully across the snow-covered terrain, pulled off his gas mask and helmet and breathed deeply, his exhaled air steaming in front of him.

Mitch had taken Grant to the medical team which had parked a dark coloured van next to the farm house.

Antonia sat next to Grant on the tailgate of the van. The door was open, and she crouched down, her hand on the engineer's knee as she gently spoke to him and handed him a bottle of water. She turned at the sound of Dan's boots on the snow, smiled and patted Grant on the knee before standing up and walking over to meet Dan.

'Okay?' asked Dan.

She nodded. As she drew closer, her smile faded and she kept her voice low. 'We need to take him with us,' she said. 'He's the only one who can protect the plant if the submarine attacks before we find it and destroy it.'

Dan lifted his chin in the direction of the van. 'Do you think he can hold it together for a bit longer?'

Antonia shrugged. She glanced at the van, then back at Dan.

'He's going to have to. There's no other way.'

Chapter 42

As he watched through the bullet-proof reflective glass of the medical treatment room, Dan drummed his fingers on the narrow aluminium window sill. The doctors dressed Grant's wounds, ran tests and spoke to their patient in calm, even voices. Machinery whirred and beeped, monitoring his heart rate, breathing and blood pressure as the medical team worked to repair his body.

He turned at the sound of footsteps echoing along the corridor behind him and saw David approaching, a frown creasing his brow.

'How's he doing?'

Dan shrugged. 'Hard to tell. The lead doctor told me to expect their report within the next half an hour, so we'll have a better idea then.'

David glanced round Dan's shoulder to see one of the doctors insert a needle into Grant's arm. 'What are they giving him?'

'Something to help with the amnesia and any breathing difficulties he'll be suffering after the drugs the kidnappers used.'

'Let's hope his programming skills haven't been affected by the last few days.'

'I know. I'm more concerned about those than getting the kidnapping details out of him.' Dan paused, and then turned away from the viewing window. 'While we're waiting for the doctors to patch him up and give us the all clear to start working with him, I want to go down to Kent – speak to the guys at the gas plant and find out what I can on the ground before we turn up with the whole team.'

David nodded. 'I agree. Find out what the likely targets there could be and what their emergency procedures are. Take Antonia with you – if she can talk with one of the engineers at the facility she might be able to understand exactly what Grant's software was designed to do – just in case he takes a turn for the worse. You've got two hours.'

'Copy that,' said Dan, and hurried from the medical rooms.

***

Dan slewed the car onto a pot-holed private road and held a steady speed down the narrow lane. The wheels churned up the loose surface, splattering the side of the car with mud and sending small stones rattling under the wheel arches.

As the road curved slowly to the left, a guard hut and high wire fencing came into view. Two guards cowered in the doorway, trying their best to shelter from the cold downpour of sleet assaulting the north Kent coast.

'I think you should move to Qatar, instead of asking me to move here,' said Antonia, her eyes following the rivulets of water cascading down the car's windscreen.

Dan grinned and slowed the car to a halt, lowered the window and held up their security clearances to the guard who hurried from the hut holding his windcheater over his head. The wind whipped at his hood as he bent down to inspect the identification. Satisfied, he nodded to Dan and straightened up.

'Go through the gates and follow the road round to the right,' he shouted over the rain. 'The Ops Manager's office is the second building on the left.'

Dan held up his hand in acknowledgement and raised the window while the guard jogged back to the hut and armed the gate controls. Dan eased off the brake as the gates smoothly slid open on tracks, and slowly guided the car through the gap.

He drove the car as close as he could to the administration building and killed the engine. Reaching down to unclip his seatbelt, he craned his neck to try and see through the office's window and whether anyone was going to let them in – or watch them drown on the threshold. He hoped the guard at the gate had phoned ahead.

After a few seconds, a figure appeared at the window and raised its hand.

'Perfect,' said Dan, and swung open the car door. 'Let's make a run for it.'

He screwed up his eyes against the sleet that hit him in the face as he climbed from the car, Antonia on his heels. A strong breeze blew in from the sea, stinging his skin. He jogged up the three steps to the brick office building, and the door opened immediately.

'Come in, come in,' urged a man. 'Quickly – otherwise we'll lose all the heat out of the building.'

Dan and Antonia stepped over the threshold and moved to one side, dripping puddles on a well-worn parquet floor as the door slammed shut behind them.

The man chuckled. 'Welcome to the Isle of Grain – what do you think of our weather?'

Dan grinned. 'It's bloody awful.'

The man held out his hands. 'Give me your coats. I'll hang them here.'

They shrugged their jackets off and handed them over. The man turned, hooked them over one of several pegs screwed into the plaster wall and turned back to them with his hand outstretched.

'Ted Harris.'

Dan shook his hand and introduced Antonia.

Harris guided them to a small office to one side of the corridor, its window facing the car park, and pointed to two chairs in front of his desk.

'Sit yourself down there. You said on the phone you were in a hurry, so where do you want to begin?' he said.

'Can you give us a run-down of how the facility works?' asked Dan. 'I mean, I know LNG tankers offload gas here, but what's the process?'

'Well for a start, we're a regasification and storage plant,' began Harris, 'which means we unload the gas in its liquid form off a ship, and then gradually heat it up so it turns back into gas. We run a few processes to get rid of any impurities, then store it. Eventually it'll get pumped into the National Grid Transmission System and can be sent anywhere around the country.'

He stood up and walked over to an enlarged aerial photograph of the facility hanging on the wall, lifted it off its hook and set it down on his desk. Dan and Antonia leaned forward in their seats to have a closer look.

'Here we've got a Q-Max tanker offloading gas from Qatar,' explained Harris. 'There are three loading arms and a vapour return arm which link the ship to the jetty and pump the liquid gas into pipes leading from the jetty to the regasification plant.' He tapped his finger on the photograph and began tracing the line of pipework which snaked across the landscape.

'The pipeline is about two miles long, and rests on concrete sleepers,' he said. 'We use four compressors at the end of that which the gas passes through before it's superheated to warm it from minus one hundred and sixty degrees Celsius to plus five degrees.'

'Is that when you pipe it into the storage tanks?' asked Dan, pointing to four large cylindrical objects located on the perimeter of the picture.

Harris nodded. 'Yes, that's right. Each one holds one hundred and ninety thousand cubic metres of gas.'

'How much of the process is managed by your SCADA system?' asked Antonia.

Harris frowned. 'All of it. The compressors, the pumps drawing gas off the ships, the valves through the pipework – everything.'

Dan folded his arms across his chest and paced the room as his mind worked. 'So, if any attack happens, the software Grant has designed can be used to shut off the gas flow through the plant to limit the damage?'

Harris nodded. 'It's like a switch – just in data code, rather than a physical switch. We can programme it to turn off the gas in different areas.'

'And Grant Swift wrote this?' asked Antonia.

Harris nodded. 'He's the lead controls engineer on the project. Our organisation employed him as a consultant. He started here a couple of months ago – he's been analysing our systems, looking for weak points and ways to implement his programme. We were only a few weeks away from the start of testing.'

'What about design drawings?' asked Dan.

Harris shook his head. 'Grant owns the background intellectual property. The organisation only owns the intellectual property for the completed system as built for this LNG plant.'

'Would it be possible for us to have a copy of the design for the final system – the ones you *do* own the copyright for?' asked Antonia, and then turned to Dan. 'I'd like to study them – as a back-up plan.'

He nodded. He understood what she was saying. If Grant didn't recover in time to prevent the submarine attack, they might have to organise a team of designers to try to reverse-engineer the schematics to try and work out the data code for the patch.

'Sure.' Harris removed a data stick from the top drawer of his desk. Inserting it into his computer, he hit a series of keys then tapped his fingers on the surface of the keyboard while the information downloaded.

Dan leaned across to Antonia. 'Do you think reverse-engineering this thing is possible?' he murmured.

She cast a glance at Harris who was removing the data stick from his computer. 'I'll get a better idea if it's possible once I see what's on that stick,' she said. 'At the moment, we can't rule out anything.'

She smiled and took the data stick from Harris. 'Thank you. I'll call you if I need anything clarified.'

Harris nodded. 'You do that,' he smiled. 'Tell you what,' he said, and looked out the window. 'That weather is easing up a bit. Let's see if I can rustle up some protective gear for you both and I'll persuade the captain of the tanker which has just unloaded to let me show you around.'

'Really?' said Dan and Antonia in unison.

Harris grinned. 'Might as well make the most of it – you're never going to get the chance to do this again.'

***

Dan reached up and ran his hand round the smooth surface of the tank. He sniffed the air, paranoid that if he suddenly moved the whole ship would disintegrate in a fire ball.

Harris laughed at him. 'You won't be able to smell it, lad.'

Dan smiled sheepishly. 'I guessed as much, but it seemed the right thing to do.'

Harris laughed and slapped him on the back. 'Come on, I'll give you the grand tour.' He walked around the tank and pointed along the ship's deck. 'There are five of these tanks on this ship. When it's full, there'll be about forty-eight million litres of liquefied gas spread between the five tanks.'

'How much energy is that?' asked Antonia, peering up at the tanks which towered above them.

'Equivalent to about fifty atomic bombs,' said Harris. 'Though the industry has never had a major accident.'

Yet, thought Dan. He turned to Harris. 'So how do you transport it to make sure it won't explode?'

Harris leaned against one of the railings on the deck and gestured over the top of the five tanks, the top of them belying their bulk beneath the deck surface.

'Once the gas is extracted from its source, it's chilled to minus one hundred and sixty degrees Celsius,' he explained. 'That stops the problem of any gas igniting at air temperature. We fill the hull with noxious gas –

nitrogen – before the liquefied gas is pumped into the tanks. It can't catch fire in that state.'

Dan frowned. 'How come no-one is allowed to have electronic devices near the tanks when this thing is full?'

Harris turned to him. 'Because there's still a small risk of vapour. We've got alarms to tell us if noxious air is escaping or there's a leak in one of the tanks, but it's all about lessening our risk of an accident. The whole ship could go up if anything caused a spark near one of these things.'

'But if it's empty now, why not just send it on its way on Tuesday without any gas in it?' said Dan. 'Let them attack an empty ship.'

Harris turned and contemplated the shipyard activity below. He leaned on the newly painted railing, the smell of the fresh blue coat stinging his nostrils. He looked sideways at Dan and seemed to steel himself before he spoke.

Harris turned and pointed across the length of the ship. 'They won't attack *this* ship, sonny.'

Dan frowned. 'They won't?'

'No – this one's a baby. They'll want to attack its big sister.'

'Big sister?' Dan felt his jaw slacken as he took in the enormity of the vessel, and then looked along the length of the jetty. He looked back at Harris. 'Where is it?'

Harris looked Dan in the eye. 'It's the one which left Ras Laffan the morning of the attack.'

'You call this one a baby? Exactly *how* big is its 'big sister'?'

'Four hundred metres long, six storage tanks, with an energy equivalent to *seventy* atomic bombs.'

Dan felt his heart lurch in his chest and looked at Antonia. 'Oh shit.'

Chapter 43

Dan knocked and entered the room.

The Vice-Admiral stopped speaking as Dan appeared, his arms crossed in defiance, his face red.

David stood up. 'Dan, glad you could join us,' he said.

Dan shook hands with him. 'What's going on?' he asked.

David gestured to the other people in the room. The Secretary of State for Defence's representative sat at the head of a beech oval conference table, while the Vice-Admiral remained pacing by the coffee machine, evidently trying to maintain his cool.

'In case the rescue mission fails, we were discussing a back-up plan,' explained David. He put his hands in the air. 'Unfortunately, it would seem we have no back-up.' He sat down in a chair facing the Vice-Admiral.

Dan walked round the table and glanced out the window at the river traffic, then turned to face the room. 'What's the problem?'

The Vice-Admiral sighed. 'Two destroyers are escorting the Q-Max tanker, which left Ras Laffan the morning of the attack, through the Atlantic as a precaution – they'll follow it up to the point it docks in the UK. The rest of the fleet are currently in the middle of a major exercise with the French and Americans in the South Atlantic,' he said. 'Unknown to the British public, our remaining assets, namely an Astute class submarine and two frigates are unavailable for defending the country at this time. '

'Wow,' said Dan. 'That's bad timing.'

'Heads will roll,' growled the Vice-Admiral.

'Where exactly are the two frigates and the submarine?' asked Dan.

'The submarine is having a refit which is running four weeks late, one frigate is off the coast of Somalia on a reconnaissance mission, and I can't tell you where the other frigate is, because that'd open another can of worms.'

Dan turned and looked out the window, letting the voices wash over him. He shivered, the cold from the bulletproof glass casting a chill which wasn't improved by the room's poor heating system. He watched a tourist boat battle a headwind and an incoming tide up the muddy waters of the River Thames, its passengers braving the elements to take photographs of the Tower of London on the opposite bank. His gaze shifted and a smile began to play across his lips as he watched a traffic helicopter hovering above the busy cityscape.

He turned to face the others, his heart racing as he fought to keep his voice calm. 'Gentlemen, I think I've found the solution to our water-based problem,' he said, jerking his thumb over his shoulder and grinning.

RAF Northolt, North London

Dan stuffed his hands into his pockets, ducked his chin into his scarf and stamped his feet as he stood outside a weather-beaten aircraft hangar. He swayed slightly as a particularly harsh thrust of wind whipped around the airfield and blew sleet in through the hangar door. He wiped his face, stepped back into the shelter of the enormous structure and turned to the man next to him.

'How much longer?'

They'll be here soon – just had to take a diversion around the M25 to miss a snow squall.' The man turned his back to Dan and strode over to a table onto which a hot water urn, tea and coffee had been set out. 'Help yourself,' he called over his shoulder. 'They'll want a hot drink when they get here. Might as well make use of the civilian supplies.'

Dan sighed, held his impatience in check and helped himself to black coffee. 'What do you mean, civilian supplies?' he asked.

'Northolt allows civilians to land here occasionally,' explained the mechanic. 'Just not when there's something special going on,' he added with a wink. 'And that includes any VIPs.'

As Dan raised his steaming mug of coffee to his lips, his ears picked up the faint sound of rotors slicing through the freezing air. He followed the other man to the hangar door and began searching the low grey cloud cover for the approaching aircraft.

The sound grew closer, and Dan's eyes scanned the horizon, waiting for the helicopter to appear. When it did, it took him by surprise, the grey hulk of a machine dropping out of the sky less than five hundred metres in front of him.

The fuselage was covered in cameras and sensors, its nose a bulbous mound of radar equipment. The helicopter banked elegantly in the air, lowered slowly to the ground and bobbed once on its wheels.

As the rotor blades slowed to a standstill, Dan peered through the downpour as the doors opened. Two aircrew dressed in identical dark green overalls climbed down to the tarmac and ran through the sleet towards the hangar.

The pilot reached the structure first and held out a hand to Dan. 'Scott Carlisle,' he said, then turned as his partner joined them, shaking water from his hair. 'And this is my observer, Rob Hamilton.'

Dan shook hands with both men and pointed towards the hot water urn. 'Better get yourself one of those before the caretaker drinks it all.'

Carlisle grinned and walked over to the table. 'So, what's the story?' he asked as he mashed a tea bag in a mug of hot water. 'I hear you have a submarine problem?'

'Just a bit,' said Dan. 'Come through to the office and I'll explain.'

He led the two men through to a small room which had been created by boarding up one corner of the hangar. A window looked out onto the hangar space while old flying club notices peeled off a corkboard nailed to one wall. A table and four chairs were set out in the middle of the room and an electric heater on its maximum heat setting battled the cold breeze wafting into the room from the main hangar.

Dan shut the door and immediately the room temperature increased by a couple of degrees. He sat down and motioned to the helicopter crew to join him. Once they'd settled, he pulled out a map of the north Kent coastline and spread it over the table.

'The situation's a little more tricky than just dealing with a submarine,' he began, 'which is why the Vice-Admiral thought it best if I spoke with you directly to see what you suggest. We've reason to believe the gas facility at the Isle of Grain on the north Kent coast is under threat. You'll have seen the incident in Qatar on the news last week.'

Both crewmen nodded.

'From the evidence currently available, it looks like a two-pronged attack. First, an LNG tanker was hit and sunk by something originating from the water – we're presuming a torpedo – which caused it to capsize while taking on gas from the facility. Secondly, when the engineers attempted to stop the flow of gas to the tanker, they discovered their computer systems had been hacked into and were unable to run their usual emergency procedures. It was only because of a recently installed programme that they were able to block the hacker from the system at the last minute and in time to prevent a major catastrophe.'

Dan took a sip of coffee before continuing. 'The original idea was to launch an attack on the submarine, but when we located its sonar signature, we found it's using other ships in the English Channel to hide behind. In the meantime, we've got a Q-Max tanker on its way to Grain to offload LNG. The tanker's about to enter the English Channel from the Atlantic, and given the number of vessels using that piece of shipping real estate, the Navy can't exactly send a couple of destroyers or frigates to destroy the submarine – we can't risk alerting the crew or their bosses to the fact we know what they're planning.'

'So what do you propose to do?' asked Carlisle, frowning.

Dan leaned forward and pointed at the map. 'Wait until they come round the Kent coastline and enter the Thames Estuary before attacking them to clear the way for the tanker,' he said. 'At which point, the Vice-Admiral suggested you'd probably be able to help.'

The pilot scratched his chin then glanced at Hamilton. 'We could certainly destroy them by using something like a Sting Ray torpedo, but it's still high risk,' he said.

'How do they work?' asked Dan. 'Don't you run the risk of hitting another ship instead?'

Hamilton shook his head. 'We'll programme our onboard weapons system with the particular submarine signature. Once we launch the torpedo, it'll locate, identify and hunt the submarine using the parameters we've set.'

'So it won't destroy another ship by accident?'

'No – if it misses the target for some reason, for instance if the submarine deploys a decoy, the torpedo will drift then recalibrate. Then it'll start a new hunt and destroy sequence. It'll keep doing that until the target's destroyed or we call off the hunt.'

'There's one other problem to consider,' said Dan.

Carlisle looked up from the map. 'What?'

'Richard Montgomery.'

'Ah,' said the pilot, '*that* old bastard.'

***

The *SS Richard Montgomery* was a Liberty-type ship built in the United States during the Second World War in 1943. In August 1944, the ship left her homeland with a cargo of munitions destined for the United Kingdom and France to help replace munitions lost in the Atlantic convoys.

While waiting for her escort to France in the Thames Estuary on 20 August 1944 off the shoreline of Sheerness, strong winds blew the ship into shallow water. Despite attempts by her crew to save her, she became grounded.

After all the crew were evacuated, a salvage operation was mounted to save the munitions needed for the war effort. After five days, with only half the explosive ordnance retrieved from the stricken ship, the vessel broke in two and sank beneath the waves, taking the remainder of her cargo with her to a watery grave.

Dan closed the report. 'It's still there – the masts stick out of the sea and can be seen from shore. There's a twenty-four hour armed patrol guarding it, but they're not going to be much use against a submarine torpedo attack.'

'How much explosives are still on board?' asked Hamilton.

'Anything between fifteen hundred and three thousand tons,' said Dan. 'As you'll appreciate, the Admiralty is a little cagey about telling us exactly how much, but if that wreck moves, or is hit by another vessel, the destruction to the surrounding area would be catastrophic.'

'What sort of explosives?' asked Carlisle.

Dan glanced down the report. 'TNT and cluster bombs, according to this,' he said. 'I spoke with the Ministry of Defence earlier this morning who confirmed the charges and detonators had been stored separately, but there're some analysts in our team concerned about the stability of the explosives – if the sea water's got to it, it won't take much to set it off. If we use a torpedo to destroy the submarine anywhere near this thing, the vibrations could very well start a chain reaction.'

'What's the scenario if she does blow?'

'We got hold of some projections which suggest tsunamis along the coasts of Kent and Essex, as well as along the Thames towards London,' said Dan. 'The shockwaves alone would cause millions of pounds worth of damage, not to mention the complete annihilation of every living being within a fifteen mile radius.'

The pilot quietly whistled through his teeth and drew a black 'x' on the map to show the *Montgomery*'s position. 'And it's only a few miles from the Isle of Grain gas facility,' he said, tracing along the coastline with his finger, 'and the oil refineries along that stretch of land.'

Dan nodded, his face grim. 'What we have to decide is *where* we're going to attack the submarine,' he said. 'Too soon, and we alert their masters we're onto them.' He paused. 'And if we're too late, we'll be responsible for one of the biggest non-nuclear explosions in history.'

Chapter 44

The armed security guard stood to one side as Dan entered the room.

David stood at the far end of the room shaking hands with Grant Swift. Both men turned to face Dan as the door closed behind him.

'Glad you could join us,' said David, who gestured to a set of armchairs arranged around a low coffee table next to floor-to-ceiling windows designed to take in the view of the river below. A laptop sat open on the table, the screen displaying a series of codes, numbers and programming script. 'Grant was just getting me up to speed on exactly what this programme of his is capable of – and how it might help us.'

Dan shook hands with Grant as he sat down. 'How are you holding up?'

'I've had better weeks,' the engineer commented as he eased himself into a chair. 'I'm going to have a lot of explaining to do when I eventually get home.'

David walked round the armchairs and stood at the windows, letting his gaze wander over the cityscape. 'Hopefully we won't have to keep you from your family much longer,' he said and turned to face both men. 'Not if this works.'

'What have you got in mind?' asked Dan, leaning forward to the table in front of him and filling glasses with water from the jug provided.

David glanced at Grant. 'This is your speciality, so I'll let you explain,' he said, and began to pace the room while he listened.

Grant leaned forward and rubbed his hand over his eyes. 'What you've got to understand is that I can't just write the code and then upload it onto the system,' he began. 'It just doesn't work like that. I've got to look at the existing SCADA – essentially what this whole controls system does. It runs the processing plant. Opens valves, records gas levels, that sort of thing.'

Dan nodded and gestured for the engineer to continue.

'What my software does is enable an authorised user to switch off the gas flow, then hunt down and destroy a hacker's access into the system. To do that, I've got to analyse the existing SCADA system and write the code within those parameters, otherwise the engineer operating this would have to re-learn the entire system, not just the application of the commands we need to control the system under stress.'

Dan frowned, leaned back and crossed his arms over his chest. 'How long will that take?'

Grant ran his hand over his hair and scratched his neck. 'The codes I wrote for Ras Laffan took three weeks,' he said. 'We'd only just got to the testing phase at Grain – it's still a raw system.'

Dan looked past the engineer and glanced at David, who was shaking his head.

Dan lowered his gaze to the display on the laptop screen. 'If we provided some people to help you, how fast would you be able to do it?'

The engineer sighed and closed his eyes. When he opened them again, he looked first at Dan, then over his shoulder at David. 'If I had a team of six engineers – and I mean on top of their game, senior controls engineers, then maybe – *maybe* – we can pull this together overnight,' he said. 'But it's going to be close. They'll get tired, make mistakes. I'll have to check everything they do, run a simulation before we even think about uploading this onto the Isle of Grain system.' He leaned forward in his chair and reached out to exit the programme and close the laptop. 'And they'll all have to sign confidentiality agreements to protect my intellectual property.'

'Working in secrecy won't be an issue,' said David. 'The CISP has some great guys working in the City at the moment on cyber security issues so they'll be up to speed on what we're trying to do. The Qataris sent their own programming expert to assist with the investigation as well – Antonia Almasi – so she'll be able to help as well.'

Grant nodded. 'Good, good – then we should get started straight away.'

***

'Okay,' said Grant, pinching the bridge of his nose and blinking. 'That's as much as we can do here.' He began handing out data sticks to each of the engineers. 'Back up your work to these and give them back to me. I'll go to the gas plant now and begin to pull everything together,' he said as he walked round the room.

The engineers began to stand and stretch, leaving the room, passing Grant on the way and handing back the data sticks. Grant glanced up, and seeing Antonia still at her laptop, called to her.

'Come on, Antonia – what's taking you so long?' he teased.

She looked up and grinned. 'Back off – I've done twice as much work as this lot,' she said as she closed the laptop and stood up.

The last of the engineers laughed as they left the room.

Grant smiled and held his hand out for Antonia's data stick as she approached him. 'You're probably right.'

'Is this really going to work?' she asked.

The software engineer sighed. 'Look – I *think* it will. The system at Ras Laffan worked well, and that had only been used in a supervised test environment before having to be used against a real attack – and a very coordinated one at that. I've spent the last two hours running simulations on a copy of the facility's system and we stand a good chance – I just can't say for certain until we're there and under attack.'

Antonia nodded and handed him the stick before slinging her laptop bag over her arm. 'I'll see you at Grain,' she called over her shoulder as she left the room.

Chapter 45

Dan stood on the cliff top next to the gas facility, his arms hugging his chest, a woollen cap pulled down low over his ears. He squinted through the sleet at the churning grey sea, the waves whipped into a frenzy by the winter storm.

Feeling a nudge to his side he looked down and took the binoculars from Mitch.

'Thanks.'

Sweeping the waters on the horizon, hopeful for any trace which might give away the submarine's position, he saw nothing, then glanced up at the storm clouds and frowned.

'Do you think they'll be able to fly in this?' asked Mitch.

'Hope so.'

'What if they can't?'

Dan turned and glared at Mitch, who held up his hands.

'Sorry. Just thinking out loud.'

'Don't.' Dan handed back the binoculars, pulled his hat lower over his ears and scowled.

Mitch looked at his watch. 'How did they come up with the attack time?'

Dan sniffed, resisting the urge to wipe his nose on his sleeve. 'Something to do with a lull in shipping movements in the Channel,' he said. 'Apparently there's a half hour window late afternoon where there's very little commercial traffic. The ferries will either be on their final approach into Folkestone or Dover or the continent. It's human nature that most passengers will be looking at the coastline they're approaching, rather than back out to sea.'

'You had to have heard that from the Vice-Admiral,' grinned Mitch.

Dan's mouth twitched. 'Maybe.' He turned to Mitch. 'In any event, it's late in the afternoon, rather than evening and,' he said, glaring out to sea, 'snowing. It's going to be relatively hard for anyone to see the actual moment of impact.'

'Subtle,' nodded Mitch.

'Not for the men in the submarine,' said Dan, 'but given the lives they've already taken, and their plans, it's very hard to have any sympathy for them.'

He broke off as his mobile phone began to ring and answered it. 'Taylor.'

'They took off from Northolt two minutes ago,' said the Vice-Admiral, his voice whipped away by the wind.

Dan turned to shelter the call from the storm and put his hand over his other ear. 'Can they see it?'

'Loud and clear,' replied the Vice-Admiral. 'It's travelling very slowly to try and disguise its signal but it just crossed behind the bow wave of the Calais to Dover ferry.'

'Jesus,' said Dan. 'That was close.'

'Good tactics,' admitted the Vice-Admiral. 'Proves your theory about them coming up the Suez by tagging onto other ships to hide their approach.'

Dan smiled. 'Lucky guess.'

The Vice-Admiral snorted, and then there was a pause at the other end of the line. 'Right. I've got to go. If you want to watch, now's the time to get yourselves in position.'

Dan hung up the phone, glanced at his watch and turned to Mitch. 'It's on.'

Mitch nodded and turned back to face the sea, the binoculars to his eyes. 'This should be interesting. How do you propose we find out what's happening?'

Dan grinned as a throaty roar emanated from further along the pockmarked track behind them, the sound growing closer.

'With this,' he said, jerking his thumb over his shoulder.

Headlights flashed at the end of the road as the ground beneath their feet began to tremble.

Mitch lowered the binoculars as he looked over Dan's shoulder, a look of shock across his face.

'You've got to be kidding me.'

Dan stepped off the narrow road and onto the slush-covered verge as a sleek black articulated truck slid gracefully to a halt next to them, its air brakes hissing, its wheels and paintwork spattered with mud and snow.

Mitch craned his neck and looked up the length of the cab. 'Tinted windows, huh?'

Dan smiled. 'Philippa organised it.'

'She thinks of everything, that girl.'

'She does indeed,' said Dan and stepped back as the engine idled then died, and the driver's door swung open.

David clambered down the stainless steel steps, turned to them, grinned and slammed the door shut behind him.

'I have to admit, sometimes I love my work,' he said.

'The helicopter's left Northolt,' said Dan. 'Can we watch the attack?'

David nodded. 'The technicians are streaming it live now – come on,' he said as he turned and began to walk towards the rear of the vehicle.

'Where exactly are we going to watch this?' asked Mitch, frowning as he followed the other men.

David stopped halfway along the length of the vehicle's trailer and looked up at a door in the side.

'Here,' he said as he reached up and knocked.

The door opened outwards and Philippa smiled down at them. 'Stand back,' she said, and unfolded a steel staircase.

'Come on in,' said David, swinging himself up and into the trailer. 'Welcome to our new office and the future of network-centric warfare.'

Mitch stood at the bottom of the steps and looked sideways at Dan. 'I suppose he wasn't technically lying to the Prime Minister when he told him he'd move his office away from the city then?'

Dan grinned. 'I guess not.'

***

As Dan clambered into the enormous trailer, his eyes gradually adjusted to the dark surroundings.

Along the length of the trailer, technicians worked at computers, their faces illuminated by their screens, colours flickering across their skin as the displays changed.

The back of the trailer housed a small kitchenette and toilet cubicle, with abandoned chairs stacked up against the wall of the trailer out of the way.

At the front of the trailer, nearest the tractor, a floor-to-ceiling screen provided snapshots of satellite imagery and real-time camera feeds from the Lynx helicopter as it powered through the icy airwaves over the north Kent coastline.

Dan looked over at David in amazement. 'You've been busy.'

'Sir, the helicopter crew report they're two minutes out from their attack position,' called out a technician.

David turned to him. 'Bring up the missile tracking software on the screen.' He turned to Dan and Mitch. 'Get yourselves down the far end and take a seat so you're out of the way of this lot.'

As Dan settled into a chair, he glanced up at Philippa who had passed a file to Mitch and was now standing over him, her eyes glued to the displays above him while she chewed on a fingernail.

'It'll be fine, Pip – they've done it before,' he murmured.

She glanced down at him and nodded. 'I know,' she said, 'but it doesn't make it any easier.'

'What did you give to Mitch?'

'The last of the financial reports we managed to track back to Hassan. The analysts have found evidence of a transaction which might explain where the submarine's weapons came from.'

She looked over her shoulder as David approached and handed out headphones.

'You can listen to our exchanges with the helicopter,' he explained. 'You'll also hear the Admiral at the London end. He has the final say on whether or not the helicopter engages the submarine.'

Dan slipped the headphones over his head, wiggled them to get the cans over his ears and turned up the volume control on the attached wire, Carlisle's voice cutting through the mild static.

'Thirty seconds,' he called.

'Copy that,' replied the Admiral, his gruff voice clipped and strained.

Dan glanced across at David, who was staring intently at the screen. 'How close do they have to get?' he asked.

'Normally they could get quite close before deploying the missile,' he said, 'but these cliffs provide limited cover – it's so flat along some parts of this coastline.' David checked his watch. 'They're aiming to fly along to Folkestone so they can use the cliffs to provide some cover from the public before firing the missile – they'll hide behind that natural ridgeline until the weapon's released, then sweep north-west to drop a probe into the sea so we get some ears under the water. Once that's set up it'll enable them to programme the torpedo. They'll try to give us an aerial view of the attack as well as an infrared reading.'

Dan nodded and turned back to the screen, crossed his arms in front of him and willed his heartbeat to slow. The pilot's voice cut across his thoughts.

'Confirm we're in position, Admiral. Awaiting your command.'

Dan stared at the screen and held his breath.

***

Ivanov held his glass of Kazakh vodka aloft and looked at the four men gathered around.

'This is for our families. For our country's future,' he said. 'Our sacrifice means economic surety through Hassan's gas venture into Western Europe.'

'Densawlığıñız üşin!' replied the men, tipping the alcohol-laden clear liquid down their throats.

Ivanov swallowed his drink and turned to Ilya. 'It is time, my friend. Let's do this.'

Ilya nodded then turned to the controls, his face pale, his hands shaking.

'Relax,' said Ivanov. 'It will be a quick, honourable death.'

The younger man swallowed. 'Yes captain,' he said, and powered the submarine forward.

Ivan turned at a sudden cry from the sonar specialist. 'What is it, Alexei?'

'I've got a signal – I think it's a sonar probe.'

Ivanov gripped the back of the seat, his knuckles white. 'What's the probe's position?'

'Three miles off our starboard side,' said Alexei.

'And it just appeared?'

The weapons expert nodded. 'One minute I had a blank screen – next minute all the alarms went off.'

'And you're sure there are no enemy ships in the area?'

Alexei gestured at the radar array. 'It's clear, look.'

Ivanov frowned. 'What's our speed?'

'Twelve knots so we can hide beside the ferry.'

'Okay. Full speed to twenty knots, and take this bearing.'

Alexei adjusted the controls, the submarine's engines vibrating through the sudden acceleration.

'Gently, Ilya. We don't want this thing to fall apart now.'

Ivanov felt the sub swing right through its axis, gradually losing contact with the ferry which had sheltered them for the past forty minutes.

'Has it locked onto us?'

'Negative.'

'Okay. Keep at this speed. Have the decoys ready to go. Let's see if we can put some distance behind us.'

Chapter 46

'Deploy torpedo.'

The Admiral's voice resonated around the walls of the trailer as all the technicians inched their faces closer to their screens, monitoring the helicopter's progress against the encroaching submarine.

'Copy that.'

Hamilton's voice sounded flat, unemotional over the airwaves. Dan found it hard to reconcile with the jovial, upbeat man he'd met the previous day. The man's detachment under pressure was chilling, his focus solely on the enemy craft beneath the waves.

'Releasing torp in three... two... one... weapon away.'

The dim interior of the trailer fell silent as the group watched in awe, a camera fixed to the helicopter's fuselage catching the flash of the missile as it released, a small plume of smoke echoing against the lens in its wake.

'Where's the probe?' asked Dan, his eyes searching the live camera feed.

David nodded. 'There.'

A second cloud of smoke momentarily obliterated one of the camera lenses.

Philippa leaned forward and tapped her finger on a second display. 'Watch here – you see where the missile's entered the water?'

Dan nodded.

'The second object is the probe. We should be picking up its signal… *now*.'

The familiar *ping* of a sonar beacon echoed through the temporary ops room.

'Beacon in place, Admiral,' Carlisle confirmed. 'Missile is tracking. Awaiting your command to arm and destroy target.'

'Copy that,' said the Admiral.

Dan jumped at a shout from the back of the trailer.

'Sir – the submarine's broken away from the vessel it was shadowing,' said a technician.

'Where are they?' growled David.

'They've swung north sir – accelerated to twenty knots.'

'They've broken cover,' said Dan. 'They know we're onto them.'

'Er… guys… I think we've got a problem,' Mitch interrupted.

The team turned to where Mitch was sitting, sheets of documents in one hand and his mobile phone in the other.

He glanced up at them, held up one of the copy wire transfers and waved it.

'There's something not right here. If Hassan stole a decommissioned submarine, it didn't have any weapons on board. So he had to get those from another source.'

'That's the money which was moved from the bank account you're holding there,' Philippa said, pointing at the paper in Mitch's hand.

'I know,' said Mitch. 'But I was just talking to one of the finance specialists. He reckons the price of torpedoes on the black market has gone up over the past two years. And this,' he said, waving the paper, 'isn't enough.'

Dan frowned. 'So you're saying Hassan has another account somewhere and we haven't found it?'

Mitch grinned. 'No. What I'm saying is, Hassan hasn't got any more torpedoes in that submarine.'

Dan slouched back into his chair and frowned.

'Think about it,' persisted Mitch. 'The reports from the engineer at Ras Laffan stated he saw the LNG ship hit twice. That's supported by the film the Sheik received on his mobile phone. Then they hit the cruise ship. Again, the captain of that reported two strikes before the ship sank. Four torpedoes in total.'

'And we've been on their case since, so they wouldn't have had time to reload,' said Dan.

Mitch took a long pull from his soft drink, set it on the table and belched. 'What if,' he said, putting down the wire transfer, 'they were never going to reload?'

Dan sat forward on his chair. 'Then they'd have to either hide the submarine, or,' he said, glancing up at Mitch as it dawned on him, 'it's a suicide mission.'

'They're not going to fire a torpedo at the munitions ship, are they?' said Mitch. 'They're going to use the submarine as a battering ram.'

'Holy shit.'

David glanced at the red flashing dot on the map displayed on the wall, then touched his radio microphone. 'Admiral – they're heading straight for the *Richard Montgomery*. Estimated time to impact…' He glanced over his shoulder at the technician, who held up his hand. 'Five minutes. We need to arm that missile *now*!'

The Admiral hesitated. 'How close is the submarine to the ferry?'

David glanced at the technician, who shook his head.

'Not clear yet.'

'We can't destroy the submarine so close to a civilian ship,' said the Admiral.

'How long do we have to wait?' David demanded.

'Another nautical mile and we'll be fine,' said the technician.

Dan grabbed David's arm. 'We can't wait that long. Philippa – contact the ferry operator. Have them tell the captain of that ship to turn away from the area and gain as much distance as he can between his location and the submarine. Buy us some time.'

He glanced at David. 'We can't let the submarine get any closer to that wreck!'

Dan glanced up at the screen and searched until he found the live feed from the camera positioned in a clear pod on top of the helicopter's rotor blade mounting.

The helicopter was hugging the coastline, keeping low on the horizon. Grey and white waves churned below the aircraft, blurred through the night vision lens, droplets of sleet and snow coursing over the surface of the pod as the machine swept through the air, following its target.

'Come on!' he urged.

'Decoy deployed.' The pilot's monotone voice dissolved in Dan's headphones.

He glanced at David, then up at the electronic feed from the underwater probe. As he watched, the submarine's decoy flashed on the screen, and the missile gave chase.

'Haul that thing back!' barked the Admiral.

'Copy that.'

A split second later, the torpedo slowed, executed a lazy arc, and began hunting the submarine once more.

Dan looked up at the nautical charts. 'We're running out of time!' he hissed.

'One more time,' said the Admiral.

'We have their signature,' confirmed the pilot.

'The ferry captain's altered course!' called Philippa. 'He should be out of range in thirty seconds.'

'Hopefully the passengers will just think it's a rough swell,' murmured Dan.

David raised his eyebrow and turned away.

The pilot's voice carried across the ops room. 'Missile re-armed.'

At his words, the beacon on the electronic display swerved left, surged forward and began tracking towards the submarine's heat signature.

As the team watched, the vessel began to slowly swerve in the water.

'They're out of decoys,' said Mitch. 'This is it.'

Dan held his breath as the submarine turned a slow arc in the depths.

'They're changing course away from the wreck,' called a technician. 'Looks like they're trying to increase their speed.'

Dan looked at David. 'Will they outrun it?'

The other man shook his head. 'Not a chance in hell.'

***

Alexei glanced over his shoulder at the submarine captain, his eyes wide.

'They've armed it!'

Ivanov remained stoic, holding onto the side of the vessel to steady himself as Ilya began to turn the submarine left and right, desperately trying to outrun the torpedo heading its way.

'Full power, Alexei – if they're going to take us out, we have to try to destroy the gas facility at the same time.'

He turned to the fourth man, older than the rest, who had emerged from the engine rooms. 'Will she hold?'

The man shrugged. 'I don't think it's going to matter, Dmitri,' he said, and pointed over the captain's shoulder to the screen in front of Alexei. 'Look.'

Ivanov turned, his eyes widening as the missile quickly bridged the gap between the probe and his vessel.

'How far away from the munitions ship are we, Alexei?'

'Four miles.'

Ivanov punched the metal wall next to him. *So close!*

As the alarms began to increase throughout the vessel, he took one last look around the controls room at his men, fear in their eyes as the realisation struck they were about to die, and their mission had failed.

'Brace for impact,' he said hoarsely, and closed his eyes.

Chapter 47

As news of the submarine's demise filtered through to the gas facility, a loud cheer chorused through the controls centre. Engineers high-fived and walked around slapping each other on the back, the relief evident in their voices and body language.

Dan walked through the small crowd and crossed the room to where Grant sat at his laptop, frowning at the screen. He looked up as Dan approached.

'Everything okay?'

Grant nodded briefly. 'We'll see. The first threat's out of the way. Let's see if the second threat is just as simple to defeat before we celebrate.'

Dan nodded and glanced out of a floor-to-ceiling window which overlooked the seaward approach from the Thames Estuary to the River Medway, then turned to one of the computer operators.

'How long before the tanker arrives?' he asked.

The man glanced at his screen, then his wristwatch, before pointing out the window and along the coastline. 'About ten minutes,' he said, 'then you'll see it come round that spit.'

Dan raised his eyebrows in surprise. 'That fast?'

The engineer grinned. 'They don't hang about when they're loaded. Gas contracts are based on supply and demand – the captain wouldn't be very popular with the owners if he was late.'

Dan snorted. 'The owners do realise they're lucky they've got a captain and ship still intact?'

The engineer shrugged, reluctant to comment.

Dan shook his head and wandered across the room to where Mitch and Antonia stood chatting with the operations manager. He stepped next to Antonia, slipped his hand around her waist and hugged her to him.

She looked up at him, her eyes glinting. 'We're halfway there,' she murmured.

He looked down at her and squeezed her gently. 'I hope this works.' He glanced over his shoulder at Grant, who was rushing from monitor to monitor, checking and re-checking the programmers' work. 'I guess we'll soon find out.'

At a shout from one of the engineers, the team looked up as one to see the prow of an enormous LNG tanker emerge from the Thames Estuary and begin its final approach along the River Medway towards the gas facility.

'Holy shit, that's a big boat,' breathed Mitch. 'Reading the dimensions off a report doesn't do it justice.'

Dan joined him at the window. 'This had better work,' he growled.

'Well, if it doesn't, you can kiss your annual bonus goodbye,' said Mitch.

Dan rolled his eyes and strode over to Grant's workstation. 'Anything?'

Grant's eyes flickered across the various displays in front of him before glancing down at his laptop, his finger hovering over the mouse, ready to deploy the anti-hacking software.

'Not yet,' he said, 'but reading the reports from Ras Laffan, they didn't even know someone else was in the system until the ship docked at the jetty.'

Dan nodded and stood behind the engineer, his arms folded as he watched the screen in silence.

Ted Harris appeared at Dan's arm. 'We've just received word from the Minister for Energy that he wants this gas pumped off the ship now,' he said. 'They've already got blackouts in Norfolk.'

Dan choked out a laugh. 'He does realise we've got a bigger issue down here at the moment?'

'Yes, but Norfolk's where his constituency is, so he's probably worried about re-election issues at the moment.'

'Jesus. I'll pretend I didn't hear that.'

'Okay people,' said Grant, raising his voice, 'take your places. Things could get interesting any time soon.'

The other engineers each ran to a desk and signed into the system.

'Antonia – you're on watch,' called Grant. 'Keep a lookout for any strange activity while these guys get that tanker hooked up and the gas piped off.'

Antonia held up her hand in acknowledgement, then concentrated on her screen, pulling up different views as her computer piggy-backed onto the engineers' systems while they worked.

'With no submarine to launch an attack, what's the hacker trying to achieve?' asked Dan, glancing down at Grant and noticing a bead of sweat working its way down the man's face.

'If anyone gained control of these systems, they could use the pressure in the pipes to damage the whole facility,' Grant explained, using the cuff of his shirt to wipe his forehead. 'Remember, the gas is cooled at minus one hundred and sixty degrees Celsius to transport it in a liquid form – this facility was designed to have that running from the ship through specially designed pipes to the processing plant. At the same time, it's gradually heated and turned back into gas.'

'It's a very, very delicate balancing act,' said Harris. He lowered his voice. 'If the hacker managed to alter the chemical and physical balances we have here, he could cause a huge amount of damage through the whole system.'

Dan nodded, understanding. 'And not just to the ship and pipework I guess – we have to protect the gas reserves stored here too, or else the people depending on it are going to die in this weather.'

'Five minutes!' called an engineer.

Dan glanced up and saw the huge Q-max tanker slowing as it crawled closer and closer to the jetty.

Grant glanced up at him. 'Decision time, Mr Taylor. Do we try to catch the hacker and attempt to lure him out by allowing him to access the systems, or do we put the programme in place straight away?'

Dan began pacing the floor behind Grant's chair, tapping his bottom lip. 'How much time will we have?'

'Depends on his typing speed,' said Grant drily.

'Okay, let me rephrase that,' said Dan through gritted teeth. 'If you spot the hacker deliberately trying to alter the pressure in the pipes, how soon after hitting the 'go' button will your programme kick in?'

Grant shrugged. 'About five seconds if all goes well.'

Dan breathed out slowly, and then turned to Harris. 'How fast does the gas travel through these pipes?'

'About one point three tons per second.'

Dan closed his eyes and moved his neck from left to right, savouring the sound of a muscle clicking into place. He opened his eyes and breathed in, then slowly out again, concentrating on keeping his heart rate steady.

'It's going to be close,' he murmured. 'Stop the attack – it's a bonus if we can catch the hacker too, but from what I understand, the forensic team can always do a search through the data afterwards and try to locate where the attack comes from.'

'We've been hit!' shouted one of the engineers. 'My system's just locked me out!'

Stepping back, Dan moved out of the way as Grant leapt towards his computer and began typing in coded information.

'Talk to me, Antonia,' Grant called. 'What can you see?'

'Typical DDOS attack,' she said, peering over her computer screen at him. 'Several IP addresses – it's going to take me a while to track down the source.'

'Okay, here we go,' said Grant, flexing his fingers and beginning to type.

Dan watched, fascinated, as Grant's computer screen blinked and flashed with the data speeding through the system. Although the anti-virus software had been explained to him, watching it hunt down the rogue codes in real time left him with new respect for the software engineer.

'Shit.'

Dan glanced down at Grant. 'What?'

'This guy's *good*. As fast as the software is finding him, he's dropping off and appearing somewhere else in the system.'

'Can you stop him?'

'We'll soon find out,' said Grant. 'I always did like a challenge.'

The engineer's hands flew over the keyboard as he parried with the hacker. Each time Grant shut a valve in the system, the hacker jumped to the next down the line, causing the valve to open and shut quickly, in an attempt to break the delicate machinery.

'Antonia – how's the system holding up elsewhere?' asked Grant.

'Getting stressed,' she said. 'We've got three of the six SCADA computers out of action – the hacker's using one of them to influence the others by the look of it.'

Grant began to type in the commands which would re-route the gas through the plant and jabbed the keys ferociously as he frantically used the controls system to close all the valves along the pipelines leading from the jetty, knowing the slightest breach would cause a catastrophe.

Dan glanced over his shoulder and out the observation window. The jetty was a hub of activity, with the ship now connected to the facility through a series of pipes. He swallowed. There were so many people dependent upon the man in front of him, and there wasn't a damn thing he could do except watch.

'Ah, now I've got you,' Grant murmured.

'Do you need my help?' asked Antonia.

'Hang on.'

Dan turned back to look at Grant's computer as the software engineer suddenly switched the view on his screen to another view of the facility's schematics and began typing furiously.

'What…'

'Don't talk to me,' growled Grant. 'Not now.'

Clenching his fists, Dan held his breath as he frowned and tried to keep up with what Grant was doing.

'Gotcha.' Grant finished typing a final string of code into the system, hit the 'Enter' key and pushed himself away from his desk.

Dan's head turned from the computer screen to Grant and back again. 'What did you just do?'

The engineer grinned. 'It suddenly occurred to me I could use the hacker's own seek and destroy code to turn it on the hacker himself. I don't know why I didn't think of it before – watch.'

Dan looked at the screens around the room as they all began to flicker, and then settle back to normal. 'Is that it?'

'Almost,' said Grant, relaxing into his seat. 'Now it's kicked the hacker out of the system, the seek and destroy code will keep working in the background until it finds the real location of the hacker's computer – it might take a few hours, but it's going to freeze the network connection and your team of specialists will know exactly where and *who* the hacker is.'

Chapter 48

'So,' said Dan, as he watched Grant sift through reporting data on his computer with a glass of champagne balanced in one hand, 'what are you doing for your wedding anniversary next year?'

Grant spluttered, sending champagne shooting up his nose. He coughed, blinked and patted his chest. 'We're going away,' he wheezed. 'A *long* way away.'

Dan laughed and began to walk around the room, shaking hands and congratulating the team.

Amid the celebrating, he looked around for Antonia. He frowned, put down the two glasses of champagne which had been thrust into his hands and wandered over to Mitch, apologising to the person he was talking to before pulling him to one side.

'Have you seen Antonia?'

Mitch glanced around the room. 'No – I thought she was with you.'

Dan shook his head. 'No.' He looked around, then back at Mitch. 'I'll find out where she is – can't have her missing the celebrations.'

'No worries,' said Mitch. He glanced across the room and frowned. 'When Grant reappears, grab him as well and I'll see you all back at the car.'

Dan threw a wave of acknowledgement over his shoulder as he left the room. The carpeted floor silenced his footsteps as he walked along the passageway, the voices of the team talking and laughing gradually fading. Dan ducked his head around office doors as he went, but Antonia was nowhere to be found. He walked a little further, and then saw a familiar figure etched onto a metal plate stuck to another door. *Ladies*.

He leaned against the opposite wall and waited with a smile on his face as he replayed in his mind the success of the mission. He frowned, glanced at his watch then eased himself away from the wall.

He turned at the sound of running feet. Mitch and Harris were approaching him fast, both with lines of concern etched across their faces.

'What?' Dan asked as they stopped.

'I tried to catch you before you left the room,' said Harris, sucking in deep breaths. 'I was talking to Grant and Philippa about the attack on our systems while you were all celebrating – they seemed to think the attack happened from *within* the controls room.'

Dan glanced at Mitch, whose complexion had paled. 'What do you mean?' he asked, turning back to Harris.

'It's Antonia,' said Mitch. 'She's the hacker.'

Dan's head whipped round to face Mitch. 'You'd better explain that comment.'

Mitch held up his hands. 'David ordered Grant to monitor her work – no explanation. I think he just had a gut feeling something wasn't right so, to protect the team, everything she worked on was recorded by Grant's laptop. Philippa was just analysing it while everyone was celebrating.'

Dan took a step towards him, glaring. 'And you *knew* about this?'

Mitch stepped backwards. 'I didn't say I liked the idea. I was under orders to let it play out in case David's hunch was right.'

'You bastard.' The skin on his knuckles split open as his fist connected with the other man's jawbone.

Mitch sank to the ground. He shook his head, tested his jaw with his hand, and looked up as Dan stalked off. 'Dan – wait!'

Dan extended his middle finger over his shoulder, pulled out his Sig Sauer and kicked open the door to the ladies' toilet.

'Antonia?' He pushed open the door a crack. 'Are you…?'

His eyes widened at the blood spattered up the walls. His heart pounding in his chest, he edged slowly into the room, his gun pointing in front of him. He swung left, checked he was alone, and then right, his grip steady, and froze.

Blood was smeared across the floor, as if someone had been dragged or had crawled across the surface. A *lot* of blood. A lot of trouble.

The blood trail disappeared round a corner. Dan stepped over the blood, swung round the wall, his gun raised, then stopped, his skin crawling.

Philippa lay on the floor, blood pooling around her body. Her neck had been sliced open, the wound still bubbling blood. Her body had been dragged under one of the wash basins, her arms cradling her stomach, her eyes wide in shock and pain.

Fighting the bile rising in his throat, Dan crouched down and pressed his fingers against her neck, knowing in his heart the woman's life had already drained out onto the floor.

'I'm so sorry, Pip,' he whispered as he searched her jacket and the belt of her jeans.

Her gun was missing.

Dan burst out of the washroom and ran up the passageway. As he moved, his mind raced. There was only one logical place Grant would be taken. He slowed as he neared the end of the corridor and edged round the corner. The double doors were open.

'Stop right there.'

His heart lurched in his chest.

Antonia sat on the edge of the central control room desk, a gun pointed to Grant's head. The engineer slumped in one of the high-back chairs, sweat beading on his forehead.

'Antonia? What the *fuck* is going on?' Dan kept his gun aimed at her.

She shook her head slowly. 'Don't, Dan. He'll be dead before you finish pulling the trigger.'

Dan kept his gun trained on her. 'Why?' His voice was hoarse, little more than a whisper.

Antonia laughed – a short, brittle laugh which didn't reach her eyes. She shook her head, slowly. 'Poor Dan. Betrayed, coerced, tricked – you didn't have a clue, did you?'

Dan's mind spun. 'The submarine?'

'A suicide mission,' said Antonia.

'The men in there – the men who just died – do you have any idea what it must have been like for them?'

She shrugged, calmly keeping her gun pointed at Grant's temple. 'Everybody has to make a sacrifice at some point.'

'If you shoot him, it's over,' said Dan. 'He's the only one who knows the data code, remember?'

Antonia smiled, reached into the pocket of her jeans, and pulled out an object. She held it up for Dan to see, turning it in her hand. 'I have a back-up.'

Dan groaned. *The data stick.*

Antonia laughed again. 'It'd be quicker if Grant programmed it in, but trust me, it won't take me long to figure it out you know.'

'But for what?' asked Dan. 'The submarine's destroyed – the system's already locked down. The gas is all piped off the ship now.'

Antonia shook her head and waved the memory stick at him, taunting him. 'This is a switch, Dan – remember? It turns the gas off *and* on.' She tilted her head. 'There's still enough pressure in those pipes to blow this place to hell if I turn the gas flow back towards the ship without them expecting it.' She lowered the data stick and placed it on the control console in front of Grant. 'This is the central control panel for the whole plant – they might've hit the 'off' switch down the passageway there as a safety precaution, but anything we do here overrides it.'

Dan's glance fell to Grant, who nodded miserably.

'She's right,' he said. 'If we release the gas here, there's nothing they can do to stop it.'

Dan looked at Antonia, his gun never wavering. 'You still haven't told me *why*.'

A cold smile played across her lips. 'Money, of course. Power. Influence throughout the OPEC leaders. *Control*. We'll have the whole world at our feet.'

'We?'

'Hassan is a very generous employer.'

'He's a madman. He thinks threatening the UK will force the United Nations to lift their sanctions on Iran,' said Dan. 'Except he's not exactly popular back home either is he?'

'He has friends of influence,' said Antonia. 'They will help him convince the leaders he is right.'

'And so you've been reporting my every move to him all this time.'

Antonia shrugged. 'We had to keep you close until we managed to speak to the genius here.' She tapped the gun on the side of Grant's head, and he flinched. 'Although you threw that plan out the window when you rescued him.'

'Which is why you wanted to be there – you were going to kill him if you got to him first!' Dan glared at her.

'Hassan will give me a generous cut of the profit he'll make from his venture.'

'There *is* no venture, Antonia. It's over. He'll dump you and run – same as he's done with everyone else involved in this scheme of his. He's using you. Please – put the gun down.'

'I can't do that, Dan.' Antonia shook her head. 'I've got a job to do. Enough talking – we're running out of time!' She dug the gun deeper into Grant's temple.

He whimpered in pain, his hands hovering about the control panel.

'Do it!' Antonia screamed.

Dan felt his heart hammering in his chest. He still couldn't get a clear shot.

'Antonia.'

The voice came from Dan's right.

Mitch.

He was standing in a second entrance to the control room, behind Antonia, his gun raised.

Antonia's head flicked round at the sound of Mitch's voice, her arm swung away from Grant's head and she fired, once.

The gunshot filled the enclosed space with a roar.

Mitch yelled as the bullet struck him in the leg and he slumped to the floor, his fingers greased in blood as he tried to stem the flow from the wound.

'No!' Dan yelled.

In the split second before Antonia turned back to face him, Dan had his shot.

He pulled the trigger.

Grant yelled and rolled to the ground, covering his head.

Antonia's body was lifted backwards across the control console with the force of the bullet. Her head rocked back with the velocity of the shot, before her body slumped to the floor.

Dan glanced across at Mitch, who held a hand up.

'I'm okay,' he croaked. 'See to her.'

Dan ran across to where Antonia lay. The bullet had entered the top right of her chest, the ragged exit wound in her shoulder pooling blood into the carpet.

He crouched down, gently turning her body towards him.

She gasped, her breathing ragged as she looked up at him, her eyes trying to focus. Blood dripped from her mouth with each breath. Her hands grasped for Dan's, seeking him out.

'I'm here,' he said and held her hands, squeezing her fingers, 'Hang on, there's a medical team on its way.'

Her mouth parted, her eyes urgent.

Dan knelt down and put his ear to her lips.

'I'm sorry,' she whispered, her eyes closing.

A last desperate gasp passed her lips before her body shuddered once, and then fell still.

Dan felt her neck, searching for a pulse.

Nothing.

A chill ricocheted through his body. He pushed past Grant, tears blinding him. He angrily wiped them away as he strode down the passageway and crashed through the fire exit doors, out into the car park.

He threw himself behind the wheel of his car and closed his eyes, forcing himself to breathe deeply. He could smell the faint signature of Antonia's perfume in the vehicle, permeating the air around him.

The nightmares would return with a vengeance this time, he was sure.

He let his head drop into his hands, and wept.

Chapter 49

'Who was she?'

David removed a photograph from his coat pocket and handed it to Dan. 'An Iranian national by the name of Yasmin Gulzar. Completed a degree in computer programming at Tehran University and was then recruited by the Iranian security service.'

The men stopped talking as a priest approached Philippa's parents, offering his condolences to the bereaved couple huddled at the graveside under a large black umbrella, their small forms dwarfed by the oak tree which cast shadows over the gathered mourners.

David sighed, his breath fogging in the cold air. 'I don't know what I'm going to do without her,' he murmured, shaking his head.

'How's Mitch?'

'The doctors saved his leg, but he's facing months of physiotherapy,' said David. 'It's not clear yet whether he's going to be able to return to field work. Whatever happens, I'll make sure he's looked after.'

As the group of mourners drifted from the graveside, the two men walked back to the Government car which had brought them to the service. The driver opened the back doors as they approached, then started the engine and began the journey back towards the city centre.

'What happened to the real Antonia?' asked Dan, settling into his seat for the ride.

'Maltese police found a body in Valetta harbour a week ago. It was badly decomposed, the face damaged by acid. They were treating it as a suspected 'honour' killing until the DNA analysis came through late yesterday afternoon.'

Dan peered out at the afternoon sky. It was getting darker, the rain beating steadily against the glass. He traced a couple of raindrops with his eyes, the car headlights in the opposite traffic lanes appearing blurred as if captured in the water streaming down the window. 'Poor kid must've suffered.' He shook his head to try to clear the thought then pulled away from the window. 'You really had no idea?'

'None.' David shook his head. 'You can imagine how embarrassed the Qataris are too.'

'Hassan's team must've intercepted her as soon as she arrived in Malta.'

'The Qataris think the Iranians were monitoring her before she even arrived. The real Antonia was meant to be reporting directly to us, so their embassy saw nothing unusual in her being out of contact. Antonia's father, the

Sheik, had left for Ras Laffan so wasn't in a position to verify what she looked like. The Qataris didn't get a whiff anything was wrong until we phoned them yesterday to say she'd been shot. You can imagine the ruckus when they sent their section chief to identify the body and found it wasn't who they expected.'

'You look tired,' said Dan.

'It's been a long week.' David held up another photograph to Dan. Its edges were blackened and curled, the image melted and creased. 'We found this in the pocket of Yasmin's jeans.'

Dan pulled it towards him. 'She found this at Hassan's villa. When I asked her, she said she hadn't found anything of significance when we were going through the ruins.'

In the middle of the photograph, a gangly teenage girl stood next to a younger Hassan.

Dan looked up at David and frowned. 'Is this who I think it is?'

'He was her father.'

'Jesus.'

'Indeed. Seems her father used her as a sleeper agent – it would appear that he had been planning this for a *very* long time.'

Dan swallowed. Putting the photograph carefully on the car seat between them, he glanced up at David. 'What happened to Hassan?'

'The Iranians are stalling. Claiming diplomatic immunity at the moment, although that won't stack up for long. My fear is they've already got Hassan out of the country.'

'How?'

'If he's got a private jet, it'll be relatively easy. The Ministry of Defence has long been complaining that because passports aren't rigorously checked at smaller airfields around London, they can't monitor who's coming into or leaving the country.'

'So he'll run.'

'I've spoken with the PM this morning. Our feeling is the Iranians will deal with him themselves. We've heard a whisper his actions weren't authorised by the Government there or the religious faction in the country, so he'll probably be punished for embarrassing them. It doesn't bode well for them trying to have sanctions lifted any time soon.'

'I can't believe we're just going to let them get away with it.'

David smiled. 'Who said anything about letting them get away with it?'

Dan's head shot up. 'I want in.'

'I thought you might. Be mindful though – if you're caught, or anyone sees you, you're on your own.'

***

His footsteps echoing along the tiled passageway, Dan glanced at each door he passed, the sequential numbers increasing as he walked through the labyrinth of the hospital complex.

Two armed guards turned to face him as he approached the last door on the right, their faces stern.

'At ease gents,' said Dan. 'Just a short visit.'

'Five minutes,' said the taller of the two guards. 'Doctor's orders.'

Dan nodded, and eased open the door.

'You better not have grapes in that bag,' said a gruff voice from the bed. 'If you've brought grapes, I swear I'm going to stick every single one of them up your…'

'Relax,' grinned Dan. 'I brought something else.' He held up the carry bag and lifted out a four-pack of John Smith's beer. 'Will these do?'

'You're an angel,' said Mitch. 'Now for chrissakes put them in the cupboard over here before the nurse finds them.'

Dan did as he was told, and then pulled over a chair to the bed. 'David tells me you're healing well.'

'Bollocks,' said Mitch. 'I hurt like hell. It hurts even more because we couldn't save Philippa.'

'Yeah.' Dan looked down at his hands. 'I know.'

'How was the funeral?'

Dan shrugged. 'David's really shaken up – more so than I expected.'

Mitch smiled. 'He always had a soft spot for Philippa,' he said. 'I've often wondered if it went a little further than the professional front they kept up. Poor bastard.'

Dan spent the next half an hour bringing Mitch up to speed on the investigation.

'So what are they going to do about it?' he asked when Dan had finished. 'They can't just let Hassan get away with it!'

Dan smiled and stood up. 'Don't worry about it,' he said. 'I have a feeling the Iranians are going to have their hands full for a while yet.'

After taking his leave from Mitch, he walked back through the hospital and out to the car park.

Turning the key in the ignition, he revved the car's engine and pointed it towards the airport. As he joined the motorway, he hit a speed dial on his mobile phone. The ringtone suggested the phone was ringing some distance away, on a foreign exchange.

After four rings, the call was answered.

'Good afternoon General,' said Dan, indicating as he swung the car right and into the overtaking lane. 'I need some of those new toys you've got stored in your barn.'

Epilogue

Somewhere near the Kazakhstan border

It began with the dogs barking, all at once, in a cacophony of noise. People looked up from their day-to-day chores in bewilderment, conversations stopping mid-sentence.

The dogs would normally bark, one followed by the others, if a stranger drove through the village, but this was different – they sounded scared, whimpering and howling.

An old woman, grey hair flecked with white tied tucked under a faded red scarf, stopped sweeping the path outside her house and leaned on her broom, mouth open in astonishment. Any dog not tethered within the confines of its owner's property was now running past her house, heading out of the village.

A faint rumble, almost an infrasound, growled in the distance. The woman felt a slight tremor in the ground under her feet. She looked up at the grey overcast sky. Rain had been forecast but no storms – no lightning or thunder to set off the dogs.

The village sat in a valley between a steep range of hills, a cluster of farming families and peripheral businesses to support them. The community was close-knit. They'd been through hardships together, flood and famine. She put up her hand to a man across the road, sitting on his tractor, the engine running, his eyes wide and staring at the animals running by. He caught her eye and shook his head in bewilderment before turning his attention back to the phenomenon.

The woman's small one-storey house was the last on the main track out of the remote village. In summer, the dust crept into the house with every breeze. As summer progressed through autumn and into winter, the dust turned to mud, caked around wheels and feet. A low stone wall formed a boundary on the opposite side of the track. She could hear sheep bleating beyond it, nervous at the sound of the barking canines.

More dogs joined the fast-moving pack as they fled down the track, eyes white with fear, tails between their legs.

The old woman's attention was caught by the sound of a loud whimpering from her neighbour's property. Looking over, she saw his dog tethered to a post outside the house. The dog was terrified, desperately trying to pull free from the rope looped around its neck and tethered to the post. Blood covered its neck where it was struggling to get its head out of the loop which held it tight.

The woman leaned her broom against the door frame and made her way slowly to the dog. She was afraid to go near it as it had a reputation as a mean animal. Something was different today though – as she approached it, the dog whimpered again, its whole body straining against the rope once more.

Another tremor. The woman looked up in the distance. The rumbling seemed to be getting closer, but there were still no storm clouds in the sky.

Talking softly to the dog, she bent down and carefully, gently, loosened the rope from around the dog's head, taking care to lift it out of the wounds which bled profusely from its neck. She lifted the rope over its neck, freeing the animal. It blinked once at her before tearing after the pack, whose barks could be heard echoing in the distance.

Easing herself upright, the old woman glanced in the direction the dogs had taken and then turned to look back at the village and the hills behind it. She frowned.

It can't be an earthquake. Not here. That's why they built the pipeline through these hills – it's safe.

A movement to her left caught her attention. She raised her hand to shield her eyes from the sun. The neighbour's land banked downwards towards a small stream which, at this time of year, was in full flow. Scrubby trees and grass covered the banks and it was here the woman's attention was drawn. She nervously rubbed her hands down her skirt and looked over her shoulder. There was no-one to walk with her.

She felt her heart racing in her chest. Taking a deep breath, she made her way down the hill, carefully lifting her skirt as she stepped over large stones and rocks in her way, trying to avoid the dung left by the grazing animals. As she drew closer to the stream, the sound of flowing water drifted up to her.

She pushed tree branches away from her face and forced her way through the undergrowth to the water. Finally, as she stood on the embankment, she started at the sound of a splash further downstream. Looking to her right, she gazed down the water course. There were ripples in the stream only a few metres from where she stood.

Frowning, she walked along the embankment until she reached the spot. She glanced down. The outline of a large boot had been imprinted into the sandy coloured mud. She looked to her right, but it seemed the man had then made sure he stepped on the rocks leading into the trees, to disguise his trail. If she hadn't heard the splash, she wouldn't have realised there was anyone there.

In the hill behind the village, the timer on the last explosive charge fixed to Hassan's natural gas pipeline dropped to zero.

Another *boom*, closer this time, made her jump. As she turned to return to her house, she let out a stifled scream.

A man's face, covered in black grease, stared at her from among the trees. His blue eyes pierced through the camouflage paint, watching her intently. As she stood still, her heart hammering, her hand across her mouth in shock, she was astonished to see the man put his finger to his lips.

Shhhh.

He grinned at her, winked – and disappeared.

Author's Note and Acknowledgements

As with any work of fiction there is often the need to bend the rules and tweak the facts to suit the story.

Anyone familiar with Malta will notice I've taken a few liberties with the geography of the place. It would in fact be impossible to hide a submarine on the coastline I've suggested, however I can highly recommend a visit to the island. It's a great place to explore.

Cyber-terrorism is a very real issue for the UK and other countries, evidenced by recent reports of different viruses and malware being used by hackers and governments alike to disrupt various utilities and power services around the world, and it seems no-one is immune. The UK's Centre for the Protection of National Infrastructure has some excellent information on its website for anyone interested in learning more about these types of threats and what the UK agencies are doing to counteract such issues.

There are a number of Government reports publicly available online to anyone interested in the security of the UK's gas supply. However, it is hoped the real UK Government is taking a little more interest in the defence of its energy supply than is depicted here.

Readers interested in the history and current threat status of the *SS Richard Montgomery* can review the latest reports on the wreck available through the UK's Maritime and Coastal Agency, which provides fascinating reading.

A number of Oberon-class submarines are now housed in various museums in England and Australia. To help with research for *Under Fire*, I visited *HMAS Onslow* at the Australian National Maritime Museum in Darling Harbour, Sydney, which helped me gain a sense of what it would have been like to work within the restricted confines of a submarine.

Thank you to everyone who read *White Gold*, wrote reviews and generally kept the flag flying in all corners of the world – I really appreciate it.

I'd also like to include a special mention here for my family and friends, who kept cheering me on when things got tough, acted as sounding boards, and reminded me not to take it all too seriously. Hopefully you have a good idea of how much it is appreciated.

See you next time.

Rachel Amphlett
Brisbane, 2013

WHITE GOLD

A conspiracy to destroy alternative energy research... a global organisation killing to protect its interests... and a bomb that will change the face of terrorism forever...

Would you know who to trust?

When Sarah Edgewater's ex-husband is murdered by a radical organisation hell-bent on protecting their assets, she turns to Dan Taylor – geologist, ex-soldier, and lost cause. Together, they must unravel the research notes Sarah's ex-husband left behind to locate an explosive device which is circumnavigating the globe towards London – and time is running out.

In a fast-paced ecological thriller which spans the globe, from London to Brisbane and back via the Arctic Circle, Dan and Sarah aren't just chasing the truth – they're chasing a bomb which, if detonated, will change the future of alternative energy research and the centre of England's capital forever.

ISBN: 978-0-646-57340-3

THREE LIVES DOWN

Dan Taylor has survived two attempts on his life. The rest of his team is missing, and now a terrorist group has stolen a radioactive isotope from a top secret government project.

Can Dan survive long enough to prevent a nuclear disaster on British soil?

With the Prime Minister determined to re-negotiate the country's place in the European Union, and deals being struck behind closed doors, Dan stumbles across a plot that will shake the country to its core.

If his mission fails, his enemies will overthrow the British government, and Dan will be a wanted man.

If he wants to succeed, he'll have to sacrifice everything.

ISBN: 978-0-9922685-9-6

ABOUT THE AUTHOR

For more information about Rachel Amphlett, and to sign up to the readers group for exclusive book news and giveaways, see www.rachelamphlett.com

CPSIA information can be obtained
at www.ICGtesting.com
Printed in the USA
LVHW08s1719120718
583385LV00004BA/720/P